The Good, the Bad, and the Pugly

Susan C. Daffron

An Alpine Grove Romantic Comedy

Book 7

Published by Magic Fur Press
An imprint of Logical Expressions, Inc.
P.O. Box 383
Ponderay, ID 83852

This is a work of fiction. All names, characters, places, and events are either the product of the author's imagination or are used fictitiously. Any resemblance to actual persons, living or dead, business organizations, events, or locales is purely coincidental.

The Good, the Bad, and the Pugly

ISBN: 978-1-61038-037-9 (paperback)
        978-1-61038-038-6 (EPUB)

Like all of my books, *The Good, the Bad, and the Pugly*
is dedicated to
my husband James Byrd,
my best friend and biggest supporter.
Thanks for everything!

<u>Books by Susan C. Daffron</u>
The Alpine Grove Romantic Comedies
Chez Stinky

Fuzzy Logic

The Art of Wag

Snow Furries

Bark to the Future

Howl at the Loon

The Good, the Bad, and the Pugly

The Treasure of the Hairy Cadre

The Luck of the Paw

Daydream Retriever

The Hound of Music

The Jennings & O'Shea Mysteries
Sensing Trouble

Sensing Secrets

Sensing Truth

Chapter 1

Grocery Trauma

Brigid stood in the serpentine grocery store check out line, leaning on her cart waiting. She looked down at the items she was buying. That tub of designer ice cream was going to be soup by the time she got out of here. In front of her, the grocery clerk seemed to be moving items across the scanner in slow motion. Was it absolutely necessary to look at every side of every single box to find the bar code? It was like the guy had never seen these things before and that each item was a huge revelation. Oh look, it's a box of Rice-a-Roni! Where do you suppose the bar code might be? Brigid dropped her head and stared at the floor as she shuffled her feet to move the cart forward a few inches. All she wanted was a little comfort food.

A shriek came out of nowhere and then a crash. When Brigid opened her eyes, she squinted up through her eyelashes at a bright florescent light and a hideous putrid green ceiling. What a disgusting color. It was probably supposed to be soothing, but it was the color of overcooked cabbage, which made her feel mildly nauseated. A woman in a white coat looked down into her face and waved at someone else in the room. "She's awake!"

Brigid said, "Where am I?"

"You're in a hospital. Do you remember what happened?"

"I was watching my ice cream melt. I swear that grocery store has the slowest checkers in the known universe."

"Do you know your name?"

"Brigid Simmons…I mean Brigid Fitzpatrick."

"Which one is it?"

"Brigid Fitzpatrick. I took my maiden name back."

"What year is it?"

"Nineteen ninety six."

"Okay." The woman grinned at her. "I think you're going to be fine. You hit your head, and we were a little worried about you. I'm Doctor Lawrence." She gestured toward another woman. "This is Sally. She's a nurse here."

"I don't remember hitting my head. Am I in a hospital? Did I get shot or something? I heard a scream. Was the store robbed?"

"No. You were hit with a shopping cart."

"What?"

"There was a little boy and he was playing. The cart sort of got away from him. There was a big bag of kitty litter in the cart, so it had some real momentum. His mother says she'll give him a good talking to."

"I was run over by a bratty kid with a shopping cart?" Brigid wanted to giggle at the absurdity of the situation, but couldn't quite muster up the energy. A comedian would have a field day with this—she could imagine the audience snickering at Jerry Seinfeld quipping, "You really know your life is in the toilet when you get run over by an out-of-control shopping cart full of kitty litter."

Doctor Lawrence leaned over and shined a tiny flashlight in Brigid's eyes. "The clerk pulled the cart off you. We checked and it doesn't appear you have internal bleeding, but you do have quite a bit of bruising."

Brigid moved experimentally. The pain in her midsection definitely wasn't funny. "I think I'd like to throw up now."

The doctor turned toward Sally, who handed her a metal pan that she thrust in front of Brigid. "Here!"

After purging the contents of her stomach, Brigid felt worse, not better. She wiped her mouth with the back of her hand. How disgusting. "I'm sorry about that."

"Now that you're awake, we'd like to run some tests and make sure everything is okay. Is there someone we should call? Husband? Boyfriend? A family member?"

"No. My husband is dead. My family is all out East and half of them hate me. Never mind. No, there's no one. Just me."

"We will need you to fill out some forms, if you're up to it."

Brigid groaned and tried to sit up. "Only if you give me some better drugs."

"Let me look you over again first."

As the doctor poked at her, Brigid tried to focus her mind on something other than nausea. She was just so tired. Tired of everything. All she wanted to do was sleep, but reality kept intruding. "Supposedly, I still have military health insurance. I've never made a claim before and I hate to think about the forms they're going to need. They'd better cough up for this—I really can't afford to be sick right now. Ouch, what are you doing? Cut that out!"

Doctor Lawrence stood up straight again. "Okay. I'm done. We're going to keep you overnight and I'm going to schedule a few more tests."

Brigid slumped down on her pillow. "This is so stupid. All I wanted was some ice cream."

The doctor put her hand on Brigid's shoulder. "I know. And I'm sorry. Sometimes accidents happen."

After Doctor Lawrence left the room, Brigid tried to roll over onto her side, but it hurt too much. Just when you think your life can't get any worse, you get run over by a shopping cart. Who knew going to the grocery store could be so dangerous?

The next day after multiple tests, exams, and what felt like four thousand extremely personal questions about every possible nuance of her female anatomy, Brigid was allowed to go home. They called a cab for her and she waited for it, sitting in a wheelchair outside the hospital entrance with her hands folded in her lap. Her car was undoubtedly still sitting in the grocery parking lot. She could get it some other time when she wasn't on heavy-duty pain killers. Although she had been given a clean bill of health as far as the shopping cart incident went, the tests revealed something else. It was unlikely she'd ever be able to have children.

She and John had talked about having kids dozens of times, but Brigid had never been ready. Particularly after he'd been deployed to Iraq, she had been firm in her decision. No babies until he was stationed somewhere in the United States. Never seeing her husband was bad enough. She didn't want to be one of those bitter military wives saddled with twelve children that she had to move all over the globe. The idea of having little kids repeatedly asking "Where's Daddy?" had always made her want to cry. Even worse, if she'd had to say, "Daddy is *never* coming home because there was a helicopter crash."

Brigid wiped away a tear. Fine. She'd never have kids. It would be okay. She'd never been particularly maternal or found children fascinating and adorable like some women did. Not everyone had kids. Plenty of women led perfectly happy lives without children. She'd just have to get used to the idea.

With her Irish temper and sarcastic sense of humor, Brigid had always worried that she wouldn't have been a particularly good parent anyway. But John would have been worse. Any kids they had probably would have ended up needing years of expensive therapy. Maybe this was actually a blessing in disguise. Although part of her was heartbroken that the choice now seemed to have been taken away from her, one thing she knew for sure was that having children with John would have been a terrible mistake.

After the cab dropped her off at her apartment building, Brigid slowly shuffled up the path to the doorway. Her whole body ached and all she wanted to do was take a few more pain-killers, crawl into bed, and go back to sleep.

She opened the door to the tiny studio apartment and gazed around the room. The sparsely furnished space was spotless, utilitarian, and about as interesting as a monk's cell. John hated knick-knacks, or "dust collectors" as he used to call them. They were just one more thing to pack when they'd had to move again.

Brigid sat down on the ugly gold sofa and put her face in her palms. When was the last time she'd actually been happy? Really happy? It felt like forever since she'd even laughed. She'd been trying for the last year to grit her teeth, go to work, and get on with her life now that John was gone and she didn't have to worry about him and their disintegrating marriage.

After John died, she went to counseling for widows like everyone said she should. Enough time had passed that the shock and pain of his death had dulled somewhat. Mostly she just felt numb and tired. They said that her nightmares would go away eventually, and thankfully, they had. Being able to sleep again was no small thing, and she slept *a lot*. Sleep was her refuge from well-meaning people and her own depressing thoughts.

Everyone had been extremely nice and claimed to understand how she felt, but they really didn't. No one did. What people didn't know was that what Brigid really felt was angry and disgusted with herself. And that, coupled with guilt for not feeling what she was supposed to feel, was more difficult to deal with than missing her husband.

At this point, the years she'd spent with John were starting to feel more like a recurring bad dream rather than something she'd actually experienced. But it still was like she was in some limbo land waiting for that bad dream to end. She'd spent most of the last year jumping through hoops and red tape, fighting with countless military offices to receive her survivor's benefits. In the end, many aspects of that bureaucratic battle had been largely futile, filled with more unwelcome surprises.

Brigid's job as a legal secretary was boring, but the people she worked with were nice enough. They had even sent flowers to her after they found out about the helicopter accident. Technically the Gulf War was over, and had been for years. Outside of the military, everyone had pretty much forgotten about it. Many people didn't even know soldiers were still in Iraq in 1995. Operation Provide Comfort was supposed to be providing "humanitarian relief" but the misleading name had just made Brigid angry. Then after

Operation Provide Comfort, the next military initiative was called Operation Provide Comfort II. Really? Couldn't they think of something else?

At least being a legal secretary was a step up from some of Brigid's past jobs, and she'd actually had enough time in one place to get promoted. It still was just a job though, and she'd more or less been operating on auto-pilot since John died, which everyone at work had undoubtedly been too polite to mention. The idea of getting yet another job had been too exhausting. Brigid's resume was a freakish mish-mash of secretarial, administrative, and random low-wage jobs, none of which had lasted more than a year. She'd been a dental receptionist, data-entry clerk, travel agent assistant, waitress, prep cook, and had even done a stint as a packager in a candy factory in that dreadful little town in the Midwest that had only three employers.

Brigid sat up straight and turned her head to look around her apartment again. Enough was enough. She didn't want to be this person anymore. The one her coworkers felt sorry for and pitied because of her empty, sad little life. What was wrong with her? Why was she even still living here? It wasn't as if she loved her job or enjoyed living in sunny Southern California. With her freckles and pallid Irish skin, she had to practically douse herself in sunscreen just to go outside. Sometimes she forgot and burned herself to the point that she looked like an overcooked Oscar Mayer wiener. The tanned, plastic Malibu-Barbie people here in the Southland gave her pale complexion and wavy out-of-control red hair a snide, knowing look, as if to say, "Get some skin pigment, woman."

It was time to start over. Before she'd met John, Brigid hadn't been this mopey useless person who was afraid of everything. In her family, she had been the sharp, funny one, always laughing and getting out and doing things. What had happened to that woman? The sad thing was that when one of the therapists had asked Brigid about her best memory, she had been so surprised and flustered that she hadn't been able to think of anything. Her mind had been a complete blank. After so many years of John berating her opinions, maybe she'd been afraid that anything she said would be written off as stupid.

Since then, she'd rolled the question around in her mind repeatedly. After some reflection, she decided that her best memories were from a trip her family had taken with friends when she was little to a little town near a lake in North Carolina. The rustic A-frame cabin had experienced some terrible plumbing problem that had frustrated her father, and Brigid remembered that she'd laughed one morning when he'd brought a mirror outside and stood in the lake next to the dock to shave. Even with the lack of amenities, it had been so much fun staying right on the water. Brigid had spent all day playing outside in the sand behind the cabin, watching people water ski and making up stories with the little girl who was staying in the cabin next door. Every day, she came in sun-baked and tired, but really happy.

Moving across the country to North Carolina didn't seem practical at the moment, but maybe she could find some place closer that was similar near a lake. Brigid stood up and grabbed an old newspaper off the table. What she really wanted was a little time to herself with no responsibilities to anyone. Not the military. Not her job. No one.

She flipped the pages to the classified ads. Little kids got to take the summer off. Why shouldn't she? After years of being the dutiful Army wife, she needed a vacation. It wasn't much, but she had some savings and her widow's pension. There was no reason she couldn't take a little time for herself to figure out what was next. Who was she, now that she wasn't a wife and was never going to be a mother? Brigid had absolutely no idea.

She looked at the vacation rental classifieds. Alpine Grove? That could work. She had gone there on a weekend trip with John when he was on leave once. They'd fought most of the time, as usual, so it wasn't much of a vacation. But she remembered Alpine Grove as a cute little town with a lake, trees, and probably thousands of hiking trails going off into the forest. Not surprisingly, John had hated the place. She grabbed a pen and circled the ad. It was perfect.

~

With all of her experience in moving, it didn't take Brigid long to find a house to rent in Alpine Grove, quit her job, and start packing. Her studio apartment was on a month-to-month lease. And because her landlord and everyone at the law office knew from the beginning that John was in the military, no one was particularly surprised when Brigid gave her notice. A well-attended garage sale at her apartment complex helped her get rid of the last of John's things and the beat-up old furniture. By the time she was done, everything she owned in the world fit in her somewhat elderly, but reliable, Honda Civic.

After turning in her keys to her landlord, she got into her car and pulled out all her maps for one last look at the route. It was exciting to be on the road at last. This move felt completely different because for the first time in a long time, the choices were all her own. The Army wasn't telling her where to go, which was both liberating and a little nerve-wracking. Suddenly, she had no one to report to, nothing she was supposed to do, and nowhere she was supposed to be.

Brigid had to keep reminding herself that the next few months were going to be a vacation. This was time she'd given herself. Time to relax, read, and just stare at the lake with no one telling her what she should be doing with the rest of her life. Although Brigid didn't remember much about the area from the one weekend she'd spent there, if the pictures in the brochures she'd received from the Chamber of Commerce were any indication, Alpine Grove was beautiful.

As she navigated the overstuffed Honda up the windy road, Brigid observed a dramatic change in vegetation as she got closer to Alpine Grove. The evergreen trees became thick and lush and she opened the window to let the crisp mountain air surround her. The breeze was charged with the scents of warm pine needles and greenery as she passed by meadows filled with wildflowers and craggy granite outcroppings dotted with moss. It was a bright sunny day and Brigid enjoyed the sensation of warm sun on her skin as she drove through the park-like scenery.

The speed limit dropped and she slowed as she approached the town of Alpine Grove itself. The sidewalks were crowded with pedestrians walking along, peering into shop windows, or chatting with one another. Pretty hanging baskets bursting with colorful flowers hung from light poles along the main street. Brigid smiled as she parallel-parked the Honda on a side street near the bookstore where she was supposed to pick up the keys to the rental house.

She walked around the corner to the bookstore. The hand-painted sign above the door said Twice Told Tales, and the window display sported a festive spring theme with lots of books and craft items. A flyer indicated that a local author was going to do a book signing there soon. As Brigid walked in, the bells on the door jingled and an older woman with short gray curly hair looked up from her post behind an antique desk. She smiled and said, "May I help you?"

Brigid returned the smile. "Are you Margaret Connelly? I'm here to pick up a key for a rental house over on Oak Street."

The woman stood up and walked around the desk. "Yes, I am! You must be Brigid. Let me get Linda's key for you."

"Thank you. I'm looking forward to seeing the house. It sounds cute."

Margaret held up a key. "Oh it's adorable. You're going to love it. Linda sold her big house and just bought this one. She got rid of her old stuff and bought all brand-new furniture for this place."

"She didn't tell me that."

"Linda isn't very talkative."

"I noticed that. But if she just bought the place, why isn't she living there?"

Margaret gestured at the shelves. "It's sort of my fault. While she was waiting for the house to close, she was helping me sort books and, well, I got a lot of travel books at an auction. I think she was inspired."

"Inspired to do what?"

"Travel. Linda is a tremendous reader and she decided she is going to spend the summer in England and visit places related to her favorite books."

"What a cool idea."

"I think so too. She wants to see the Yorkshire moors from *The Secret Garden* and the Brontë books. And of course, Shakespeare's birthplace in Stratford-upon-Avon. She's also talking about going to Agatha Christie's house in Devon, Beatrix Potter's Lake District cottage, and Jane Austen's house at Chawton in Hampshire. In London, she plans to visit John Keats's place, the only surviving London home of Charles Dickens, and of course, Sherlock Holmes's famous flat on Baker Street. She's also making a special point to see the Paddington railway station because she loved the Paddington Bear books."

"That's going to be quite an involved trip. No wonder she's renting the place to me for the whole summer." Brigid grinned as she took the key from Margaret. "I can certainly understand wanting to take a vacation. That's why I'm here. My plans are nowhere near that ambitious though."

"Linda told me you were here to relax and I think that's wonderful. I think many of us tend to work too hard. Most people don't take enough vacations—I know I certainly haven't. But I have a trip all set up for later in the summer when my daughter will be available to take care of the store."

"Could you tell me where the house is?"

"Oh, it's just a few blocks from here." Margaret gestured as she described the streets and landmarks. "If you enjoy walking, you can easily walk back here to the store. Do you like to read?"

"I have some novels in the car, but I'm sort of at a crossroads in my life, you might say. I was thinking after I have settled in a little bit, I might get some books to help me figure out what I'm going to do next."

"Oh dear, I'm sorry. I can talk about books forever and you are probably anxious to see the house." Margaret waved her arms in a shooing motion. "Enjoy! But please come back and I'll show you some of my favorite self-help books." She chuckled. "I think I have probably read them all. If you need anything at the house, just let me know."

Brigid clutched the key in her hand and said goodbye to Margaret. People certainly were friendly here. She couldn't remember ever having a conversation like that with someone at a big box bookstore. It was clear that the little shop was well-loved. She'd definitely be back.

As she strolled back to her car, Brigid looked up at the huge maple trees that lined the side street. The leaves were a brilliant spring green, creating dappled shade on the sidewalk. It was so peaceful here and so far away from her life in the city that it was like a different world. She drove the few blocks to the address and stopped in front of a small house with light-brown siding and white trim. The little bungalow was constructed in a quasi-Craftsman style with big windows and a single dormer upstairs. The tidy front porch had white painted railings and a wooden rocking chair sat next to the bright red front door, practically inviting her to sit down and relax.

Brigid ran up the path to the door, unlocked it, and walked inside. The living room had rich dark brown wood floors, and as Margaret had said, the furniture was obviously all new. It didn't look like anyone had ever sat on the sofa in front of the fireplace. Brigid stepped into the kitchen, which was a "U" shape with sparkling white cabinets and shiny new counter-tops. She opened a drawer and found rows of shiny silverware organized into tidy compartments. The whole place was immaculate. She went upstairs to the bedroom and walked over to the dormer window. Standing in-between the slanted ceilings, she gazed out at the street and the maple tree that shaded the front yard.

Unable to stop grinning at having found such a happy little house, Brigid ran back downstairs and started bringing in her things from the car. She couldn't quite believe she was going to spend the whole summer here. It stretched out ahead of her like a tranquil green oasis in the desert of her troubled life.

~

After Brigid unpacked and put away her few possessions, she realized it had been quite some time since she had eaten anything. The next item on her to-do list needed to be a trip to the grocery store. It would be a relief to shop at a different store—one where she had not had an accident requiring hospitalization.

The local Save-a-Lot in Alpine Grove was smaller, older, and far less shiny than the grocery where Brigid had been run over. At least kids wouldn't have as much surface area to get up to ramming speed. Since the shopping cart incident, Brigid had kept a much closer eye on unsupervised children who might be "helping" their mothers shop for food.

Brigid needed staples like milk and butter, so she went toward the refrigerated section. In front of one of the dairy cases, two women were laughing so hard they seemed to be having trouble breathing. A petite woman with long, dark wavy hair was leaning on the shopping cart and trying to catch her breath as the other woman, wearing a skin-tight red dress, burst into song, interspersed with choking laughter and some strange disco-like dance moves that would have made John Travolta weep.

Brigid looked around. No one else seemed to be in the aisle witnessing the performance. People certainly seemed to have a lot more fun grocery shopping here than she did. As she walked toward the case, she smiled politely at the woman in the red dress and said, "Excuse me. I just need to grab some butter."

The woman flipped her huge mop of curly brunette hair, yelped, "Butter!" and pointed at the other woman. "If you're not gonna let me make cookies out of a tube, I need that, right?"

The other woman giggled and nodded. "And sugar. Oh, and brown sugar too."

Brigid stood and waited as the curly-haired woman launched into a medley of songs related to sugar, including *Brown Sugar* by the Rolling Stones and *Sugar, Sugar* by the Archies. Brigid groaned mentally. Now that stupid song was going to be stuck in her head all afternoon. Maybe the rental house had a stereo, so she could purge the Archies from her brain.

The other woman moved her shopping cart and said, "Maria, you need to get out of the way."

Maria stopped singing, apparently realizing that she was blocking access to the shelves. "I'm sorry!" She turned and pointed at a package of biscuit dough that appeared to have exploded out of the end of the tube, leaving a pale cylinder of dough drooping off the shelf of the refrigerator case. "But look at that."

Brigid smiled slightly and tried to repress a giggle. It looked like the Pillsbury Dough-boy had some kind of unfortunate dysfunction going on.

Maria shook her finger at Brigid. "See there, I can tell by your face. I know *exactly* what you're thinking! It's not just me. My friend Kat here says that I have a dirty mind. But I'm sorry—that is a very sad limp situation and I just don't like to see that because it reminds me of a few extremely disappointing evenings."

Kat leaned on the shopping cart and wiped a tear of laughter from her eye with her fingertip. "Please, please don't sing *Tube Snake Boogie* again. I'm begging you."

Maria put her hand on her hip. "It was totally appropriate and you know it."

Brigid pointed at the refrigerator case, "I just need to get some butter."

"Don't touch the tube snake. You don't know where it's been." Maria said.

"Or who it's been with," Kat said.

"This is the dairy case." Brigid said, "Maybe it's got the jack."

"And who knows what else!" Maria whooped and pointed at Brigid. "I like you! You just gotta love a woman who can intersperse obscure AC/DC lyrics with her cheese."

Brigid transferred a box of butter to her cart and said, "I guess now that we've shared dirty song lyrics, I should introduce myself. My name is Brigid and I'm renting a house here for the summer."

Kat held out her hand. "It's nice to meet you. I'm Kat and this is Maria."

"I haven't lived here long either," Maria said. "But Kat believes that by this point, I should see if my oven is functional. And I believe that cookies are the only reason anyone would ever want to turn on an oven. So now we are discussing the merits of prefabricated cookie dough in a tube versus the old-fashioned hard way."

"It's not hard!" Kat said. "The recipe is right there on the bag of chocolate chips."

Brigid nodded. "They are so good when you make them from scratch."

Maria rolled her eyes melodramatically. "Cooking from scratch is not something I have any desire to do. Why would they bother to put things in pretty packages if you're not supposed to eat what's inside?"

Kat held up a tube of cookie dough. "See that? Artificial flavor. I don't think there's anything wrong with avoiding artificial stuff."

"The engineer is turning you into a health nut, isn't he?" Maria said.

Kat put the tube back in the case. "No. I was a vegetarian before I met Joel, remember?"

"That doesn't make you a health nut. Potato chips are vegetarian. You cook now and you know it." Maria pulled the cookie dough back out of the case. "I refuse to yield to that level of domesticity."

Kat took the tube and put it back. "All right! I'll make the cookies for you. Just to prove to you how easy it is."

"I knew you'd cave." Maria smiled smugly. "Now that we've settled that issue, we need to look at new toys for my possessed cat."

"Your cat is not possessed." Kat said.

Maria gestured toward the pet aisle. "She's hiding the seven thousand toys I bought somewhere, so I'll keep buying more. You don't live with Scarlett, so you don't understand. I think you need to board her at your place to be sure she's not actually the devil's spawn."

"How many times do I have to tell you? I don't board cats." Kat rolled the cart forward out of the way of another shopper. "Get a dog. There's a really cute one at the vet that needs a home."

Maria turned to Brigid. "How do you feel about cats versus dogs?"

Brigid shrugged. "I love both really. We had dogs and cats when I was growing up, but it's been years since I've had any pet at all."

Maria pointed at Kat. "She is opening a boarding kennel, but she's discriminating against felines."

Kat sighed. "That's because it's going to be a *dog* boarding kennel."

Brigid said, "Hanging out with dogs all day sounds like it would be fun."

"It depends on the dogs, but usually yes, I enjoy it." Kat said. "Everything will be a lot easier when we finish building the kennels."

"So far, everyone who boards their dog there ends up getting a date, which I think is not fair to the cat ladies of the world. Particularly me, because I seriously need some action." Maria waved toward the canned biscuits. "You know the situation is getting dire when even limp biscuits can bring back memories."

"Get a dog." Kat repeated. "The little dog at the vet is there because her owner died. It's so sad."

"Why is it at the vet?" Brigid looked at Kat's blue eyes. They were a pretty cornflower color. It was unusual to look eye-to-eye at another person, since most people weren't as short as she was. "Is the dog hurt or sick or something?" She couldn't stand the idea that the dog had lost its family and was also in pain.

"No. The dog is fine. Just homeless. They're trying to find someone to adopt her, but right now, she's just stuck in a cage at the clinic. I'm not sure what kind of dog she is, but she's adorable. Her name is Gypsy. I would love to take her, but I think Joel would kill me."

Maria snickered. "Yeah, the engineer draws the line at five dogs and five cats, I guess."

Brigid said, "That's a lot of pets. How did you end up with so many?"

"It's a long story," Kat said. "You seem like a dog lover. Why don't you adopt Gypsy? I'll give you a free weekend of boarding if you do. She's so sweet. The vet is just down the road. Tell them I sent you."

"I don't know." Brigid shook her head. "It's probably not a good idea for me to adopt a dog right now."

"Just go look at Gypsy. I think she'd be perfect for you." Kat looked at her watch and then at Maria. "I've got to get back. Let's get the rest of the cookie ingredients and get out of here."

Maria pushed a clump of curly hair away from her face. "Okay, but first we need to stop by the kitty toys." She gave Brigid a knowing smile. "Adopt the dog and then board it out at Kat's place. You won't be sorry."

"Spending so much time in the advertising business is turning you into quite the promoter," Kat said to Maria. Turning to Brigid, she said, "It was nice to meet you."

Brigid said goodbye to the women and rolled her cart toward the milk case. As she grabbed a carton, she stopped and turned to look back at them. Given the peals of laughter, they'd found something funny in the pet aisle too.

Maybe they were right. Why shouldn't she adopt a dog? The house she had rented allowed pets. Although she wasn't sure what would happen after the summer, one thing she did know for sure was that she wouldn't be moving overseas again or dealing with complicated rules and quarantines. Now that she thought about it, the truth was that she missed having animals around. She loved hanging out with the dogs she'd had when she was a kid. And dogs were always glad to see you. That would be a novel change after so much time alone. If nothing else, maybe she could stop by and visit Gypsy. The poor little dog was probably lonely. Brigid could sympathize, since she certainly had a lot of experience with that emotion.

～

Brigid put away her groceries, and looked at the clock. The veterinarian's office probably wasn't closed yet. Maybe she could just stop by for a short visit. She looked up the address in the thin Alpine Grove phone book, grabbed her keys, and got in the Honda.

She parked in front of the building, which seemed to be a rather popular place. A woman with curly reddish hair walked out with a rotund Labrador retriever who looked delighted to be exiting the veterinary clinic.

If they were really busy, maybe this was a bad idea. But it seemed silly to have driven over for nothing. And little Gypsy was probably still lonely. Brigid got out of her car and went inside. The receptionist looked up at her and smiled. "May I help you?"

Brigid looked around at the various people waiting. "I'm sorry, it looks like you're really busy, but I met a woman named Kat who said you have a little dog here that is lonely."

The woman nodded her head vigorously and leaped up, her straight blonde hair sweeping her face. "We do! Come with me." As she walked away, she turned her head and smiled. "I'm Tracy, by the way."

Brigid followed Tracy into another room that had rows of metal cages with various animals in them. Some appeared to be asleep and others were very, very awake. A hound began baying as Tracy approached. She crouched down in front of the cage. "Oh Roscoe, it's okay. Your dad will be here soon."

Brigid peered into a cage with a card attached to it that said *Gypsy*. In the back, a small, furry caramel-colored dog was curled up on a little bed. "Oh my gosh, she's so cute!"

Tracy stood up. "She's a little shy, probably because it's so noisy here. I can tell you for sure, she's not too fond of Roscoe's barking. He has a little trouble shutting up. It's a hound-dog thing."

"I just wanted to visit her for a little while. Kat said she's lonely."

Tracy gestured at the cage. "Do you want to hold her? There's an office over there where you can spend some time getting to know each other. Dr. Cassidy is busy with appointments, so she's not using it right now."

"Could I?"

Tracy opened the cage and the dog stood up, stretched, and yawned. "C'mon Gypsy. You have a visitor." She pulled a leash out of her pocket, clipped it onto the dog's collar, and handed Gypsy to Brigid. "Actually, she hasn't been out in a while and I've got to get back out front. Could you take her out? It's just through that door. Then you can visit in the office for a while."

Brigid just nodded as she snuggled the dog to her chest. "She's so soft."

"I know. I brushed her earlier while Dr. C was doing surgery. Gypsy loves being brushed. I wish I could adopt her, but my dachshund doesn't like her. I think Roxy is determined to remain an only child." Tracy pointed to the door. "The yard is right through there."

"Okay." Brigid stroked the dog's head as she walked toward the exit. "Are you ready for a little walk?" Gypsy looked up at her with round brown eyes. The dog really did look kind of lonely.

Outside, Brigid put Gypsy down and walked slowly with her, watching as the dog sniffed at the grass. "You probably wonder what happened to your mama, don't you?"

After the dog had finished, she stood and stared up at Brigid with those soulful eyes again. Gypsy had pointy ears and a curly fluffy tail that did an impressive job of helping her express her various moods. The way the dog tilted her head and smoothed her ears back against her head almost made it look like she was asking a question. Brigid giggled at the dog's inquisitive look. "Well look at this. You expect me to pick you up, don't you? Aren't you the demanding one?" The dog continued to stare and Brigid reached down for her. "All right. I'm guessing you were a little spoiled, weren't you?"

She took Gypsy into the office and sat on the floor with the dog in her lap, stroking her head and talking to her. Later, the door opened and Tracy smiled down at them. "You're still here. We're about to close up."

Brigid got to her feet and looked up at the clock. "I'm sorry. I had no idea it was so late."

"It's okay. I'll just put her back in her cage."

Brigid handed the leash to Tracy. "All right."

Tracy bent down to pick up the dog. "Are you ready for your dinner, Gypsy?"

Brigid followed Tracy as she settled Gypsy back into the cage. Tracy went to a cabinet and began putting food in a bowl. Brigid said, "I guess I should be going. Thank you for letting me visit."

Tracy said, "Feel free to come back. Until she finds her new home, Gypsy needs all the loving she can get."

Brigid glanced at the cage where Gypsy was standing, just staring at her again. Those expressive brown eyes seemed to ask, "You aren't leaving me here are you?"

Brigid walked up to the cage and put her fingertips through the bars. "No Gypsy, I'm not."

Tracy walked up with the food bowl. "What did you say?"

"What do I need to do to adopt Gypsy? Do I need to fill out forms or anything? I'll take her. Right now."

"Are you serious?" Tracy grinned as Brigid nodded, and she handed over the food bowl. "Let me go get Dr. C. She's going to be thrilled."

Tracy returned with a tall thin woman wearing a long white lab coat. She had curly brown hair and dark circles under her eyes. The veterinarian was probably tired and Brigid felt a little bad for making everyone work late, but there was no way she was leaving without Gypsy.

Holding out her hand, the woman said, "I'm Karen Cassidy. I hear you want to adopt our fuzzy guest."

"Yes, I do. I had dogs when I was growing up, but I've never seen a dog that looks like Gypsy." Brigid pointed at the cage. "I was curious if you know what breed of dog she is."

"She is some type of mix and we've been guessing maybe Papillon, Pomeranian, or spitz might be in there. She's too big to be a Pom, but she has that kind of foxy face and similar coloring. Really, we have no idea. All we know is she's small, very furry, and healthy. I gave her a full workup and she's up to date with all her shots." The veterinarian handed over some papers. "Here's a copy of Gypsy's records. The top paper also is a form I'd like you to fill out with your contact information."

Brigid put the papers on the counter and pulled a pen out of a cup. She looked at the vet. "I hope this isn't a problem, but I'm just here for the summer. I'm renting a house."

Dr. Cassidy leaned on the counter. "The rental takes pets, right?"

"It does, and it has a fenced yard too. The owner is really nice. But after the summer, I have no idea what I'm doing next. I'm sort of in transition, I guess you'd say."

Tracy nodded as she handed Brigid Gypsy's leash. "Been there."

"I suppose I should ask you a bunch of questions to make sure you're a good person, shouldn't I?" Dr. Cassidy said as she ran her fingers through her hair. "But from what Tracy said, you seem to love Gypsy. Just update us once you know where you'll be. And if you decide to move away from Alpine Grove this fall, we'd like to give Gypsy a check-up before you go."

Brigid looked up from the form. "I promise I'll give her a good home and I'll be sure to let you know when I move."

Tracy crouched down next to a cabinet, pulled out a variety of items, and put them in a paper grocery sack. "When Gypsy arrived, she came with quite a few toys and a crate where she used to sleep. I'm also giving you some food to get started." She held up a bag. "She really likes these treats too. Once she gets to know you, she'll be easy to train."

"She seems so quiet." Brigid glanced at the cage. "When I was petting her, she hardly moved."

Tracy dropped another toy into the bag and stood up. "I think she's depressed. Gypsy was a lot more animated when her owner used to bring her in. Small dogs can be more demanding than you might expect. My doxie is a little snot."

Brigid laughed. "I'll keep that in mind."

"Yeah, Roxy spends most of her day with my boyfriend making sure no one enters his office without her consent. When she gets too snotty, we do a few training sessions to remind her who pays for her dog food." Tracy opened the kennel, put the leash on Gypsy, and snuggled her up for a hug. "Are you ready to go home? I'm going to miss you, little dog."

Gypsy wagged her feathery tail and licked Tracy's cheek. Tracy handed her to Brigid and said, "You be good."

Brigid took Gypsy in her arms and stroked the soft fur on her head. "Do I owe you any type of adoption fee? I didn't really notice, but is this an animal shelter in addition to a vet clinic?"

Dr. Cassidy crossed her arms. "No. Well, it's not supposed to be anyway."

Tracy grinned. "Dr. C is a soft touch. Alpine Grove doesn't have an animal shelter."

"Where do people take lost dogs?"

Tracy glanced at the vet. Dr. Cassidy shrugged and said, "Technically, you're supposed to take strays to the police station. But the dogs can't stay there long because there are only a couple of kennels. That's basically the "dog pound." After their hold time is up, the dogs are transferred to a place that doesn't, well, *keep* dogs for very long."

"Everyone knows what that means, so people avoid the pound," Tracy said.

Brigid snuggled Gypsy a little more tightly. "So they end up here?"

"Sometimes. If they aren't picked up as strays by the police or the county sheriff." Tracy said. "I know quite a few people who have dogs that ended up on their doorstep. When they couldn't find the owner, they just kept the dog."

"We really don't have the space here to handle stray pets. We can't take every dog that people find or want to give up, particularly big ones." Dr. C gestured at the cages. "I mean, look at those cages. They aren't ideal. And Tracy and I are pretty busy caring for people's pets. There's only so much we can do."

"That's terrible," Brigid said.

Tracy said, "As more people move here, it's becoming more of a problem."

Brigid put Gypsy on the floor. "Thank you both for helping Gypsy. And for letting me adopt her. I promise I'll try to be the best dog mom I can be."

Dr. Cassidy smiled. "I know you will."

Chapter 2

Introspection & Judge

Over the next few days, as Tracy had predicted, Gypsy started to come out of her shell. As the little dog began to settle into her new home and daily routines, her shyness subsided and she followed Brigid around everywhere. It didn't seem like Gypsy had received any training in her last home, so Brigid wanted to teach her some basic commands. Having a little furry shadow was flattering, but it would be good to teach Gypsy the down-stay, so she didn't get stepped on while Brigid was cooking in the kitchen.

When Brigid was about thirteen, she had taken her shepherd mix to obedience class, but it had been years since she'd done any dog training. She needed to talk to Margaret about a pet deposit for the rental house anyway, so maybe she could get a couple of dog-related books while she was there, along with the self-help ones. After leashing up Gypsy, they set out for the bookstore.

At the door, she picked up the little dog, since dogs probably weren't allowed in the store. If Gypsy's dainty paws didn't touch anything, it might be okay to at least talk to Margaret for a minute.

Brigid leaned on the door and the bells jingled as she walked into the shop. Margaret was talking to a tall man who was holding a battered leather cowboy hat in front of him with his fingertips.

As the pair turned to look at her, Brigid pointed at Gypsy. "I have my dog with me. I hope that's okay that I brought her inside. I need to ask you a question."

Margaret waved her over. "My dog Arlo comes in here all the time. As long as the dog doesn't relieve herself on the merchandise, it's fine."

Brigid smiled as she walked toward the desk. "No, I don't think Gypsy would do that."

The man backed away from Margaret, holding up a paperback. "It looks like you're busy. I'll just be going now. Thank you for getting the book for me."

Margaret waved. "Don't run off, Clay. This is Brigid. She's renting a house down the street for the summer from a friend of mine." She pointed at the man. "Brigid, this is Clayton Hadley."

He smiled and nodded at her.

Brigid said, "It's nice to meet you. Do you live around here?"

"I have a place north of town," he said in a deep low voice.

"Oh it's an amazing ranch!" Margaret said. "With all the gorgeous horses grazing out in the green pastures, it's like a photograph on a calendar. My friend Jill and I went for a trail ride there last fall and it was lovely."

He grinned, "Well, that's kind of you to say since it's not that much of a ranch anymore, but thank you."

Margaret put her hand over her mouth in surprise and dropped it as she exclaimed, "Oh my goodness, Clay, your teeth look fantastic!"

Brigid turned her head to look at both of them. She'd missed something here. Although the rest of him seemed somewhat weathered, the man did have nice, straight white teeth.

Clay laughed warmly. "Yeah, I used some of that movie money to get them fixed."

At Brigid's confused expression, Margaret said, "Clay was on the rodeo circuit for a while and, well, the last time I saw him, he was missing a few teeth."

"If you fall off a horse, don't land on your face," he said.

Brigid readjusted Gypsy in her arms. Clay had light-brown wavy hair and given his tan, he evidently spent a lot of time outside. He had a serious scar on his chin and his hands were chapped. Although the tiny wrinkles around his deep-set eyes gave him a somewhat weary look, it was easy to imagine him galloping a horse across a vast expanse of ranch land.

After putting Gypsy on the floor, she stood up and took a closer look at his face. His eyes were a rich walnut brown with striking topaz flecks around the pupil. She gestured toward the hat in his hands. "I've never been to a rodeo. What did you do?"

He shrugged. "Mostly trick-riding shows."

"I know your poor parents were worried sick about you the whole time you were doing that," Margaret said. "On the trail, you told us some great stories about the horse training and stunts you did in Hollywood too. I can't believe you met Steven Spielberg and went to Tunisia. I've never met *anyone* who has been there."

"It's hot."

"Jill and I had so much fun. We want to go riding again! I'm so glad you came back home."

"Yeah, I missed Alpine Grove more than I thought I would when I left," he said.

Margaret nodded. "I think that happens to many people who grow up here. My daughter is thrilled to be living here part of the year again, which given her attitude in high school, is nothing short of remarkable."

"It's hard to imagine little Beth all grown up," Clay said. "The last time I saw her I think she was probably eight or nine years old."

"I guess that's around the time you left town." Margaret said, shaking her head sadly. "But did you hear? Beth is getting married. We've been doing lots of wedding planning and it will be so much fun. I can hardly wait."

"That sounds nice," he said, picking the book back up off the counter. "It's been great catching up, but I should go."

"Please give your parents my regards," Margaret said.

"Will do." He turned to Brigid. "It was nice meeting you."

"You too."

As she and Margaret watched, he put on his hat and strolled out of the store. Brigid smiled to herself. Alpine Grove was an interesting place. Maybe it was just the hat, but how often did you get to meet an actual cowboy?

Turning to Margaret, she cleared her throat. Time to get down to business. "As you can see, I have a dog now. So I need to give you a check for a pet deposit to give to Linda."

"All right." Margaret gestured toward a pile of books on the desk. "I was hoping you'd come back, so I pulled out some books for you to look through. These are some of my favorites from the self-help section."

"If you could point me toward the pet-care books, I need to read up on dog training too."

Margaret pointed toward the side of the store. "They're on that wall over there. My dog Arlo can be a bit of a problem child, so I've spent quite a bit of time with those books as well."

Brigid picked up Gypsy again and gave her a hug. "They warned me at the vet clinic that Gypsy would start to behave differently once she was more comfortable. But I think she might be a little too comfortable now. She's on the high road to spoiled rotten."

Margaret reached over to pet Gypsy. "Oh, but she's so cute."

"She's well aware of that. And that I adore her."

~

After spending far too much money, Brigid walked Gypsy back home, carrying a big bag of books on positive reinforcement for both humans and dogs. As Brigid opened the door to the house, she said, "Okay Gypsy, if we follow the advice in all these books, we'll be unstoppable. You'll be the best-behaved dog in the world, and I'll never have another crummy job, bad relationship, or even get angry again. I'm going to know what my life's purpose is and we're going to be blissfully happy. You'll see. It's going to be great."

Gypsy looked up at her with wide eyes. Brigid smiled as she bent to unclip the leash from the dog's collar. "I'm kidding! You always look so serious."

Apparently sufficiently convinced that all was right with the human, Gypsy ran off into the house and plopped down into her dog bed, ready to settle in for a nap. Brigid curled up on the sofa with the books and started flipping through them, trying to determine which problem to focus on first. Good thing she had the whole summer to figure everything out. Deciding what she wanted to do career-wise and rebuilding her battered confidence could take a while.

A few hours later, Brigid's brain had reached self-help overload. She couldn't stand pondering her own life anymore and her thoughts began wandering to all the people she'd met in Alpine Grove. Her mind drifted from possessed cats, to cowboys, to upcoming weddings, to the stray dogs at the police station. Considering she'd only been in Alpine Grove a short while, it suddenly seemed like she knew quite a bit about a lot of different people and things. After living in cities for so long, she was used to being insulated in a cocoon of anonymity. It was odd for her to have met so many people who were so open about what was going on in their life.

Over the next few days, Brigid went out to the lake and checked out a few hiking trails with Gypsy. Not working had a lot to recommend it, but she could feel herself getting antsy for something else to do. Sitting home all day pondering her psyche was not in her nature.

In the past when she hadn't been able to find a job or was in the process of looking, she'd volunteered with various groups. She'd helped at food banks, libraries, schools, and animal shelters. Volunteering had given her structure and a much-needed sense of accomplishment. It also helped her to meet people after she moved yet again. Even though she'd only be in Alpine Grove a few months, there was probably some place where she could help out. It wasn't any different from the many short-term locations she'd experienced as an Army wife. The recurring theme had been to meet people, get to know them a little, and then say goodbye.

As Gypsy continued to blossom into a happy little dog, Brigid couldn't stop thinking about the stray dogs stuck at the Alpine Grove dog pound. They must be scared. Who fed and walked them? Presumably, the employees were busy with other things, weren't they? Was someone in charge of the dogs? If so, who?

Questions roiled in her mind and finally she was too curious not to find out. The worst thing that could happen was that some law enforcement officer would tell her to get out and mind her own business. After dealing with so many people in the military for years, she certainly wasn't going to be intimidated by a uniform.

Gypsy was happily napping, so Brigid figured it was a good time to investigate the situation. She drove the short distance to the town's municipal buildings and parked in the lot next to the large square brick edifice.

She walked inside the police station and found a young officer of the law leaning back in a chair reading a magazine. The Alpine Grove criminal element must be busy doing something else at the moment. He pushed a lock of black hair off his forehead and put his feet on the floor with a thump. "Can I help you ma'am?"

"I hope so. I was told that stray dogs are brought here if they are picked up by law enforcement." She looked at the sign on the desk. "Are you Officer Reynolds?"

"Yes ma'am. Are you missing a dog? There aren't any here right at the moment."

"I'm glad to hear that." Brigid tried to suppress her annoyance. He was being polite, but all this ma'am-ing made her feel like a decrepit crone. Okay, she was obviously quite a bit older than the officer, but sheesh, she wasn't *that* old. "I would like to see where the animals are kept."

A look of confusion crossed his face. "You wanna look at empty cages?"

"I'm curious about the stray dog situation here." Brigid stood up straight, trying to exude confidence. "I've volunteered at animal shelters in the past."

"You gonna report us for cruelty or something?"

Brigid waved her hand in the negative. "Not at all. I'm hoping I can help. You must be very busy here. Who takes care of the dogs?"

The officer pushed the errant lock of hair off his forehead again. "Well, it depends. Sometimes we get the budget to get a kid in to help clean, but right now, mostly we kinda take turns. It depends on who is on desk duty. We put a schedule on the white board when there are dogs here. But like I said, there aren't any right now."

"I'd still like to see where they are housed." She leaned toward him and raised her eyebrows. "Are you terribly busy doing something else?"

He glanced at the magazine. "No, um, I suppose not." As he stood up, he pushed the chair back with his foot and called out to someone in another office. "Hey Ronnie. I gotta go out back for a minute. Keep an eye out front will you?"

A voice of assent came from the office and Brigid followed Officer Reynolds down a long hallway through the building toward the back.

They walked outside the back of the building to an area that seemed to be a maintenance yard. There was a pile of gravel, equipment, and some pieces of road-maintenance machinery in the fenced-in area. At the far end, the dog pound building was nestled in a corner. They walked over to where empty chain-link kennels were set up in the back of an outbuilding that looked like it had once been a storage shed. The cages were about two feet wide by four feet long with concrete floors. Officer Reynolds waved his hand at the cages. "There ya go. Empty cages, just like you wanted."

Brigid looked around the bleak environment and thought about how it must feel to be a lost dog tucked away back here scared and alone with no one around. No wonder they were transferred out quickly. Although from what she had heard at the vet clinic, being transferred didn't seem like a particularly promising fate either.

At one of the animal shelters where Brigid had volunteered, dogs that weren't claimed often went to foster homes. People would bring the dogs into their homes on a temporary basis, caring for the animal until a permanent placement was found. It didn't seem like they did anything like that here.

She looked at the tall young man, who was fussing at his hair again. "I'm here for the summer and I'd like to help. When you get a dog, I'll come in and clean the cage, feed, and walk the dog. You could have the summer off from dog duty. It won't cost anything. Just call me and I'll help. I live very close by. Could I give you my number?"

Office Reynolds grinned widely. "Well, that would sure make my life easier. I have to clear it with the chief, but I'll give you a call in a few hours and let you know what he says."

Brigid put out her hand. "It's a deal. Thank you, Officer. I look forward to working with you."

"Yes, ma'am!"

∽

After returning from her excursion to the police station, Brigid went out to the back porch with Gypsy to enjoy the rest of the afternoon. The house had a small but very peaceful back-yard. Gardens were set up in front of the weathered wood-plank fencing, which coupled with all the trees and vegetation, made the space seem completely private.

Gypsy ran around the yard and rolled in the grass for a while. Then, having exhausted herself, she lay flat on her side snoring in the sun. Brigid brought some of her new books outside along with a notepad.

Although the books varied in their take on what to do when people were faced with uncertainty and change, they did have one thing in common. They all suggested that readers spend some time taking stock of what had happened in their life and what they wanted to happen in the future. A few even had worksheets, and Brigid was determined to force herself to answer the questions.

Brigid closed her eyes and let the sun warm her face as she pondered her answers to questions like, "What if you were going to die in the next year? What would you do?" Or "Where do you want to be in five years?" "Are you happy right this second?" "Are you passionate about your life?" "What is your life purpose?"

All of this investigation didn't lead to much insight because most of the answers Brigid came up with were along the lines of "I have no clue." In reflecting on her past, it was becoming obvious that most of her existence had been defined by external influences.

Up until now, her parents, her husband, the military, or some combination had decided her fate. Brigid had mostly been along for the ride, which was a depressing realization. Intellectually, she knew she had been unhappy and should change some things, but she'd never really had a feeling deep down that things *had* to change. Her disastrous marriage was ample evidence of that. With the benefit of hindsight, she felt stupid for letting things with John get as bad as they had. She'd felt stuck and incapable of doing anything about it. Everyone said marriage required work and commitment. But nothing should take *that* much work. It made her tired just recalling the experience. Years of loneliness and strife were worth forgetting.

Making changes was like losing weight. Everybody knew what they *should* do: eat right and exercise more. But often people didn't decide they had to change until something drastic happened like a heart attack. Then eating right evolved from something a person *should* do to something a person *had to* do. Brigid had definitely reached that point in her life.

Maybe it took being slammed by a shopping cart to wake her up to the fact that floating aimlessly wasn't really an option anymore. She'd spent too long in a weird, guilt-laden stasis after John died. Even if she didn't know what was next, she was glad she'd left all that behind. Now it was time to do something new and move forward.

The big question was: toward what? There were no guarantees she'd like whatever was next any better than what she'd just lived through. But at the moment, she felt better about the fact that she had at least done *something*. Going to the police station and offering to volunteer was a first baby step. Doing something was always better than doing nothing. One thing that had come out of all the reading and reflection was that Brigid discovered that she craved a sense of accomplishment and feeling like she was making a difference. Even if she could make a difference for one dog in one kennel in one little town, it was a start. She could build up her confidence from there.

Brigid was still writing notes and enjoying the late-afternoon sun when the phone rang in the house. She jumped up and ran inside to answer it.

Officer Reynolds greeted her and continued, "I talked to my supervisor, ma'am, and he says volunteering is A-OK. Also, we just got a dog-running-at-large call, so if you want to come by tomorrow morning and get started with this critter, that would be great."

She agreed on a time to meet the next morning and hung up the phone. Gypsy was standing below her, looking up with the questioning look in her dark-brown eyes again. Brigid picked up the dog and snuggled her to her chest. "Don't worry, everything is okay. But it looks like I have something to do tomorrow other than cater to your every whim." Gypsy wagged and licked Brigid's neck enthusiastically.

The next morning, Brigid went back to the Alpine Grove municipal buildings. Officer Reynolds was apparently still on desk duty. He smiled when she walked through the glass door. "I'm sure glad to see you this morning, ma'am!"

"Please call me Brigid, Officer Reynolds. When you call me ma'am, I feel like you're talking to someone's grandmother. I'm not your grandma."

"Oh, okay. Sorry about that. You can call me Jake." He got up from his chair. "Come on back."

Brigid followed him down the hallway again and he turned around to look at her, so he was walking backwards.

"So I was wondering something. How much do you know about dogs?"

"I have owned dogs, walked dogs at animal shelters, and I just adopted a little mixed-breed dog the other day. So about as much as most people, I suppose. Why do you ask?"

"Because this one's got some kind of problem. It's kinda gross actually."

"Does the dog need to see a veterinarian?"

"I don't know. I was hoping maybe you'd know. The dog is super-friendly. Maybe he's just a funny breed that's got weird fur or something. Like those hairless cats? Have you ever seen pictures of those things? Man, they are really ugly."

Brigid pointed at Jake to indicate he was going to walk backwards into a door. He turned around, opened the door for her, and continued his description. "The dog's skin is kinda scraped up too. I don't know. Maybe it got into a fight."

Brigid walked up to one of the cages, where a dark-brown dog leaped up onto the gate barking loudly. He was probably part retriever mixed with something else. Maybe a lot of other somethings. It was difficult to even hazard a guess what breeds made up the mutt. She stepped back and then bent her head to get a better look at the dog's stomach while he was on his back legs. Although the retriever mix certainly had a healthy voice, Jake wasn't wrong about the dog's skin and fur. She spoke softly, encouraging the dog to settle down, and then turned to Jake. "Do you have a leash? And some type of collar?"

Jake pointed to the wall where chains and leashes hung on hooks. "Yeah, I'm thinking maybe this guy is a medium." He walked over, looped the chain through the ring, and handed it to her. "Here ya go."

Brigid had grown up around a number of exuberant retrievers and this one was no exception. Years ago, a friend's dog had jumped on every person she met until Brigid convinced the dog that jumping on *her* was not a good idea. She'd also recently spent a lot of time reading dog training books again, so she had a few tricks up her sleeve.

Once Brigid was inside the cage, she kept turning away from the dog when he tried to jump on her. She quickly looped the collar over his head, snapped the chain, and said, "Sit" in a firm voice. The dog looked startled for a moment, but sat and wagged his tail. She stroked a small patch of fur on his head and told the dog that his knowledge of the sit command was an utterly brilliant achievement. In response, the dog curled himself around so he could scratch at his neck.

Jake said, "Hey Brigid, this is great! You really know your stuff. But I gotta run. The judge is coming over here later and he's gonna be all kinds of pissed-off if I don't have his coffee going for him."

"Would it be okay if I take this dog to the vet?"

"I guess so. If his owner comes looking, I'll tell him you're over talking to Dr. C."

"You know Dr. Cassidy too?"

He opened the door to go back inside the building. "Heck, every single person in this town who has a dog or cat knows Dr. C. Be sure to say 'hi' to Tracy too. I miss talking to her. Since she's been hanging out with that geeky boyfriend of hers, she won't give me the time of day."

As the door closed, Brigid clipped the leash on the dog and breathed a small sigh of relief. Jake certainly did like to talk, and that was more than she needed to know about his amorous intentions. She ruffled the dog's ears and smiled as he soaked up the affection. "Ah, young love. Spring is in the air, isn't it?"

The dog whipped his scraggly brown tail back and forth in agreement.

~

After walking the dog around the neighborhood for a while, Brigid had decided to give him the name "Judge" for the time being, since "hey you" wasn't particularly effective. She also was pretty sure Judge had some type of serious skin problem, so taking him to the vet was probably a good idea. The dog's skin and coat were, for lack of a better word, disgusting. He had bald spots all over his body and whatever was wrong with him was itchy, so he had scabs, sores, and scrapes from scratching. He also didn't smell particularly good, although that could have just been from wandering around lost.

Once Brigid got Judge settled back into his kennel and gave him fresh water, the dog looked far more relaxed. She asked to borrow the phone and then managed to convince Tracy to squeeze in an appointment for Judge with Dr. Cassidy at the end of the day.

After another relaxing afternoon of napping and occasional bursts of introspection, Brigid got ready to go back to the station. She gave Gypsy a hug, told her to behave herself, and went to pick up Judge for his appointment at the vet clinic. Not surprisingly, the dog was, once again, over-the-moon thrilled to see Brigid. Even if Judge wasn't the prettiest dog in the world, he was very sweet. He didn't know how awful-looking he was, and Brigid liked his enthusiasm. It was nice to feel appreciated for a change.

At the clinic, she opened the door and Judge leaped into the waiting area. An older woman with a cat carrier on her lap leaned away from the bounding bundle of canine energy with a look of horror on her face. As Brigid tried to get the dog under control, she smiled weakly at the woman. Tracy looked over the counter at Judge and said, "Wow, you weren't kidding." She pointed at the hallway. "Take him into exam room two. Dr. C will be right there."

Brigid sat on a bench in the exam room and convinced Judge to sit in front of her. She stroked the fur on his head— what little there was of it. There were pink patches of exposed skin all over his face and body, which gave him an odd mottled appearance. Judge bent over to chew on a back leg. Poor guy. It was like he had the worst case of eczema ever.

Dr. Cassidy walked into the room and gazed down at Judge. Running a hand through her curly brown hair, she sighed. "Hi, Brigid. I didn't expect to see you back here again so soon. Who is this?"

Brigid stood up and Judge leaped around her. As she bent to try to settle him back down, she said. "Well, he doesn't really have a name. He's a stray from the police station. I'm calling him Judge."

"Do they know you have this dog?"

Brigid straightened. "Oh yes. I told them I'd volunteer to walk and feed the dogs. And clean out the kennels too. Officer Reynolds cleared it with his boss. Then Judge came in and I knew he needed to see you." She waved her hand toward the dog. "I mean, look at him. What is wrong with his fur? He looks horrible."

Dr. Cassidy sat down on the bench and Judge scuttled up to greet her, wagging his whole body back and forth at the exciting new human. The vet snapped on some latex gloves and put her hands on both sides of his head, holding him still so she could take a closer look at his skin. Judge continued to wag the back half of his body happily, enjoying the attention. The veterinarian looked up at Brigid. "He has some type of mange. I need to do a skin scraping for verification, but given the symptoms he's presenting, I believe it's demodectic mange."

Brigid made a face. "I have no idea what that means. Is it contagious? My hair isn't all going to fall out is it? That would be just my luck. I try to help a dog and go bald."

Dr. C laughed and stood up. "No, transmission to humans is almost unheard of, so all that red hair should remain on your head."

"Well, that's a relief."

"This type of mange is caused by Demodex mites. Dogs all have small numbers of mites on their skin without it being an issue because their immune system keeps the mites from getting out of control. However, some dogs don't have the antibodies that defend against an infestation." Dr. Cassidy put her hand on Judge's shoulder. "That's what's going on with our friend here."

"The poor thing. He must be uncomfortable."

"I need to do a more thorough exam, but at first glance, other than the skin problem, he seems very healthy. Demodex usually affects puppies, old dogs, or dogs that are ill. Their immune systems aren't working at their usual capacity for some reason, which allows the Demodex mites to get a foothold and get out of control."

"Puppies get this?"

"They do if they're unlucky. Often when they are tiny, they get it from their mother during the window of time when their immune system isn't completely developed. The mites live in the dog's hair follicles and the rapid reproduction of the mites causes the follicles to become inflamed and the dog's fur falls out. This guy only looks to be about five or six months old. Being a stray probably didn't help his immune system either."

"Can other dogs get this from him? He's in one of the holding kennels now. What if another dog comes in?"

"As long as the other dog is healthy, it's probably not a problem." She grabbed a stainless-steel tool from the counter. "Hold him as still as you can for a minute. I just need to do a little scraping here. It won't hurt him."

Brigid followed the vet's instructions and watched as she performed the procedure and took the skin scraping over to the counter. She did something with a slide and bent over the microscope. "I thought so." She gestured to Brigid. "Take a look. There is evidence of Demodex mites and nymphs."

"Is it gruesome? I'm not much of a scientist. I practically flunked chemistry in high school."

"No, it's not particularly objectionable, but you can see that there's definitely something there."

Brigid looked through the eyepiece and saw little cone-shaped critters moving around. "Okay. I guess that's a thing. Eww." She pulled away from the microscope and looked down at Judge. "So you've got those icky things on you, huh?" The dog wagged in response and Brigid looked back at the vet. "What is the treatment for this?"

"A couple of treatment options exist, but because we don't know his breed make-up and you won't be there to monitor his reactions closely, I'd advise that we dip him. It's a somewhat unpleasant option because you'll have to dip him every week."

"What do you mean *dip?*"

"You give the dog a bath with a special shampoo and then apply the dip solution with a sponge. You need to wear gloves when you apply it, and you don't wash it off. The solution is designed to kill the mites, and you need to be very careful to measure and dilute it correctly since it's nasty stuff."

Brigid leaned back on the counter. "Wow, I'm not sure what to do. He's not my dog. I didn't think about it before, but am I legally allowed to have him treated? I have no idea."

"Technically he's not your responsibility. In this state, the stray holding period is three days. I'm surprised they let you bring him here today actually."

"I think Jake was a little disturbed when he saw the state of Judge's skin."

"I don't think I've met a dog named Judge before. That's an unusual name."

"I suppose. Jake said he was worried about getting coffee for a judge, and I have to call this dog something, so I named him Judge. I'm not sure Jake thought about the legality of me taking the dog. Mostly he was worried about the coffee. I only met the guy yesterday, but he doesn't really seem to be the sharpest tool in the shed."

Dr. Cassidy chuckled. "I've met Jake. For a while he was hanging around here drooling over Tracy, until she finally told him to get lost."

"Well, I guess that explains what he said about her." Brigid raised a hand in a Boy Scout oath sign. "Don't worry,

I promise I'll pay for this appointment. But what should I do about treating Judge?"

"Since he's here and we're closed now anyway, I'll show you what to do. Even just doing one treatment and giving him a bath with the medicated shampoo will help his sores and probably make him feel better as far as the itching."

Brigid smiled. "That would be great. If Judge's owner shows up to claim him, I can explain everything."

"I wouldn't count on that, but yes, that would be a good idea."

The two women worked together to bathe and dip Judge, who took the whole process with remarkably good humor, particularly considering how bad the dip solution smelled. Brigid was glad she was wearing thick rubber gloves. The stuff was just as noxious as the vet had warned.

While they were working on Judge in the bathtub, Brigid finally asked the question she had pondered earlier. "When I volunteered at animal shelters before, they had foster programs where people took in dogs temporarily. Is there anything like that here? If Judge isn't claimed, maybe I could foster him and try to find him a new home after his treatments are done."

"No, there's nothing like that here. You should set up a program."

"Me? I can't do that. I'm just visiting."

"Even in just one summer, you could do a lot of good for these homeless dogs. I can introduce you to some other people who might be willing to help. A few people have complained to me about the situation, but nothing has ever happened. You have a lot of ideas and experience from volunteering at other shelters. If you can get a foster program going, maybe someone else can take it over when you leave."

"Maybe."

"Or you could just move to Alpine Grove permanently." She grinned. "People do it all the time."

Brigid sponged some more dip solution onto Judge's leg. This was a lot of information to take in. "Okay, I'll think about what you said."

"In the meantime, let's get this guy cleaned up, so you can take him back for his dinner."

～

The next day, Brigid walked to the police station to tend to Judge in the morning and evening. No one had come forward to claim the dog and Jake had been unconcerned about the fact that the veterinarian had treated the dog. Mostly, he'd been pleased to hear that this type of mange wasn't contagious. Judge was thrilled to see Brigid and seemed somewhat less itchy, which was encouraging.

In a way, it was a relief to Brigid that she hadn't gotten in trouble for taking the dog to the vet, but it was also a little heartbreaking to find out that no one was looking for Judge. He was such a sweet dog and Dr. C had made it sound like it was unlikely anyone would ever claim him.

Brigid had volunteered at enough shelters to know that sometimes dogs with medical issues seemed to "get loose" when their former owners didn't want to deal with the problem. In two days, Judge's hold period would be up and he'd be shipped off somewhere. Sadly, Jake didn't seem as impressed by Brigid's idea of foster care as the veterinarian had been. It was something different and mostly he seemed confused by the concept.

The conversation with Jake had been somewhat aggravating and Brigid needed some time to decompress. Since she wasn't ready to go home yet, she turned down the main street of Alpine Grove to explore a little. She walked slowly and stopped to look in the window of a gift store. It had closed for the day, but she made a mental note to return, since the window display was filled with lots of pretty things she'd like to check out. At the sound of a whooping noise, she turned to look across the street.

It was the women from the grocery store again. Maria was dancing in front of Kat, gesturing wildly about something. Or maybe it was a dance move. It was hard to tell. Kat looked across the street and waved to Brigid.

Did small-town protocol dictate crossing the street to chat? Brigid wasn't sure, but she waved back and tried to look friendly. Maria said something to Kat, grabbed her hand, and dragged her across the street toward Brigid.

They walked up to her and Maria said, "Hey, I heard through the grapevine that you adopted that dog at the vet and you're going to adopt another one."

Brigid raised her eyebrows. "That's a serious grapevine."

"You have no idea," Kat said.

Maria put her hand on her hip. "Well, I work in that ad agency across the street there. And the man who owns the building—his name is Michael, and if you haven't seen any pretty men lately, I recommend you stop by and take a look. Anyway, he rents office space to another guy named Rob, who is Tracy's boyfriend."

"Tracy from the vet clinic?" Brigid asked. "So that means Rob is the geeky guy?"

"Yes he is! I'm impressed." Maria patted her arm. "You are already starting to be in the know. Anyway, that means I get all the vet dirt from Rob."

"You know, it sounds disgusting when you say it like that." Kat said. "She means she hears stories about what's going on at the vet clinic."

"So, two dogs in less than a week is really sort of over the top," Maria said. "I'm guessing there's a story there."

Brigid shook her head. "I did adopt Gypsy, but I haven't adopted the second dog. He's a stray down at the police station. I just took him to the vet."

"He's in one of the cages down there?" Kat said. "That's not good."

"I know. I decided to volunteer to help out." Brigid gestured toward the station. "I live really close by and I felt bad for those dogs stuck there all sad and alone. No one has claimed Judge and he has a skin condition that has to be treated. He's only got a couple of days left."

"That's nice of you to help out before they get sent away." Kat said.

Brigid glanced at Kat and grinned as an idea flashed into her mind. "I want to take you up on your offer of dog boarding."

"You want to board Gypsy already?" Kat said.

Maria raised her eyebrows. "Uh oh, I think I see where this is going."

Brigid wanted to jump up and down with excitement. "No, not Gypsy. Judge! The stray dog."

"The dog you just took to the vet because of a skin condition?" Kat looked dubious. "I don't think that's a good idea. The new kennels aren't built yet and the one space I have isn't exactly ideal for a sick dog."

"It's an ugly outbuilding that leans kinda funny," Maria said.

Kat shook her head. "I've got five dogs of my own and I have to think about them too. I'll be able to disinfect the new kennels, but they aren't done yet."

Brigid said, "The problem isn't contagious. It will be fine. Will you do it? It will just be for the two days you promised if I adopted Gypsy. I'll figure out something else after that."

"We're in the middle of construction," Kat said. "My place is kind of a mess right now, so I haven't taken any dogs in the last couple of weeks. Pouring concrete and dealing with plumbing and electrical stuff is more complicated than I thought it would be."

"Hey, that part is done," Maria said and turned to Brigid. "You might think that the word *construction* would imply sexy guys wearing hard hats with washboard abs, but let me assure you, it does not. I checked. It's more like creepy dudes with beer guts wearing grimy baseball caps."

"I just need a couple of days to find a better placement, so I'd like to use my free boarding," Brigid said evenly.

"You did promise," Maria shoved Kat's shoulder. "You always do this kind of thing."

"I know. My life would be a lot simpler if I just kept my mouth shut." Kat sighed. "Okay, fine. Bring him over when his hold period is up. I'll give you directions."

"Thank you!" Brigid really did jump and down this time. She clapped her hands. "It will be Sunday. I just need to get permission. This is so exciting. Judge is the sweetest, *sweetest* dog. You'll see."

"I guess I will," Kat said and then mumbled to Maria, "You realize Joel is going to kill me for this, right? Do you know how many people I turned away for Memorial Day weekend? We agreed to hold off on boarding any more dogs until after the major construction was done."

"Oh, he'll get over it." Maria waved toward Brigid. "So why are you wandering around here all by yourself? Everything is shut."

"The guy at the police department irritated me. I just wanted a little time alone I guess before going home. Gypsy is very sensitive to my moods," Brigid said.

"I'm alone too and that's why Kat and I are out here on the mean street of Alpine Grove. It's Friday and I need some action. So we're about to take this town, such as it is, by storm!" Maria opened her arms expansively. "It's time to get out there. Want to come with us?"

Kat added in a mocking voice, "Yeah baby, we're on fire here on this single, solitary mean street. You'd better watch out for us."

Brigid couldn't help but smile. "Okay. Where are you going?"

Maria's pointed down the street, "Well, you've got your choice of two dive bars. After careful consideration, we've opted for the Soloan, rather than the 311."

"We flipped a coin," Kat said.

Brigid looked in the direction Maria had pointed. "The Soloan? That's an odd name for a bar, isn't it?"

"Actually it's the Mystic Moon Soloan, which sounds more poetic than the place actually is," Maria said.

"It's not poetic at all, and it offends my writerly sensibilities," Kat said. "A long time ago, a couple of drunk guys put up the sign and failed to spell *saloon* correctly. No one ever fixed it."

Brigid said, "Are you kidding? That's hilarious."

"Actually, it's lame," Maria said. "But it's a bar, so we're going because my social life has reached an all-time low. Oh, and just to warn you, the bartender is missing teeth. I try not to hold that against Fred, but it disturbs me. Dental hygiene is important, you know."

"Huh, that's the second man I've heard about here with dental problems." Brigid said.

"Yeah, don't remind me. I don't wanna talk about it. It's not like there aren't dentists here." Maria took Kat's and Brigid's arms in hers and began strutting down the street. "Let's hit it, ladies. Happy hour awaits!"

They crossed the street in front of the bar, which truly did have the name spelled wrong on the sign. Somebody probably got in big trouble for that way back when. They opened the door and Brigid looked around the dimly lit area. Lots of mirrored signs advertised a wide range of beers and the neon beer sign above the bar seemed to have some sort of problem that caused it to flicker erratically. A few people were standing around pool tables in the back of the room, leaning on their pool cues and looking irked at one another.

Maria gestured toward the bar with a flourish. "Welcome to Alpine Grove night life."

Brigid walked up to one of the bar stools and tried to smile politely at the huge bartender. With his leather vest and bandanna, he looked like he was ready to jump on his motorcycle and ride off into the sunset. As Maria and Kat settled into their bar stools, he put a napkin in front of each of them and said, "What can I get you?"

Given John's drinking habits, Brigid had always been the designated driver and she hadn't been out since he died. She glanced at Maria and Kat.

Kat said, "Just a club soda. I've got to drive home later."

"I'm walking." Maria said, "What's the most complicated drink you can make, Fred? I wanna see what you can do."

"Maria's still proud of her Queen's Park Swizzle," Kat said.

"Yeah, top that!" Maria said.

Fred grinned, revealing the gap in his teeth, and Brigid was glad she'd been warned. Alfred E. Neuman of *Mad* magazine fame had nothing on Fred. The bartender gestured dismissively at the row of bottles, "Oh c'mon—that's child's play. Let me think for a sec." He turned to Brigid. "What can I get you?"

"Well, I'm walking too, and I don't know what a Queen's Park Swizzle is." Brigid looked past Maria to Kat. "Do you have any suggestions?"

"Well one time Maria made me an iced tea that was great," Kat said. "Mmm."

"That's a *Long Island* iced tea, Fred," Maria said.

"Gotcha. I kinda figured that," he said as he reached for a bottle of liquor.

"So, you need to wow me with some mixology here. What can you do?" Maria said.

"Well, if you're into layered drinks, how about a B-52?" He pointed at the bottle of Bailey's behind the bar.

"Okay, not bad." Maria gestured toward the bottles. "Show me your stuff while I try to get the lyrics to 'Rock Lobster' outta my head."

"It's better than 'Love Shack,' baby," he said as he poured the Grand Marnier on the top of the liquids in the glass and handed it to her.

Maria cringed as she took the glass. "Oh noooo...that was just cruel."

Brigid smiled as Maria commented on Fred's bartending technique while he poured drinks for other people. The woman was really pulling out all the stops, flirting wildly with the guy, which he seemed to appreciate and reciprocate. Maria had warned them she was on the prowl, but for Brigid it was impossible to imagine even wanting to get a man's attention like that anymore.

After John died, she'd sworn off men for good. Some people were good at romantic relationships, but Brigid had ample proof that she wasn't one of them. At first, it was kind of worrisome to discover that she had zero interest in meeting anyone. For a while, she was afraid there might be something wrong with her. But now, after all this time, she was more than fine with her single status. Life was a lot simpler when you didn't have to worry about someone else. Well, except for Gypsy, but she wasn't particularly demanding and she was *always* glad to see her.

Although Brigid would never say it out loud to anyone, even after such a short time the sweet little dog was a whole lot easier to love than John ever had been.

Brigid looked down the bar at Kat, who seemed to be quietly amused by Maria's exuberant coquettish behavior. Kat's long dark hair fell around her face as she sipped her club soda and methodically folded her straw wrapper into a tiny square, and then unfolded the accordion. Brigid wondered what Kat was thinking and if she should go talk to the woman. There was no doubt Kat had been annoyed with her earlier. Now she was obviously a little bored, but resigned to wait out the evening to make sure her friend made it home okay.

Brigid hadn't had a best friend like that since high school. Moving around a lot wasn't good for establishing deep friendships. She'd made a lot of acquaintances, but no good friends. After John died, people seemed to shy away because they didn't know what to say to her, which was fine, since she mostly just wanted to be left alone.

Fred walked toward her end of the bar and raised his hand in greeting, "Clayton! Thanks for stopping by. How's my horse?"

Brigid looked to her right and found Clayton Hadley leaning against the bar. He was wearing a beat-up old leather jacket, a white t-shirt, and faded jeans. He transferred his hat to his other hand, reached into his pocket and pulled out a piece of paper that he handed to Fred. "That horse may be getting up in years, but he's still a sweetheart. And his hooves are all trimmed up nice and pretty now. I'm not sure your poodle is too fond of me though. He barked his head off."

"Yeah, Charlie likes to defend the ole homestead. Sorry about that. Let me get you the check. Want a beer?" Fred said. "On the house."

"I don't think I can say no to free beer." Clay set his hat on the bar, took off his jacket, and sat down next to Brigid, giving her a cordial smile. "Hi again. How's your little dog doing?"

"Gypsy is doing very well. Thank you for asking." Brigid noticed the scar on his chin again and another long scar that stood out on his tanned forearm. Maybe that had happened when he fell off the horse and knocked out his teeth. Riding a 1200-pound animal had to be dangerous. The whole thing about getting back up on a horse after you fell off had always struck her as idiotic. If a horse didn't want her on its back, she'd take the hint and stay off.

The whole male tough-guy thing caused men to do unbelievably stupid things. She'd seen plenty of testosterone poisoning among the military men she'd met. Maybe it was true of the rodeo crowd too. Half of them intentionally got on animals just so they could be thrown off. How dumb was that?

Fred returned with a pilsner glass full of beer and placed it on the bar in front of Clay. "Here you go."

Clay thanked the bartender, took a sip of the beer, and shook some foam off his hand. He put down the glass and said, "Are you enjoying your stay in Alpine Grove?"

Dragged back from her surly thoughts about the male of the species, Brigid looked down at her iced tea. Clay was trying to be polite, but she wasn't in the mood to talk. "It's pretty here. I haven't really seen the sights yet though. I've only done a little bit of exploring. Mostly, I've just been here in town."

"The Soloan isn't one of our prettiest sights."

The deadpan look on his face was priceless, and Brigid laughed in spite of herself. The sound was so unfamiliar that it seemed to echo in her head like a sharp bark. How embarrassing. She clapped her hand over her mouth and then dropped it again quickly. Good thing it was so dark in here because she had to be blushing like an idiot. "No, I suppose it's not. I haven't been to a bar in a long time, but I'm pretty sure the last one didn't look like this." She took another sip of her tea and gestured toward the women seated next to her. "I met Maria and Kat and they invited me to join them for happy hour."

Clay tilted his glass slightly toward Maria. "Well, one of them looks happy anyway."

Peering around Kat, Maria waved at them enthusiastically. "*Outstanding*! Check it out. Indiana Jones is here. Hi Indy!"

Clay looked momentarily confused, but nodded slightly at Maria.

Brigid smiled. "Maybe it's the hat."

"I suppose. Did you get any good books the other day?"

Brigid sipped her drink as a stalling tactic. Talking to someone you had nothing in common with was hard and she was out of practice. But no matter how pathetic she was at this, there was no way she was going to mention all the self-help books she'd purchased. "I wanted to learn a bit more about dog training and Margaret recommended some books. What book did you pick up?"

"It's not the type of book I normally read." He looked down at his glass. "I mean, it's kind of a romance. But a bunch of people said I should check it out, so Margaret set a copy aside for me."

"That's quite a few disclaimers. What's the title?"

"It was some best-seller last year called *The Horse Whisperer*. There's talk that it will be turned into a movie."

Brigid lifted her drink at him in a mock toast. The combination of realizing that he was just as uncomfortable as she was, along with the Long Island iced tea, were helping her relax. "So the horse guy has to read the horse book?"

"Something like that."

"Did you like it?"

"I liked some aspects of it."

"You liked the horse, didn't you?"

With a slightly sheepish look, he nodded.

At his expression, Brigid laughed again. It sounded more normal this time, which was a relief. "I understand. When I was a kid, someone told me I should check out *Old Yeller* because it was a dog book. Fortunately, I asked the librarian about it first. After she told me the story, I vowed never to read it."

"I had to read it in school, but I didn't like the ending too much."

"See! Everyone says that. There's no way I'm *ever* reading it." Brigid sucked on her straw and peered over the glass at him. "Life is hard enough. I'll stick to happy books, thanks."

"I can't say I disagree."

Brigid tried to think of something to say as she sucked down the last of her drink. She should just go home. Why was she even talking to this guy? She sat up straight and looked around, trying to figure how she could best extricate herself.

Clay pointed at the glass. "Do you want another one? You're not driving, are you? Margaret said you live nearby."

Brigid looked at him and then at his beer glass, which was still three-quarters full. It would probably be rude to say no and just leave in the middle of a conversation. "I walked here. The Long Island iced tea was very good, but I should probably go. I have to get up early and walk a dog."

"I guess that little dog is an early riser, huh?"

"Oh no, not Gypsy. She's happy to just hang out and wander in and out through the doggie door. I am volunteering at the pound."

"Really? That's a kind thing to do, particularly since you're on vacation."

"I'm not very good at just sitting around." She sucked on her straw again, even though the glass was empty. "The dog who's there now—Judge—he's so happy to see me. It just melts my heart."

"You sure you don't want another? I'm buying."

Brigid hesitated. She should say no, but something about the timbre of Clay's low voice was soothing and he was obviously trying to be nice. What the heck? Like he said, she was on vacation and Gypsy was probably just snoring away at the house anyway. "Well, okay. Thank you."

Clay waved to Fred and ordered the drink. He looked at her. "So tell me about Judge. That's an interesting name for a dog."

"Well, it's not really his name. Or I don't know—I named him. So far, his owners haven't claimed him, and I'm not sure what's going to happen to him. I guess they ship dogs off to other facilities after their holding period is up."

"Yeah, I've heard that."

"But Judge has a skin condition. I took him to the vet and found out it's treatable. But he looks terrible right now.

It's so sad—he's such a sweet dog. And he doesn't know he's hideous."

"Has he got mange or something?"

Brigid slapped her hand on the bar. "Yes, that's it exactly! It's some type that isn't contagious, I guess. Dr. Cassidy assured me I won't go bald and other dogs shouldn't get it either."

"I'm glad to hear it." He smiled. "It would be a shame to have all that pretty red hair fall out."

"I'm worried about Judge and I'm thinking about fostering him after his hold period. I'm not sure they'll let me though." She turned to look up at Fred, who handed her another tall glass full of alcohol tea. She took a long sip from the straw. This stuff was potent. Maybe she shouldn't have gotten a second one. She really needed to be quiet. Why was she telling Clay all this?

"Why wouldn't they let you take the dog?"

"I don't know. The guy I talked to seemed confused by the idea."

"Find out if it costs them money to ship the dogs."

"Maybe." Brigid sat up straight and looked into his eyes. "Wait, that's brilliant! If a foster program saves them money, why *wouldn't* they do it?"

"I can't think of any reason. But I'm not a cop."

"Assuming I can get Judge released, I have a place for him for two days. But it's really temporary." Brigid slumped back down. "I'm honestly not sure how it could work. The place I'm renting is just beautiful. Everything is new and for Gypsy it is fine. She's small, healthy, and well behaved. But Judge, well, he has these sores and he kind of bled all over my Honda when I took him to the vet. It was nasty. I don't care about my car because it's old and crummy. But I really shouldn't take him to the house, since it's not mine. And what will happen when they get the next stray dog? I'd need to find more foster homes because the strays are only held for a short time."

Fred walked up and pointed at Clay's glass. "Are you gonna want another one?"

Clay shook his head at Fred. "No thanks." He turned to Brigid. "Can't you find some place else to put the dogs?"

"Where? Most towns have an actual animal shelter for strays. I think I found the only person in the area who actually has a dog kennel. It's not like people have that kind of thing just lying around."

Fred gestured toward Clay. "Well, you've got that huge empty barn and all those rolls of fencing that aren't doing anything."

Brigid looked at Fred and her eyes widened. "I never thought of a barn. That's a wonderful idea."

"It's for cows," Clay said.

"You don't have cows anymore, and you said you never want to see another one. I believe it was something along the lines of you'd have to be an idiot to run cattle again." Fred shrugged. "Do you think a dog would care that cows used to live in that barn?"

Brigid looked at Clay. "Do you really have a completely empty barn? How far away is it? I could come over every day and take care of the dogs in the barn. It would only be temporary until I find them foster families. But then I could get them out of that horrible police station and they wouldn't go off to…well, wherever they go, which no one wants to talk about. But I'm guessing it's bad."

Clay made a face. "Well, I sure wouldn't want to get sent there."

Fred nodded. "C'mon, man. That barn is just sitting there. You've got plenty of space for the horses and that whole other open shed for hay storage. You're not using the cattle barn for anything anymore."

As Fred moved down the bar to check on Maria, Brigid turned to Clay, "Please, could you help? Judge's time is running out."

"All right. But it's temporary. That barn isn't set up for housing dogs and it's not exactly empty. It's a mess and would take some work to set something up." Clay grabbed his glass, drained his beer, and set the glass down on the bar with a thump.

"But it's big enough and you have fencing, right? I'll help! I've got a little reprieve since Judge will be at Kat's place for a couple days. And I'll also work on finding Judge a foster home or maybe even get him adopted. Dr. C said she knows people who want to help the dogs." She drummed her palms on the bar in excitement. "This is going to be such a good thing. I just know it."

Clay put his hand over hers to still the drumming and Brigid jerked her hand into her lap in surprise. He said, "I should go. Are you going to be okay getting home?"

"I'll be fine. I came here with Kat and Maria and like I said, I live nearby."

"Okay, good. Let me give you my number and directions out to the ranch. We can meet and you can see what you're dealing with. You might change your mind once you see it. I'm there pretty much every day working. Just give me a call and let me know when you want to come out."

Brigid nodded mutely and looked into his dark eyes. In the light of the neon bar sign, the topaz flecks flashed in his eyes in an oddly compelling way. What had she just gotten herself into?

~

The next day, Brigid set up a meeting with the police chief to talk about Judge. She was determined to get the dog out of there before he was shipped off to points unknown. It really bugged her that no one ever said where or what the place was. After hearing about it repeatedly, she was afraid to ask.

She went to the police station and greeted Jake, who told her to head back to the chief's office. Even though the chief's desk was huge, Kirby Russell was a large man who took up a lot of real estate behind its expansive mahogany surface. It was a beautiful desk, unlike the standard ugly beige metal desks found in municipal buildings everywhere. He stood up and held out his hand. "You must be Brigid."

"It's very nice to meet you. I appreciate you taking the time to talk to me about the dogs."

He gestured for her to sit. "Well, you're doing us a favor by helping out. What can I do for you today?"

"I'd like to see about setting up a foster program after a dog's holding period is up."

He folded his hands on the desk. "I'm not sure what you mean."

Brigid had relived her conversation with Jake the day before so many times in her head that she knew exactly how to describe what she wanted to do. "Well, I have lived in a lot of places because my husband was in the military. Many shelters have what they call a foster program to help homeless animals find new homes. After the stray holding period is up, the dogs are taken in by volunteers on a temporary basis until the dog can be placed in a permanent adoptive home. I'd like to put the dog you have now into foster care."

"That animal is scheduled for transport."

"I know. Does sending the dogs away incur costs? Because what I'm suggesting would cost the town of Alpine Grove absolutely nothing. It's all done on a completely volunteer basis. I have arrangements made for this dog now. All you have to do is say yes."

Chief Russell leaned back in his chair and put his folded hands on his stomach. "Well, you make a compelling argument. Transport and the agreement we have in place does have budgetary implications."

"We can try this with the dog that's here now if no one claims him. I believe this is his last day. I can pick him up tomorrow morning, and if my foster idea doesn't work, I'll figure something else out or adopt him myself. There's no risk to you. But if this test goes the way I hope it will, I'd like to continue to take new dogs that come in and put them in foster care when their holding period is up. If no one claims them, these dogs deserve a chance to find new homes."

The chief put his hands back on the desk. "All right. We'll give this a shot. The timing is good since Monday is a holiday, and it would be good to have that dog gone to free-up space, just in case. I don't know why, but dogs always come in on holidays. I'm going to need you to fill out some transfer forms for this animal before you take him."

Brigid smiled. "I'd be happy to do that. Thank you so much! You are doing a wonderful thing for these dogs. I'm sure of it."

Chief Russell seemed to warm to her enthusiasm. "Well, the truth is I've got a couple dogs of my own. I'm glad to see you doing this, and I honestly hope you can make it work."

Brigid stood up and held out her hand. "I'll do my best."

The next morning, Brigid arrived precisely at eight to pick up Judge. She couldn't stop smiling as she signed the forms and loaded him into the back-seat of her car. It seemed like a miracle that everything was working out. For the first time in a long time, she'd done something really important and useful.

The sense of excitement made her feel like she'd had too much coffee in a way, but without the jitters. Judge seemed glad to be away from the pound. He poked his nose out the window, seemingly excited to be headed off to new places with new scents to sniff.

Kat's place was quite a ways north of Alpine Grove, or "out in the sticks," as she'd put it. Thank goodness Brigid didn't have to go out there every day. While Judge was being boarded, she'd have time to work on getting everything set up at Clay's ranch. Although Brigid was a little apprehensive about working with someone she barely knew, it was for a good cause. He seemed nice enough anyway. She smiled at Judge's reflection in the rear view mirror. What an incredibly happy dog. For someone without a job, Brigid certainly was keeping herself busy. Her mom always used to say, "Better busy than bored." It was true. Bored she definitely was not.

After driving what seemed like a long way through acres upon acres of forest, Brigid turned down a driveway that was covered with a thick layer of light-gray gravel. The long driveway snaked through the huge trees and at one point, Brigid wasn't sure she was in the right place. The dog was sniffing furiously behind her, deeply absorbed in the fragrance of so many evergreens. "Sorry Judge, I might have turned down the wrong driveway. I hope I didn't get us lost." But as she looked ahead, she saw a collection of old pick-up trucks off to one side, where the driveway seemed to fork. Kat had told her to continue straight toward the house.

Brigid looked over her shoulder at the dog. "Okay, it looks like I didn't take a wrong turn, after all. We're here!" She parked under a large tree near an outbuilding. Maria had been right. It did sort of list a little bit to one side. Oh well, it was just for two days.

The front door of the log house opened and with a wave, Kat walked down the steps toward Brigid's car. As Brigid got out, Kat was peering into the back window. She gestured toward Judge. "That's one hairless dog."

Brigid opened the back door and clipped the leash onto the new red buckle collar she had purchased for Judge. She'd even gotten a temporary ID tag and written her phone number on it with permanent marker. Judge leaped out and began sniffing the air. Brigid pulled him a bit closer in an effort to contain his exuberance. The light breeze was incredibly earthy, filled with the scents of pine and forest debris. To a dog, it was probably an outrageous olfactory experience. "I think the dip helped him. You wouldn't know it, but I think he does look a little better."

"I read up on demodectic mange and it takes a while to treat, I guess," Kat said, taking the leash from Brigid.

"Thank you again for taking him." Brigid looked back down the driveway toward the collection of pickup trucks. A tall man was walking toward them. She gestured toward the trucks. "I see what you mean about the construction. That's quite a group you've got assembled over there."

"I know. And I've discovered there's a wide range of motivation among people who work construction." Kat smiled at the man as he walked up to them. "Brigid, this is Joel. He lives here too."

"You must be the engineer Maria mentioned," Brigid said. In his beat-up jeans and thrashed t-shirt, at the moment he didn't look much like an engineer. Mostly he looked grumpy, so Brigid went for her most ingratiating smile. "I've heard a lot about you."

Although he smiled, it seemed forced and the look in his forest-green eyes remained serious. "I hate to think what Maria said. Don't worry though. We'll take good care of your dog." His gaze shifted to Kat. "I need to talk to you when you get a second." He raised his gloved hands. "I'm going inside to wash up. It was nice to meet you."

Kat and Brigid watched him for a moment as he strolled off toward the house. Brigid said, "I guess he's helping with the construction?"

"Yes, although I think working two jobs is starting to get to him. I'm sorry if he was a little short with you."

"No problem. I was married for quite a while. I'm well aware of the unpredictable nature of the male psyche."

Kat laughed. "I'm glad to hear it. Men always say *women* are hard to understand. Give me a break. They have no idea what we deal with!"

~

After Brigid left, Kat took Judge for a walk around the forest and settled him into the outbuilding, which she referred to as the Tessa Hut because her golden retriever Tessa had stayed there when Kat inherited the house from her great aunt. Although the outbuilding was old, the kennel inside was secure and a number of dogs had stayed there without any problem. Compared to the kennels at the police station, it was undoubtedly a big step up in accommodations.

Judge had done so much sniffing on the walk that he was practically hyperventilating. Apparently, that level of intense nasal activity took a lot of energy because Judge was significantly more subdued by the time they returned. After taking a long drink of water, the dog seemed ready to settle in for his morning nap.

Kat walked up the steps to the house and was greeted by the sounds of loud barking from her own dogs. She went inside and looked down the stairs at the dogs. They were in the hallway behind a gate at the bottom of the steps to the daylight basement. Five tails wagged at her as she encouraged them to be quiet. Joel was in the kitchen leaning against the counter eating a sandwich. He raised a hand in greeting and continued chewing.

She walked over to him and looked up at his face. "You said you needed to talk to me? What's up?"

Putting the sandwich down on the plate with a sigh, he said, "You aren't going to like this."

"More delays?"

"Remember how we only got a partial order of the block?"

"Yes."

"It still hasn't turned up. I'd like to send everyone home."

Kat pressed her hands together and tried not to jump up and down with glee. "You mean we'd be *alone?* With time to ourselves? Just us?"

"Exactly. Well, except for the extra dog with the bad fur."

"He's no trouble at all. Just a little stinky. I'm looking forward to a vacation from the sound of rusty old diesel pickups in my driveway."

Joel wrapped his arms around her. "I'm looking forward to a few days of seeing only you."

Kat leaned her head on his chest. "Me too. I'm a little tired of the rest of the world."

With a final squeeze, he released her from the hug. "There is one more thing though. You need to pull more money out. The next payment is due on Tuesday."

"Are you kidding? I just did that."

"Sorry. You wanted to add all that plumbing so you could wash dogs in the second building."

"This is getting so expensive. I think I need another antacid."

He bent to kiss her. "I'm going to give everyone the bad news that they're laid off until the blocks are off back order. Then maybe I'll actually try to get some programming done. I'm unbelievably behind on that project."

"That reminds me. The Las Vegas folks called for you. I left a note on your desk."

Joel snapped, "What? Why didn't you tell me before?" He glanced at Kat and rubbed his eyes with his fingertips. "I'm sorry. I need to call them, since they're probably wondering where their software is. My friend John is going to regret ever recommending me for this contract."

"You've been doing a great job for them for months. They have nothing to complain about."

"That's nice of you to say, even if it isn't true." He gave her a peck on the lips and put his plate in the sink. "See you later."

After Joel left the house to return to the construction mess, Kat went to the bathroom, took her antacid, and returned to the kitchen to make herself a cup of chamomile tea. Once she was armed with a relaxing herbal beverage, she took her mug and went downstairs to her office to face on her latest freelance article. Given the delays and additional construction costs, she needed to make as much money as possible as soon as possible. After sending an email to her editor asking about her next writing assignment, she felt a little better although her stomach was still letting her know she was anxious about more than just money. She was worried about Joel.

After almost a year of living together, Kat had come to rely on Joel's calm, quiet nature. To have him be so irritable about even little stuff was jarring.

The worst part was that she couldn't help with most of the things he had to do. It wasn't as if she could program software for him. And her construction experience was pretty much zero as well. He justifiably didn't really trust the guys working on the new kennels enough to just leave them alone out there. In fact, he had suspected that someone might have stolen some of his tools, which really infuriated him.

They'd even had to fire one guy who had kept pitting Joel against her, which had led to some touchy conversations over dinner at the end of the day. After they compared notes, it turned out Leon had been playing some type of bizarre mind game with them.

Leon would complain to Joel that Kat wouldn't make a decision or they couldn't move forward because of some problem related to a choice she'd made. Even worse was that when Leon didn't like her answer to a question, he'd turn around and ask Joel, hoping to get a different reply that would make his job easier. The guy practically defined lazy.

After they'd figured out what was going on, they met with Leon and fired him together. Kat had never sent anyone to the unemployment line before and it had been awful. Sure Leon was a jerk, but the whole experience definitely showed that she and Joel needed to work as a team on this project. She'd read that parents needed to present a united front to their kids. Apparently, the advice went double for guys who worked construction.

After weeks of dealing with mud, culverts, driveway rock, concrete, and countless contractors, Kat just wanted everything to finally be done. But trying to rush finishing it probably would just increase their stress level.

When Joel came back inside, she'd talk to him and see what he thought. The kennel construction was a long way from finished and his stress level wasn't going to get any better unless something changed.

Later, Kat was working on her article when Linus came over and thumped his huge brown canine muzzle on her thigh. He tilted his head up slightly, gave her an imploring gaze, and wagged his tail. Kat ruffled one of his big ears. "You want to go outside?"

The dog leaped backwards to show his support for the idea as the other dogs came into the office and crowded around to make sure Linus had successfully alerted the human about the need for their afternoon walk.

The front door opened and Kat could hear Joel stomping around upstairs before coming down the steps to the walk-out basement where their offices were located. A few minutes later, he appeared in the doorway, surveying the milling canines around her desk. "I guess it's walk time?"

"Linus was nominated to let me know." With a thud, Kat put down the user guide she'd been looking at on a stack of other books. "Is everyone gone?"

"They all left, and my old hammer magically appeared. It was just sitting there on a half-built wall. I think the person who ripped it off thought better of the idea after we canned Leon."

Kat paused in her book rearranging. "Well, that's good. You were pretty upset."

"Those tools are practically the only thing I have left of my father's. It's probably sentimental and stupid, but I've built a lot of things with that old hammer."

Kat got up and gave him a hug. "I know, and I don't think that's stupid at all. I'm glad it turned up." She leaned back to look up at him. "And even more glad we canned Leon. Want to go for a walk with us?"

"Okay. I could use some forest time."

They leashed the dogs and went out the back door to the trail into the woods. Kat held Chelsey's leash in one hand and Joel's hand with the other. Lady the collie mix and Lori the border collie chased each other, circling around Linus and Tessa, who were attached to each other using a harness and leash arrangement. Linus acted as the "boat anchor" to keep Tessa from running off after something, since the boisterous golden retriever had the attention span of a fruit fly.

The sun was shining and Kat could feel her muscles relax as they meandered along the sun-dappled trail through the tall evergreens. She squeezed Joel's hand. "I need to talk to you."

He glanced down at her. "You're not going to tell me something bad, are you? I'm really not in the mood."

"I know. That's what I want to talk about. Having all these people here working all day, every day. It's too much."

"Too much what?"

"Too much everything. Too much work for you. Too much noise and humanity for me. I think we need to look at the schedule again. Maybe slow it down."

He stopped and turned to face her. "But we talked about this. The faster the kennel gets built, the sooner you can take dogs and start making money. People keep calling. It's not like you're going to have a shortage of clients."

"I know. But making ourselves miserable isn't worth it. As long as the kennel is done before it snows, I'll be happy."

He smiled. "It's May. I think that's doable."

"Maybe we could take this week off, so you can get caught up with other stuff. Monday is a holiday anyway. I feel bad that you've been roped into becoming a full-time general contractor."

"Well, I did agree to do it."

"I know. But I think we underestimated how much work it would be for you."

"Probably."

Kat squeezed his hand again. "I don't want you to be unhappy. I love you and I miss having you across the hall doing whatever nerdy things you do on your computer."

"I love you back. Let's go home and figure out a way to make this work."

Chapter 3

The V Bar H

The next morning after tending to Gypsy, Brigid called
Clay to let him know she was heading out to his place.
The ranch was close to Alpine Grove, located north of town
off the highway past the Kmart. Clay said it would probably
take her about fifteen minutes at the most to get there, which
was a relief after taking the long trek out to Kat's place.

Brigid turned on V Bar H Ranch Road, which was a
long gravel road that traversed rolling meadows that were
almost an electric green with yellow wild buttercups dotting
the landscape. The road wound around through a heavily
wooded area and then opened out into a clearing where a
house and a number of outbuildings sat near a pasture lined
with white wooden fencing. Several horses grazed in the field,
giving the place a picturesque, bucolic feel. The scene looked
like a picture on the cover of an equine magazine.

The house was a two-story farmhouse with reddish cedar
siding and a wrap-around wood porch. Behind it rose a huge
red gambrel-style barn that had to be at least three-stories
high. White lettering above the huge sliding doors said *V - H.*
Clay was walking a horse toward a single-story red barn that
had a large opening on one end.

Brigid parked in front of the house and waved at Clay as
he walked back toward her from the barn, having apparently
stowed the horse inside somewhere. As she got out, he walked

up to her car, took off his hat, and rubbed his hair with his hand. He put the hat back on and said, "Welcome to the V Bar H ranch."

"I've never been to a ranch before. It certainly does look the part. This is like something out of a movie set."

"Not the sets I was on." He shrugged, "It's not much of a ranch either. When I was growing up, we ran 250 to 300 head of cattle."

"Do you own all the land up to the highway?"

"Not anymore." He gestured toward the pasture where the horses were grazing. "This is pretty much it now. I've got sixty acres. It used to be four sections, but my father sold off the other two thousand acres, and this is what's left."

"Sixty acres seems like a lot of land to me."

"It's enough."

"So who owns the rest of it now?"

"As it turns out, where our cattle used to graze is an important wildlife corridor, so a conservation organization came knocking. Now it's part of a habitat-preservation deal for some bird."

"Well, at least it won't be subdivided or turned into condos."

"That's kind of unlikely for Alpine Grove. But since it's off the highway, they'd probably build an ugly big box store like the Kmart or a fast-food joint. So yeah, I'm happy the land is going to remain the way it has been forever." He gestured toward the barn with the gambrel roof. "That's the barn I'm not really using anymore. I tried to clean out some of the junk this morning, but it's still a mess. I'm not sure you're going to want to deal with it."

"I'm sure it will be great. I've had lots of practice cleaning from moving many times."

"I hope you don't like those clothes because cleaning out a barn isn't like cleaning a house. If it's greasy, grimy or smells bad, it's probably in there."

Brigid looked down at what she was wearing. "That's okay. These jeans are old anyway."

They walked out of the sun and into the barn, which even in the dim light Brigid could tell was enormous. When she drove up, she hadn't realized exactly how big it truly was. She tilted her head to look up at the loft. "Does hay go up there?"

"Not anymore. It's in that open building back behind the horse barn. After the cows were sold off, I didn't have to use the loft anymore. As you might imagine, hay is easier to deal with when you don't have to move it up and down. I don't miss that."

"Well, there's certainly enough space. You could fit ninety-five kennels in here."

"How about we start with one?" He pointed toward the far wall. "I looked around and found some old gates"

Brigid peered into the dim space, where a number of large, complicated rusty-looking machines were lined up. "You certainly have a lot of equipment."

"I've still got enough pasture to do a little haying in the summer." He smiled. "And I don't think anyone else could fix those old things at this point."

"So where do we start?"

"I was thinking we could clean out this corner near the front door here and set up a kennel for the dog you have now." He pointed at a huge pile of wood. "But we need to move that over back behind the equipment."

Brigid walked over to get a closer look. She bent to pick up a log and startled a large black spider that went scurrying into the darkness under the woodpile. Dropping the log, she made a shooing motion with her hands. "Do you have gloves?"

"Over here." He walked toward a door and indicated she should follow him. "This is the work room. If you need tools or gloves, they're probably in here or in the tack room. That's in the other barn with the horses."

After Brigid had donned some oversized leather gloves, Clay went over to an ancient tractor, climbed up, and started it. The machine coughed out a plume of diesel exhaust, rumbled, and snorted a few times.

Brigid waved her hand in front of her face. "Ugh, that's horrible."

"I'll move it outside and it will clear out in a minute," Clay shouted over the noise of the tractor. "If we throw the wood into the front loader, it's a heck of a lot easier to use the tractor to move it to the back of the barn than to walk it over there yourself."

"I suppose so."

With a roar of the engine, Clay drove the tractor outside and turned it around to face the door. In the light, Brigid could tell the machine had been green once. Now it was green and rust-colored with a thick coating of grayish-brown dirt. Clay parked it and turned it off. With a final snort, the tractor sat in grumpy silence again.

"Are all farmers deaf?" Brigid said.

Clay yanked something out of his ear and held it up for her to see. "Earplugs."

They worked together throwing logs from the pile into the tractor's front loader. Many trips later, the pile of wood had been relocated and Brigid's arms felt like they were made of Jell-O.

Clay handed her a rake. "Here. See if you can clear out any, well, whatever's there while I go get the fence. I have some three-quarter-inch rock that we can throw into that space."

Brigid wasn't sure about the rock, but she raked the dirt, clearing away various bits of wood and probably disrupting lots of well-established spider homesteads. She was completely exhausted and ready for a nap and yet Clay seemed utterly unfazed, which was irritating. Didn't the guy ever rest? There was no way she was going to let him see how tired she was.

As Clay pounded posts into the dirt with a tube-like contraption, Brigid backed away from the loud clanging sound. He wasn't kidding about earplugs. What a horrendous noise.

He disappeared with the tractor and came back with a load of gravel, which he dumped into the area. Then he stretched the fencing around the posts and attached one of the old gates.

Brigid gazed at the new enclosure, then at Clay, who still seemed to have barely exerted himself. How could he not be tired?

He gestured toward the gate. "Ta-da! It's a kennel."

"Isn't rock going to be uncomfortable?"

"It's better than dirt as far as keeping it clean. This is drain rock, so, well, that means it drains. You said Judge is getting baths, so he'll be wet. This way, he won't turn into a ball of mud."

Brigid smiled. "Good point. So is it really all ready for him to come out here tomorrow?"

"Yup. Mission accomplished. You look like you could use a drink of water. Do you want to come inside for a minute? My dog probably wants out by now."

Brigid pulled off her gloves. "I wouldn't mind washing my hands too."

They walked toward the house where behind the glass door a pretty yellowish dog with goofy ears was bouncing happily. Clay opened the door and the dog whooshed by them out into the yard.

Brigid said, "Is it okay for him to be out loose like that?"

"It's fine. He won't go anywhere. Scout needs to go check on his cats."

"His cats?"

"There are some barn cats that live here and he thinks they're his responsibility. Scout plays with them and herds them sometimes."

"I didn't see any cats."

"They're really shy. After they showed up, I trapped them and got them fixed. They aren't too excited about people, but they are best buddies with Scout."

Brigid washed her hands at the kitchen sink and took the glass of water Clay handed to her. He gestured toward the table inviting her to sit down. She tried not to sigh audibly with relief as she settled into the old wooden chair.

Clay sat across from her. "So have you spent much time around horses?"

"No. My best friend in junior high took riding lessons and I begged my mom for weeks to let me take lessons too. Finally, she gave in. But I took one lesson and the teacher was so mean, I never went back."

"You got on a horse once? That's it?"

"Yes and it was awful. I had to ride in a circle and this big mean old woman sat on an upside-down five-gallon bucket holding a riding crop and yelling at us. I had no idea what I was doing. By the end I was just trying not to let her see me cry."

"I can see how that would have ruined it. But riding can be fun."

"I'll take your word for it." Brigid took a sip of water. "I'd probably just fall off."

"Well, I don't recommend that, but maybe you can give riding another chance sometime." He leaned forward, putting his elbows on the table and cupping his large hands around his water glass. "In the meantime, you saw the horses out in the pasture. That's Dusty, Willy, Chico, and Peppy. They're old cow horses, kind of in retirement you might say, except for the occasional trail ride. They wouldn't hurt a fly. My horse Hank is a bit more energetic, so just be a little careful around him. But the most important thing is that sometimes I board horses that I'm training. Any horse that isn't familiar, you need to stay away from, okay?"

"That's fine with me." Brigid said. "I'm here to deal with dogs, not horses. It's just temporary, and I promise I'll stay out of your way. Thank you for doing all this work."

"Well, I keep saying I'm gonna clean out that barn and use it for an indoor arena, but I never do it. Now at least one corner is a little cleaner."

Brigid brightened. "Yes, and tomorrow Judge has a place to go! Kat is going to be thrilled. I should get going, call her, and then continue with my efforts to convince various officers of the law that stray dogs now have a temporary home until they can be fostered or adopted. I don't think they really believed me."

"Well, if they need verification, you just have them give me a call."

"I will." Brigid stood up and tried not to wince as her rapidly stiffening sore leg muscles let her know how much work they'd done today. "Thanks again. I guess I'll see you tomorrow."

"I guess you will."

~

After she got home and took a long, hot shower, Brigid left a message on Clay's answering machine and also talked to Kat to let them know that she would be able to pick up Judge the next afternoon and take him out to the ranch. Kat seemed pleased and volunteered that the dog had been a well-behaved guest during his stay so far.

With a sense of satisfaction, Brigid curled up on the couch with Gypsy and the stack of self-improvement books. She didn't appear to have burned any bridges with Kat, which was a relief. A woman in the process of building a bunch of dog kennels was someone Brigid needed to remain on friendly terms with if she wanted to get more dogs adopted into new homes. It was easy to imagine needing temporary boarding again. Even if she had to pay, it would be worth it to get those dogs out of the police station.

Although she was determined to try to find people to adopt the homeless dogs of Alpine Grove, Brigid was quickly discovering she had no idea what she was doing. Volunteering at an animal shelter wasn't the same as starting something new like this. Shouldn't she have forms? There were probably legal implications to adopting dogs as well. Most organizations were nonprofits. Maybe she needed to look into that too.

After the holiday weekend was over, she needed to go to the bookstore and the library and learn more about nonprofit organizations, pet care—pretty much everything. It was both overwhelming and exciting. For the first time in a very long time, she felt like she had a purpose.

The next morning, she took Gypsy out for a long walk on a trail near the lake. It was another beautiful blue sky day and the gentle spring breeze was energizing. Both Gypsy and Brigid were getting in much better shape with all the exercise and fresh air. After they returned home, Gypsy settled into her dog bed for some serious afternoon nap time while Brigid got ready to pick up Judge.

During the drive out to Kat's house, Brigid considered what Dr. Cassidy had said about not leaving at the end of the summer. Even though she'd been living in Alpine Grove for only a few weeks, she felt more settled than she had in years. It was easy to imagine staying for the foreseeable future.

Remaining in Alpine Grove also made her plans to help the dogs by starting a nonprofit more feasible. How could she start setting it up and then leave halfway through the process? It just wouldn't work. She needed to stay at least for a while until something was established. Maybe she could find a job. Even little towns needed secretaries or clerks. She had such an eclectic work history, she'd undoubtedly be able to find something she was qualified to do that could pay the rent before her savings ran out.

As she turned the car into the driveway, she was flooded with an overriding sense of optimism and hope. The good weather probably helped, but finally letting go of the past and making a decision about her future was mentally freeing. It was like a great cloud had been pushed aside, so she could see more clearly what lay ahead.

She parked the car under a tree near the outbuilding and got out. Judge was barking furiously from within. Brigid turned at the sound of the front door of the house opening. Kat walked up to the car and gestured toward the building. "I think Judge has figured out you're here."

They walked inside and Brigid spoke softly to Judge as she opened the chain-link gate. He settled down enough that she could clip the leash on. She then told him to sit before opening the gate and letting him out.

Kat said, "Hey, good for you making him sit. I'm sure improved manners will help him find a new home."

"Along with some new fur. I need to figure out how I'm going to bathe him out at the ranch."

"I know the feeling. This house has a tiny bathroom. After a few unfortunate dog-bathing experiences, I decided to add a grooming area into the new kennels."

"When will the construction be done?"

Kat made a wry face. "Well, we're figuring that out. It may take longer than we were expecting."

"Oh, I'm sorry to hear that."

"Gypsy is a sweetheart and I could probably board her in the house if you really needed to, but I'm not going to take any more large dogs until the kennels are finished."

"Okay." Brigid tried not to sigh at the not-so-subtle warning that Kat was going to say no if she asked to board another homeless dog. "I hope to set up more kennels at the ranch. There's tons of room in the barn. And find foster homes. Please let me know if you think of anyone who could foster a dog. Oh, and if you know of anyone hiring, let me know that too. I'm going to try to stay here in Alpine Grove if I can find a job."

"That's great. I'll keep that in mind. If I hear anything, I'll let you know."

Brigid said goodbye to Kat and loaded Judge into the car. He was, as usual, enthusiastic about whatever his next adventure might be. She turned on the radio and as the strains of upbeat music filled the car, Brigid realized she felt the same way. She was looking forward to seeing the ranch again and enjoying the result of the hard work she and Clay had done. Sure, it was just one kennel, but it was going to give Judge more time to find a new home with a family who would love him.

The ranch looked exactly the same as when she'd left. Horses grazed in the pasture and all was quiet and peaceful. As she got out of the car, the dog she'd seen the last time she was here came racing out of the horse barn, barking at her. Judge started barking from within the car as the dog skidded to a stop in front of her. He seemed to realize that he'd already met her and wagged his long feathery tail. Brigid held out her hand, "Hi Scout. Remember me?"

Clay opened the door to the house and whistled loudly. Scout leaped away from Brigid, ran up the steps, and shot across the porch and through the door into the house. Clay closed the door and waved at Brigid as he slowly ambled toward her.

She opened the back door of the Honda, clipped the leash onto Judge's collar and let him out. The dog bounded to the ground and stopped. He looked around and raised his snout into the air, enjoying the novel ranch smells. The equine scents were obviously quite thrilling.

Clay put his hands in his pockets and looked down at the dog. "That's certainly not the most attractive animal I've ever seen."

"I told you—he has a skin condition." She stroked a patch of fur on Judge's head and the dog wagged his tail happily. "But see how sweet he is!"

"I'm sure he's a nice dog. Do you want to get him settled into his new digs?" Clay gestured for her to follow him and started walking toward the barn. "I made a platform for him to sleep on, out of some old wood. I hope he's not a chewer. It was all I had lying around."

They walked into the barn and Brigid led Judge over to the kennel, which was set up with the wooden platform bed and an old blanket in the back corner. She turned to look at Clay. "This is wonderful. I can't believe you made this for him."

"Well, you seemed a little worried about him sleeping on the gravel."

Brigid busied herself getting Judge settled. "I need to get his food out of my car. Where should I put it?"

"The tool room over there. I'll go get a metal can out of the tack room for you to put it in, so the mice don't get to it."

"Mice? Eww. Okay. Good idea."

Brigid walked back to the car and opened the trunk where she had a forty-pound bag of dog food. Levering it out of the trunk, she heaved it over her shoulder, straightened and returned to the barn. She dropped the bag on the floor with a thud.

Clay walked in behind her, carrying the metal can. He put the can down and put his hand on her shoulder. Startled, Brigid leaped away from him and crashed into a wooden bench, causing some large rusty things to fall off with a clang. Ow. She was going to have quite a bruise. Her heart was hammering in her chest and she gasped for air, as if a hand were gripping her throat.

Clay reached out as if to steady her, but she backed away. He said, "Are you okay?"

She nodded, but didn't say anything, squeezing her eyes shut for a second in an effort to try to will her heart rate to return to normal.

With a shrug, he took off the metal lid, opened the bag of dog food, and dumped the contents into the can. "You sure are jumpy."

Brigid could tell her cheeks were probably thirty-nine shades of red. She put her hand up to her face and felt the mortifying heat. At least she could breathe again. "Sorry."

"I was just gonna say that you're pretty strong for such a small person."

"I've been doing things myself for a long time."

"I see." He bent to pick up the rusty artifacts and put them back on the bench.

Brigid wasn't sure what to say. The expression on his face indicated he definitely did *not* see and that she should probably explain herself, particularly after he'd been so nice and even made Judge a bed to sleep on. But she didn't want to. Better that he just think she was weird.

She turned to leave the room. "I, um, I should feed Judge and get out of your hair. I need to get his bowl out of the car. Oh, and he's already had a nice long walk today. I'm not sure how this will work exactly. I'll come back in the morning. Maybe you could check on him before you go to bed though. Just to make sure he's okay?"

Clay nodded and leaned against the bench, crossing his arms across his chest. "I can do that."

"I'll be right back." Brigid practically ran back out to her Honda. Pulling the bag of dog paraphernalia out of the trunk, she took a deep breath. The beating of her heart was stubbornly refusing to slow back down to a normal rate. What was wrong with her? Not every man was like John. She needed to get a grip on herself. Clay had been nothing but polite to her and he was doing her a favor.

Slamming the trunk lid with an air of finality, she mentally gave herself a shake. It was time to get over this problem. Fifty percent of the world was male, and some of those men might touch her in a friendly, non-threatening way.

She walked back into the work room and said overly brightly, "This won't take a minute. Then I'll leave you alone."

"You don't have to keep reassuring me you're gonna leave." Clay put his hands on the bench and pushed himself forward. As he walked by her, he said in a soft low voice, "Relax, Brigid. It's fine. I'll see you tomorrow morning."

She turned to watch him leave and looked down at her hands, which were still shaking. For her, relaxing wasn't as easy as he might think.

~

Brigid was sitting at the table eating breakfast when the phone rang. Carefully stepping over Gypsy, who was supervising the eating activities, she walked across the room and picked up the handset. "Hello."

"Hey Brigid, it's Jake down at the police station. We've got another dog here."

"Okay, I'll be right over."

When she walked into the police station, she greeted Jake, who waved toward the back. "You know where everything is."

Brigid smiled. "I do. Can you tell me anything about the dog?"

"He was hanging around a farm south of town. He's a skinny thing and seems kinda depressed. He hasn't wanted to eat anything yet and I don't think he likes men very much."

"Okay, thanks." Brigid walked outside and went to the cages. The dog was a black greyhound who looked extremely unhappy to be there, curled up in a tight ball in the back corner of the cage. Brigid spoke softly to the dog. "Hi there, sweetie." The dog lifted his head and pointed his long nose at her. "You're very pretty. Would you like to go for a walk?"

She grabbed a leash and collar off the hooks and opened the gate as quietly as she could. The dog stood up and slinked over to her with his head hanging low. He was wearing a collar, and she bent to stroke the fur on his shoulder, which was more gray than black, thanks to a fine layer of dirt and dust. "I want to look at your collar, sweetie." The dog pressed his forehead against her leg, which Brigid took as an affirmative, so she unbuckled the nylon collar. The ring where tags would go was empty, but the collar had a brass nameplate riveted to it that said *Nugget*. Why would someone put the dog's name on the nameplate and not a phone number? Brigid stroked the smooth fur on his head. "Are you Nugget?"

The dog moved his head away and looked up at her, his dark brown eyes expectant. Brigid smiled. "I think you are Nugget, aren't you? You certainly are quite a snuggler." She put the collar back on and said, "Let's go for a walk."

After walking Nugget, Brigid put him back in the kennel and reassured him that she'd return later. The dog seemed unconvinced and curled up in his corner again. Brigid sighed as she closed the gate. The pretty greyhound obviously had lived in a home once. Someone had even bothered to buy him a special collar.

Nugget still had a couple more days and Brigid hoped someone would come looking for him. She couldn't think about this dog right now though, since she had to haul herself back out to the ranch and deal with Judge. She was later getting out there than she'd thought she would be. Maybe Clay wouldn't notice.

When she got out to the ranch, Clay was out doing something with a horse in a fenced-in area. He seemed to be making it run in circles, then stop. It was hard to tell what they were up to. Maybe it was some training thing. Brigid waved at him and went into the barn to tend to Judge, who barked in hysterical joy at the sight of her. She clipped on the dog's leash and they walked back out into the sunlight. Glancing over at the corral where Clay had been, she noted that it was empty. He and the horse had disappeared. She stopped and turned around, wondering where they could have gone so quickly. Was that one of his horses? She couldn't remember what he said about which ones were his. It was simpler to just avoid all of them.

She walked down the driveway with Judge, letting him sniff and snuffle all he wanted. The four horses were in the pasture again. Maybe Clay was doing something with his horse. Hank? Whatever. Not her business.

Judge turned around and woofed at a huge buckskin-colored horse walking toward them. Clay was riding the horse bareback and Brigid cringed at the thought. Wasn't that uncomfortable? You'd think it would rub various tender body parts the wrong way. But Clay seemed perfectly content and tipped his hat at her as the horse walked closer to them.

Brigid attempted to settle Judge, who did not seem to appreciate the equine presence. But after the initial notification woof, he just stared at the large beast in wonder. "Judge, you need to get used to horses. They're everywhere here." She probably needed to take her own advice. It was quite possible Judge had more horse experience than she did. Horses were just so *big*.

Clay dismounted and held the horse's reins in his hands as they walked closer. "How are you on this fine morning?"

"I'm okay. Which horse is that?"

He stroked the horse's nose. "This is Hank. We were having a conversation about bags."

"Bags? What kind of bags?"

"Terrible, scary, horse-eating bags. I was gonna throw away that empty bag of dog food last night and I guess I got distracted. I think Scout dragged it out here and this morning Hank was pretty sure he didn't like it."

"I thought he was one of the good horses."

"He is. But he's sensitive to new things and still pretty young, so he doesn't have a lot of years of experience with new smells and scary bags sitting where they're not supposed to be. Once he found out I was okay with the evil horse-eating bag, he was less worried about it. But we had to have that discussion and then I had to wait until his curiosity got the better of him and he checked it out himself."

"So he's not going to freak out or anything, right?"

Clay looked at the horse's head, then at Brigid. "Does he *look* like he's going to freak out?"

"Well, no. I guess not. I'm just checking."

"Horses aren't so different from people. Some are more sensitive than others, that's all."

Brigid tried to decide if he was still talking about the horse or not. "I guess that makes sense."

"If we keep standing here, Hank will probably start falling asleep." Clay scritched the horse's cheek below one of his half-closed eyes. "I don't think you have much to worry about at the moment."

"Okay."

He moved and the horse stepped forward toward Brigid, who stepped back, pulling Judge with her.

Clay studied her face for a second. "Well, let me know if you need anything." He grabbed Hank's mane, swung his leg back, leaped up on the horse, and turned the huge animal around. "See ya."

"Wait! I forgot. I need to ask you something."

He turned Hank back around in a tight circle to face her again. "What's that?"

"Another dog came in. Can we build another kennel here?"

He set the reins down in front of him on the horse's neck. "I suppose. How many are you planning on having here? I thought you had other ideas."

"I do. But in three days, this beautiful greyhound will be shipped off. His name is Nugget and he's a little scared, but he snuggles up to you. It's the cutest thing."

Clay chuckled. "Well, okay then. How could I possibly refuse a snuggling greyhound?"

"I can help you now, if you've got time. I just need to get back to town later to walk Nugget again at the station."

"All right. I'll let Hank hang out with his buddies in the pasture. Then we can get started."

"Thank you."

He tipped his hat again. "No problem. I'll meet you at the barn."

Brigid continued walking Judge down the driveway. Clay had asked a valid question. How many kennels were they going to set up? This situation could get completely out of hand quickly. She was just one person, and eventually he'd say no to more dogs. It was definitely time to get some help, given that she was already feeling like she was in over her head. More stray dogs were going to come in whether she was ready or not.

⁓

By the time Brigid returned from her walk with Judge, Clay had already pounded in some posts and fired up the stinky old tractor again. She waited outside the barn with Judge while Clay used the tractor to dump some gravel into place.

After the tractor was silent again, she returned Judge to his enclosure. The dog happily nestled himself into the blanket on his platform for a nap.

Brigid held the fencing while Clay attached it to the posts. He had to be one of the least demanding people she'd ever met. Somehow, he seemed to know that she was out of her element, but her silence didn't seem to bother him as he efficiently worked to finish up the fence and attach the gate.

Picking up his toolbox, he looked at her. "Is everything okay? You seem upset."

"I guess I'm just still thinking about what you said. You're right. How many kennels can we realistically put here? I'm not sure what I've gotten myself into. I can't just keep putting dogs in your barn."

He grinned. "I'm glad you're figuring this out now and not when you have thirty five animals in here."

Brigid couldn't help but smile back. "Thanks for being so nice about this. You probably think I'm some kind of dog nut."

"No, although you do seem to be wound a little tight." He leaned against the door frame of the tool room. "Usually when I've got a problem, I go for a ride. It helps me think."

"I told you, I don't ride."

"Want to try again? I promise I won't yell at you." He gestured toward the pasture. "Willy is the most mellow horse you'll ever meet. And now in his retirement, he's kind of a slug. I'm not sure you could get him to gallop, even if you wanted to."

"I'm not sure."

"If you're going come out here every day, you need to get used to being around horses."

Brigid was dubious, but he did have a point. "All right. But only if we go really slowly."

"Willy will like that idea. Slow is his favorite speed. Let's go get them."

"Me too?"

"Yes, you too."

Clay grabbed some halters with lead ropes off a hook and they walked past the barn out to the pasture. The horses all came over to the fence to see what Clay was up to. He walked through the gate and spoke softly to each horse as he rubbed its neck. Brigid couldn't hear what he was saying as he threw a rope over the neck of a brown and white horse, put the halter over the horse's nose, and buckled it behind the horse's ears. She said, "I hope you're telling him to be gentle with me."

Clay walked through the gate with the horse. "Meet Willy. He's not going anywhere, but hang onto the rope for me for a second."

Brigid reached out her hand to take the rope and Willy turned his big head toward her. "What's he doing?"

"Relax, he's just *looking* at you."

More than a little embarrassed, Brigid held the rope near Willy's neck as Clay had instructed and tried to regain her composure. She was being such a wimp.

Clay walked out with the buckskin horse he'd been riding earlier and closed the gate again. "Okay, time for a little horse safety information. When you meet a horse, always approach him from the left and from the front if you can. Horses have monocular vision, so there are blind spots where they can't see you. They can't see right in front of their nose or directly behind them. You can think of their field of vision as like the shape of an hourglass on its side or butterfly wings. Since you don't want to sneak up on or surprise something as large as a horse, you want to approach from an angle. And always scratch or stroke the horse, but don't slap him. Try not to make sudden movements or noises either. Got it?"

Even though it seemed like a lot to remember, Brigid nodded in agreement.

"Okay, let's go to the barn and get them saddled up. A lot of this stuff is just common sense. I'm sure you don't like people running and screaming around you. Horses are the same way."

Brigid led Willy and walked with Clay and Hank to the barn. Too bad no one had explained horse safety to the screaming kid with the shopping cart at the grocery store. As they walked, she reached with her other hand to stroke the horse's neck. "Be nice, Willy. You're a lot bigger than I am."

In the barn, Clay tied up the horses and explained to Brigid how to pick the hooves, brush the horses, and saddle them. Brigid liked the grooming part. It was relaxing and Willy seemed to enjoy it too. He swished his tail at a fly, but other than that he stood almost completely still while she ran the brush over his body.

After Willy was saddled, Clay gently stretched each of the horse's front legs out in front of him. When Brigid asked why, he said it was to make sure there wasn't any folded skin under the cinch that might be uncomfortable or pinch the horse.

Clay tightened the cinch again and moved Willy next to a yellow plastic mounting block. With a flamboyant gesture, he encouraged her to come near the horse. "Your mount is ready m'lady."

Brigid stepped up on the block, put her left foot in the stirrup, and threw her other leg over Willy's back. She tried to put her right foot into the other stirrup, but couldn't reach it. "It's really long."

"You're really short," Clay said as he readjusted the length of the stirrups. "Okay. Try that."

Once her feet were in the stirrups and she was settled in the saddle, Brigid looked around the barn while Clay dealt with saddling Hank. The ground seemed extremely far away, but as long as she was just sitting here motionless, she wasn't likely to fall off anyway.

Clay got on Hank, turned the horse around to face her, and gave her some basic riding instructions. "We're just going to walk, so you don't have to do much except follow me and Hank. Willy knows the way, so it's the next best thing to a pony ride."

Brigid followed his directions and they walked out of the barn. Willy seemed content to go slowly, which was a relief. Now that she'd spent some time grooming him, the horse didn't seem quite as intimidating. Willy methodically plodded along after Hank, and as they went across the road up into the trees, Brigid started to enjoy the view from up high. "Where are we going?"

"National forest land. I've got a special permit to take people for rides back in there. It goes for miles." He waved to indicate she should ride alongside him. "The trail widens out here. C'mon up next to me."

Brigid gave Willy a little kick and almost had a mini-heart attack as the horse jolted into a speed-walk to get up next to Hank. Clay smiled. "Good boy, Willy."

Brigid said, "We're not going to go fast, right?"

"Nope. I just thought you'd have more fun if you got to look at something other than Hank's butt."

Brigid chuckled, "Well, he's got a nice butt. It's very muscular."

"Aw, you'll give him a big head." He stroked the horse's neck. "He's a good horse, and coming along nicely. He just needs some more miles on him."

"This is really beautiful back in here."

"It is." He glanced at her. "You're looking a little more relaxed too."

"I am, although I'm still worried about what I'm going to do. Thanks for taking me out."

"Sometimes getting away can be helpful."

"This must have been an amazing place to grow up. I can't imagine it."

"Well, it wasn't all trail rides on pretty sunny days. This was a cattle ranch then, so mostly it was work. Half the year you're out there freezing your toes off getting cows fed and dealing with calving. Then the rest of the year there's fence and equipment to repair, building projects, cleaning corrals, haying." He gestured dismissively. "It's boring, hard work. You don't wanna know."

"Is that why you left?"

Clay glanced over at her quickly. "I guess you heard that at the bookstore. Yeah, it's a long story, but that's some of it. I left here when I was eighteen, a while after I graduated."

"From what Margaret said, it sounds like you were very successful."

He laughed. "I don't know about that. More like young and stupid."

"I can understand that. I left home pretty young too. And I was definitely stupid."

"It seems to me you're doing the best you can with the dogs. Trying to help them while you're on your vacation is admirable. I don't think I've ever met anyone who would do that."

Brigid gripped the reins more tightly. "I don't think I'm doing a very good job of it. I have this habit of following my heart instead of my head. You'd think I'd know better by now."

"What did you do before you came here?"

Brigid looked straight ahead, wishing she could gallop off without falling off and breaking her neck. Of course, Clay was such a good rider, he'd just catch her anyway. Drat. "I, um, had a lot of jobs. I moved around a lot because my husband was in the military."

"I get the impression you're not married now."

"No. He's dead."

"I'm sorry."

"I'm not." Brigid looked at Clay in horror. She'd actually said it out loud. "I mean, I know that sounds terrible. And it is. I don't mean I'm glad he's *dead*. Just that he's not in my life. I uh, we didn't have a good marriage…we were about to split up. I still shouldn't have said that though. That was horrible. I…um…my husband…he had some problems."

"You feel how you feel." Clay glanced at her. "I think I understand."

"No! No, you don't. It's not like John was a bad person. We just fought all the time. Together we were just awful to each other. Hateful. I can't believe I said the things I did. If he hadn't been overseas so much, we would have split up before he did what he... I mean...well, it would have been sooner."

"I'm thinking that's why you were terrified when I touched you, isn't it?"

"What? No, of course I wasn't."

"You were shaking like a leaf."

"I am very grateful to you for letting the dogs stay at the ranch."

"That's nice of you to say, but I know that look in your eyes wasn't gratitude."

Brigid shook her head even though she knew he wouldn't believe her, particularly since he was right.

Chapter 4

On the Trail

Brigid stared fixedly at the trail ahead as they rode in silence, the only noise the sound of hooves crunching on dry pine needles. It was easy to blame her failed marriage on the military. Everyone knew that being an Army wife could be difficult and that any marriage required work. But getting married young to someone you barely knew was a recipe for disaster.

Brigid had known as little about John as he'd known about her. Neither of them had any clue about marriage or the amount of dedication life in the military required. Even when John hadn't been overseas, all they did was argue. They fought about big things and small things. There were endless disagreements about everything from the right way to wash the dishes to the latest temporary duty assignment. Brigid didn't miss the never-ending barrage of bitterness, sulking, and hateful words.

She scowled at Willy's pointy ears. Being around Clay was becoming more uncomfortable, since in his quiet way he seemed to be able to tell what she was thinking. It was downright creepy. How did he know what had happened with John? Maybe someone told him? But that was impossible, since no one here knew her. It certainly wasn't like she was going to volunteer that information to anyone.

Most people just ignored her and stayed within the comfortable realm of small talk, which was a lot easier. Clay didn't seem to deal in small talk much at all. It was odd. What was wrong with the guy? He either said nothing or said things that made her uncomfortable. Maybe spending so much time around horses had damaged his social skills.

She glanced to her right, where Hank was still slowly clopping along. She moved her gaze up to Clay and gasped. "What on earth are you *doing*?"

Clay was standing on the horse's back with his arms outstretched above his head. He actually looked sort of peaceful or bored like he was waiting for a bus. "Horse yoga." He'd removed his boots and they were hanging from a strap on the saddle.

"Are you insane?"

"Not the last time I checked." He leaned forward, placed his hands on the horse's neck, and stretched a leg out behind him, pointing his toes. "I'm not suggesting you do this, but it's good for balance. And relaxing once you get into the rhythm of the horse's movement."

"This is the horse that is afraid of dog food bags! What if he bolts off? You could kill yourself."

"I suppose." He sat back down on the saddle and put on a sock. "Maybe then you'd finally get out of your head and stop brooding."

"I am *not* brooding. I'm riding."

"You're festering on something and it's eating you up. Maybe you don't want to talk to me, but you need to talk to someone about whatever happened to you."

"No I don't! And, not that it's any of your business, but I did that. I went to counseling. And groups. After my husband died, I did everything everyone said I was supposed to."

"But you didn't really let it out, did you?" He stretched forward onto Hank's neck so he could turn his head back and see her face. "You said what you thought they wanted to hear, not the whole story."

Brigid wiped an errant tear from her eye. "It's been a year now. I'm over it. *Totally* over it."

"If you don't want to talk, that's okay." He sat straight in the saddle again and busied himself putting his socks and boots back on. "You know, the great thing about horses is that they never lie. They're honest to a fault. Whenever I have a problem with a horse, the first thing I have to ask is why. What is making the horse do this? Because if you pay attention, the horse will let you know what's going on. And once you understand the problem, you've taken the first step toward solving it."

Brigid glared at him. "Are you *actually* comparing me to a horse? A thousand pound beast of burden? You've got to be kidding me. This is beyond insulting. You've really got a lot of nerve."

"I suppose I do, and right now I'm thinking there might be some truth to that whole thing they say about redheads having a temper. Maybe getting mad at me will help." He hooked a leg over the saddle horn so he was sideways, facing her. "Everybody has problems. A past with things you wish were different. I know I do and it took me a lot of time riding out here to reconcile myself to it."

Brigid pushed her hair back behind her ear in frustration and stared at Willy's ears again. "I don't need to reconcile anything. I'm fine. Can't we just talk about the weather or something?"

After a long pause, Clay moved his leg, so he was facing forward in the saddle again. He looked up at the deep blue sky and said, "It's sure a nice day for a ride. Almost like it's apologizing for last winter. I know you weren't here, but it was sure a wicked one. Half the county lost electricity during a freak Thanksgiving blizzard, then there was the cold and more snow. Mother Nature really had herself quite a party."

She looked over at Clay and met his gaze. The sympathy in his dark eyes seemed to melt the hard knot of anger and tension in her chest. "Yes...yes it is beautiful today. So beautiful." She collected the reins more tightly and Willy started to attention. "I...I, think I need to get off now."

Clay moved Hank in front of her, so he could grab Willy's reins. With a fluid motion, he dismounted and held both horses as Brigid removed her feet from the stirrups and slid down to the ground. She leaned her forehead against the saddle and let herself cry as she stroked the smooth hair on the horse's neck.

Clay touched her back and rubbed it slightly. He said softly, "I'm so sorry, honey." Brigid turned around and squeezed her eyes shut as she clutched his shirt and pressed her face into his chest, sobbing uncontrollably.

He smelled like horses, hay, and warm skin. For the first time in far too long, she felt the warmth of human contact as he wrapped an arm around her shoulders and let her cry.

After a few minutes, there was a snuffling noise and something tickled her ear. Brigid pulled her head away and looked up at Clay's face. "Was that you or Willy?"

"Willy. I might need a shave, but my whiskers aren't *that* long. He's just making sure you're okay."

She smiled tentatively. "I'm so sorry about this…I barely know you. This is really embarrassing. I don't know what happened. I haven't cried like this before."

He rubbed her back gently again. "Maybe you needed to."

As she stepped away from him, he straightened his arm and dropped it to his side. She looked down at Willy's hooves. "I guess so."

Clay reached out and tilted her chin up with his fingertip, so she was looking into his eyes, then dropped his hand again. "Sadness is nothing to be ashamed of or to be embarrassed about. But I hope you can let it go in time."

"I don't understand why you are being so kind to me."

He glanced toward the sky again and looked back at her. "Well, I don't know exactly. Partly you seemed like you could use a little kindness. And at the bar, you were so set on saving that dog. You don't see that level of compassion often, and it struck me."

"More like stupidity. If it weren't for you, I'd have a house full of dogs."

"Instead, I have a barn full of dogs." He grinned. "I'd say that was a good move on your part."

Brigid smiled involuntarily as she wiped her eyes. She probably looked all blotchy and horrifying by now. "I'm not sure what to do though. I keep flip-flopping between hope and despair. I'm unemployed and don't know anyone. In all my enthusiasm or compassion or whatever you want to call it, I haven't exactly planned ahead and it's going to be the dogs who lose out."

"Given that you're in Alpine Grove, it's probably only a matter of hours before you meet more people. Soon you'll know everybody. More than you ever wanted to know, in fact."

"Spoken like a true native."

"I confess that is part of why I left. But it's also why I came back. In a small town like this oftentimes people are willing to help out. You just have to ask."

Brigid looked down at her feet. "I guess I'm not very good at asking."

"You asked me."

"That's true. But it was a weird situation and probably half the reason I did was because the bartender was encouraging me. And the spiked iced tea didn't hurt either. Most people aren't like you. What if they say no?"

"You go ask someone else."

She reached out to pet Willy's brown forehead. "I am planning to go to the library and get books, so I can learn more about nonprofits and fundraising."

"It sounds to me like you've got some good ideas and the start of some plans."

"I've also decided to stay here. I don't really have anywhere else to go. If I can find a job, I won't need to leave at the end of the summer and then I can do this right."

"There are worse places to live."

Brigid smiled. "I know. I've lived in some of them. It's so nice to have a choice now."

"I suppose that's a downside of the military life."

"When I got married, I was so excited to see the world. A life of adventure going to from place to place. And I did get to spend some time in Europe and travel a little seeing the sights. But mostly I ended up living near Army bases that weren't necessarily in places I would have wanted to visit, much less live."

Clay chuckled. "I can imagine. When I was doing movie work, I found out that for every exotic location you go to, like a castle in Germany, there's three backwoods places you end up at where it's 400 degrees and full of bugs."

"Well, it sounds like fun anyway."

"At the time I did enjoy it, although it's tiring. There's more standing around and waiting than you might expect and a lot of long hours." He patted her horse. "So are you ready to get back up on Willy before he falls asleep on you?"

"Okay. He's been great about putting up with my lack of riding ability." She went to Willy's left side and looked at the stirrup. There was no way she could get her foot up there. "I think I have a problem."

"Grab the horn." Clay interlocked his fingers and bent to hold his hands down near her foot. "Now, go for it."

Brigid put her left foot in his hands and he hoisted her up as she swung her leg over Willy's back. After she was seated and had her feet tucked back in the stirrups, Clay put his hand over hers on the saddle horn. "You okay up there?"

"Yes. Better than okay." She put her other hand on top of his and squeezed. "Thank you."

∼

During the ride back to the ranch, Brigid chatted with Clay about some of the places she'd lived. Because he'd been on the rodeo circuit, he knew even some of the more obscure areas of the country where she'd been stationed, particularly in the

West. They both agreed that neither of them ever needed to see Oklahoma again, and he implied that there were aspects of rodeos he wished he'd known at eighteen, but didn't. Given the expression on his face, Brigid didn't ask for specifics.

Periodically, Clay made riding suggestions, like keeping her heels down. Easy for him to say. He looked like he was glued to the horse, whereas she felt precariously perched, about to tilt off to one side half the time. The guy clearly had some kind of astounding sense of balance that she lacked.

She could already tell that after she dismounted, her legs were going to let her know that she didn't use some of those muscles for anything else. Riding was harder on the body than it appeared. The idea of going any faster than a walk was laughable. She had a new appreciation for all those Old West cowboys. Riding the range must have been a lot tougher than it looked on TV. And John Wayne must have had legs of steel to play cowboys in the movies for so many years. Ouch.

Even though she was tired from the ride and her emotional meltdown, Brigid felt better than she had in a long time. Probably years. Clay was easy to talk to and didn't seem to think she was a nut, even after she'd wept all over his shirt.

Everyone said that Army wives forged unique bonds because they had to move so often. Supposedly, these women had deep friendships that lasted through the ages. But that wasn't the case with Brigid. She'd always worried that there was something wrong with her because she felt like an outsider looking in at a party she hadn't been invited to attend. Maybe it was because she was afraid they'd find out what her marriage was really like. It was a relief to know that here, for once, she wasn't going to have to move and leave her nascent friendships behind.

She had no idea why, but she'd had more interesting conversations since she'd been in Alpine Grove than she'd had in all the other places she'd lived with John. Maybe she could ask Kat and Maria to come over to her house some time. They seemed to enjoy getting out, and it would be fun to laugh with girlfriends about silly stuff.

After returning to the barn, Brigid successfully navigated Willy next to the mounting block and managed to get off the horse without her rubbery legs flying out from under her, causing a humiliating incident. Clay took Willy from her, unsaddled him, and explained where everything was supposed to be put away in the tack room.

The old clock on the wall indicated that they'd been out riding for quite a while. Clay was undoing the cinch on Hank's saddle when she walked over to them. "I should feed and walk Judge again and then go back to town and tend to Nugget. Poor Gypsy is going to wonder what happened to me. I'm glad she has a doggie door at the house. She loves sleeping out on the back patio in the sun. It's so cute."

He pulled the saddle off the horse and walked to the tack room with it. "You're gonna put a lot of miles on that car coming out here so much."

"I don't care. It's already old and tired."

As he unhitched the horses, he said, "I know the feeling."

"You're not old."

"Sometimes it feels like it." He walked by her and smirked, "I'm pretty sure I'm a whole lot older than you are."

"I don't know about that." She hustled up to walk alongside Willy as Clay led the horses toward the pasture. She looked around Willy's nose at Clay. "When did you graduate from high school?"

"1975."

"At least you didn't have to worry about getting drafted."

"I would have been 4-F anyway. Medical deferment."

"For what?" She looked at him. "You're in incredible shape." Particularly compared to her.

"I ride better than I hike." He pointed toward the large red barn. "When I was at the doctor one time, they told me I have flat feet."

She looked down at his boots, which revealed nothing. "Oh."

"You need good feet to tramp through jungle swamps I guess." He looked at her. "When did you graduate?"

"1983. See! You're not *that* much older than I am."

He glanced at her. "You sure look young. I don't suppose you skipped a few grades, did you?"

"No. It's because I'm so short. Everyone thinks I'm in junior high."

"Well, I didn't think you were *that* young. I'm not some creepy old guy like in that book everyone had to read in school."

"You mean *Lolita*? Eww." Brigid pushed her hair back behind her ear. "Personally, I don't think I look that young. When I actually *was* twelve or thirteen, I looked like Pippi Longstocking."

Clay chuckled. "With freckles and pigtails?"

"Yes, and buck teeth. I got braces when I was fourteen to fix that. And the freckles on my face faded as I got older, which helped lower the Pippi effect."

He opened the gate to the pasture, removed the halters from the horses' heads, and let them run into the vast grassy area to graze. Turning to her, he smiled. "You certainly don't look like Pippi now."

"I'll take that as a compliment."

"It was meant as one."

Brigid wasn't sure what to say. Was he actually flirting with her? It had been so long, she didn't even know how that dynamic worked anymore. Maybe it was just friendly conversation. It had to be.

Clay gestured toward the house. "Do you want something to drink before you walk the dog? Riding can be pretty tiring if you don't do it often."

"I noticed. I may not be able to walk upright by the time morning rolls around."

They walked companionably toward the house. Once again, Scout was standing behind the glass door looking eager to come outside. Brigid turned to Clay, "Does he ever go out on rides with you?"

"Usually he does. But new riders can find a dog running around distracting. I figured it was better to let him continue his nap."

Clay opened the door and the dog shot out toward the horse barn.

Brigid laughed, "Is he heading for his cats again?"

"Yup, Scout has his routines and you don't want to get in the way. Working dogs need to get their jobs done. He takes his responsibilities pretty seriously."

"Do you think he'll be okay with Judge?"

"Yeah, he'll probably just ignore him and the greyhound too, if the dog ends up here." Clay handed her a glass of water. "Scout is mostly interested in his cats, not dogs."

Brigid sat down and her tired muscles seemed to all relax at once as if they were melting into the chair. The urge to put her head down on the table and take a nap was considerable. The old farm house had a comfortable lived-in feel that was calming. Although the oak kitchen cabinets had obviously seen a lot of use, all the wood made the room seem warm and inviting.

She was curious about what it was like for Clay to return after growing up here. Although he'd mentioned it during their earlier conversation, it also seemed like there was quite a bit he wasn't saying.

Clay put down his glass. "Well, I've got to go and deal with a horse with bad feet. Make yourself at home."

Brigid scrambled to get up. "I'll just walk Judge and get going."

"Don't worry about it. Take as long as you need. I might see you tomorrow, depending on when you come by. If I'm not here, just do what you need to do. You know where everything is now."

As he grabbed his hat and walked out the door, Brigid was surprised to find she was sorry to see him leave. It had been an odd, exhausting, but surprisingly good day and she was looking forward to returning tomorrow.

~

After walking and feeding Judge, Brigid returned to her house, ate, gave Gypsy a big hug, and went to the station to tend to Nugget. Not surprisingly, the dog was still there. It bothered Brigid that no one had come for him. Someone had obviously loved this dog, and Nugget's owners might be frantically looking for him, for all she knew.

On her way out, she detoured toward Jake's office. He was eating a hamburger and as she approached the desk, he swallowed quickly and gave her an odd look. Brigid looked down at her dusty clothes. Maybe she should have changed. Oh well.

He put the burger down on its paper wrapper. "Hey Brigid, how are you?"

"I'm fine. I was wondering what you do to get the word out about the dogs here."

"Uh, what do you mean?"

"If I had lost my dog, how would I know he's here?" She gestured toward the back of the building. "That greyhound has a fancy collar with his name on it. Don't you think his owners are looking for him?"

"Maybe. The truth is, dogs don't usually get claimed."

"Do you advertise?"

"What do you mean advertise? Like in the paper?"

"Yes—ads, flyers, posters. Something that says a dog was found."

Jake shook his head. "We don't have time. Everyone knows this is where strays go."

"What about people visiting here? Tourists? How would they know?"

"I dunno. Maybe they could ask someone?"

Brigid sat on the corner of the desk. "I think something needs to be done about that. You must keep track of where the dogs are picked up, right?"

"Yeah."

"I could make flyers and put them up in the area."

"I guess. If you want to."

She stood up again. "Okay. That's what I'll do. See you tomorrow."

Jake picked up his burger again and waved it. "See ya."

After Brigid returned to the house, she collapsed on the sofa in exhaustion. Gypsy jumped up next to her and sniffed at her blouse. "I know, Gypsy. I'm disgusting. I probably smell like a horse, but I suppose that could be interesting to you. To me, I just stink. Tomorrow I'll ask Clay if you can go out there with me. You might like it." Gypsy settled in next to her hip and curled up in a small ball.

Brigid jerked awake at the sound of the telephone. Gypsy stood up and hopped off the couch as Brigid stumbled over to the phone. "Hello?"

"Hey Brigid, it's Jake. I'm just calling to let you know we got another dog in, so don't be surprised tomorrow morning when you find another one here. After a holiday weekend, that tends to happen."

Brigid mumbled her thanks and hung up. She looked down at the dog. "Okay Gypsy, tomorrow I promise I'll get my act together. I have so many ideas swirling in my head right now, but I'm too tired to think about any of it, so I'm taking a shower and going to bed." The little dog wagged her tail and followed her up the stairs.

The next morning, Brigid got up early and took another very hot shower in an effort to soothe her sore muscles. Then she sat at the dining room table and made a list of all the things she needed to do, the people she needed to call, and the things she needed to buy.

The yellow legal pad was full by the time she finished doing a brain dump of everything she'd been thinking about over the last few days. One daunting prospect was that she really should get a computer and printer so she could make flyers. The list on the pad was ample evidence that no one could read her handwriting, except her. A computer would make it easier to create forms and documents as well.

After going to the station and the ranch to tend to the dogs, the next thing she needed to do was research, so a trip to the Alpine Grove library was on the agenda.

Brigid was disappointed to find that Nugget was still at the station and Clay was nowhere to be seen at the ranch. The new stray dog at the station was a short, round, female Shetland sheepdog mix that had been found wandering around the H12 motel parking lot in town. The stout sheltie's most notable quality was the desire to eat everything in sight. When Brigid fed her, the dog wolfed down the kibble so quickly that it was a little disturbing. After looking her over, Brigid considered the possibility that the dog may have been doing some serious dumpster-diving at the motel, given the pieces of food and stains on her sable coat.

After coming home and eating lunch, Brigid ventured out to the Alpine Grove library, which was located on the other end of town from her house. As she walked up the concrete steps, she admired the brick building, which was obviously old and had been restored. Maybe it was a historic landmark or something.

She walked through the glass door and looked around. Across the lobby, a woman with curly reddish-blonde hair sat at the checkout desk. She looked up from her book and smiled. "May I help you?"

Brigid said, "Could you point me to the books on nonprofit organizations and fundraising?"

The woman got up eagerly. "Fundraising is in the 360s, right over here. Follow me. Then I'll show you where the information on nonprofits is located. It's in a different section." She looked behind her at Brigid. "Are you planning to start an organization? I'd be happy to help you do some research."

Mildly startled by the woman's enthusiasm, Brigid said, "Yes, I am. I want to set up a nonprofit to help the homeless dogs here."

The woman stopped by a shelf and pointed downward. "This is what we have on raising money. I know I've run across some good information online too."

Brigid crouched down and looked at the titles. "Thank you. This looks like it will be helpful."

Bending down to hold out her hand, the woman said, "My name is Jan. I have a dog that was my mother's and if I hadn't been able to take her, Rosa would have been homeless too. I think what you're doing is wonderful."

Brigid shook her hand and stood up. "Thank you. I'm glad you feel that way. But I haven't really done much yet."

"Getting more information is the first step. I'm so glad you stopped by. I just read a study that said more than four million animals entered animal shelters in 1995. And I can tell you that this town has very little as far as animal control or services. It's becoming a problem."

"Actually, you're not the first person to say that to me."

Jan backed down the aisle toward the desk. "Well, I'll leave you to browse and see what I can find online for you. When you're ready, I can show you where the other books are too."

"Thanks. That would be great." Brigid crouched down again and looked at the book titles on the shelf. What a gung-ho librarian. By the time Brigid left here, Jan probably would have unearthed every tidbit about animal welfare available on the Internet.

After the trip to the library, Brigid didn't feel the need to get any more books at the bookstore. Maybe later, but for right now Jan had loaded Brigid up with a vast quantity of material to read. It was time to start digging in. She settled on the back porch with Gypsy, who was continuing to work on her tan, flat on her side, snoring contentedly in a big patch of sunlight streaming through the leaves of the big maple tree.

Brigid skimmed a few books and took notes, trying not to panic about the overwhelming amount of work ahead of her. This was like starting a business, except with volunteers instead of employees. That meant she had to get people to work for free. How was that supposed to work? She skimmed some sections on volunteer recruitment. Maybe people in Alpine Grove were big-hearted animal lovers. She'd better hope so, or she was in trouble.

Later that afternoon, Brigid returned to the station. No one had claimed Nugget, so it was looking more likely he'd be heading out to the ranch to join Judge in the barn. She leashed up the new sheltie for her walk, but it seemed like something was wrong. When Brigid had arrived, the dog had been pacing around her kennel panting. Now she didn't want to go out. Brigid held out a treat to try to entice her, but the dog wasn't interested. Then she started to whine plaintively. It was pitiful to hear and Brigid wasn't sure what to do. Maybe the poor little dog was really sick.

She put the sheltie back in her enclosure, closed the gate, and ran into the station. Jake wasn't in his office, so she scribbled a note on a pad on his desk and went back outside to get the dog. The little sheltie cried as she was hoisted into the back-seat of the Honda and Brigid thought her heart would break. "I'm so sorry! It will be okay. We're going to the vet. Hang on. It's really close."

At the vet clinic, she snuggled the dog to her chest and turned to push the door open with her back. Tracy looked up from her desk. "Hi Brigid. I didn't see you on the schedule. We're about to close."

"I'm sorry! It's an emergency. I think there's something wrong with this dog."

"Another one? Where did it come from?"

"The police station. She's another stray. This morning she was starving, trying to eat everything in sight. Now she won't eat and she's panting and crying like she's in pain. I don't know what's wrong with her."

Tracy came around the desk and took the dog from Brigid's arms. "Okay, I'll take her to Dr. C now. Stay here. I'll be right back."

Brigid sat in one of the chairs in the waiting room with her hands clasped between her knees, hoping that the dog wasn't really sick or dying. She wasn't sure she could handle that.

A few minutes later, Tracy returned to the desk. "Well, we know what's going on with your dog."

Brigid hurried over to the counter. "Is she okay?"

"Yes, she's fine. And she's being quite a good mommy."

"What?"

"She's having puppies."

"Oh. Wow. That's...unexpected. And it would certainly make me whine too. So, is she all right?"

"She's fine. But we should probably keep everyone here for a while. Could you tell the local law enforcement where she is? They tend to get upset when we run off with their dogs."

"I couldn't find Jake and I was in a rush, so I left a note." Brigid rested her elbows on the counter, put her forehead on her palms, and groaned. "What am I going to do with *puppies?*"

Tracy smiled. "Well, when they get big enough, find them homes."

"Dr. C said she knows people who might want to help. Do you think you could get a list together of people I might call? Right now, I've got to go back and walk Nugget, then go out to the ranch to take care of Judge." Brigid handed her credit card over the desk. "Here you go."

"Thanks. If you talk to Jake, I'll talk to Dr. C."

"It's a deal."

～

After leaving the vet clinic, Brigid returned to the police station to walk Nugget. Tracy said that she would call her the next day to let her know how the new momma and her puppies were doing. Brigid was still somewhat shocked at the day's events. Who knew the dog was pregnant? Not her, obviously. Utter panic had apparently turned her into an idiot. She also needed to think of a name for the little wanderer. Maybe Tracy would come up with something.

Jake met her at the door and held up the note. "Hey, I wondered where you were. I can't read this. You 'tamed a duck and want to vote?' What's that supposed to mean?"

Brigid sighed. "I'm sorry. I was in a rush. It says I took the dog and went to the vet."

He looked down at the piece of paper. "Really? Wow, I didn't get that."

"I'm sorry, but the dog was acting strange and I thought she might die. It was an emergency."

"Did the dog have some type of attack or seizure or something?"

"No. She had puppies."

"Oh wow. We aren't set up to deal with that at *all*."

"I know. They are at the vet clinic for the time being."

Jake crumpled the paper in his hand. "You probably figured this out, but we don't have the budget for any medical-type stuff. All we do is give the dogs shots when they come in."

"I know. Don't worry. I'm paying for it." Her credit card was really getting a workout.

"Well, maybe I should call Tracy tomorrow."

"No, that's okay. She wanted me to talk to you."

"Oh. All right."

Brigid went back, took Nugget out, and apologized for being late. The dog was extremely glad to see her and did his head-snuggling thing again, which Brigid found completely endearing. What an adorable dog. Why wasn't anyone looking for him? What was wrong with people? Who wouldn't be frantic about losing a dog like this?

After giving Nugget his walk, some affection, and dinner, Brigid went out to the ranch. Thinking about careless, irresponsible people had darkened her mood, but seeing Judge's wagging tail helped cheer her a little. He was such a happy hairless fellow. She leashed him up and they had walked down the driveway a little way when an old and very dented tan pickup truck appeared from out of the trees.

Clay slowed, rolled down the window, and stopped the truck next to them. "Hey there. How's it going?"

"Okay." She glanced at the back of his hand, which was resting on the steering wheel, bleeding. "What happened to you?"

He wiped his hand on his jeans, leaving a long smear of blood on his thigh. "Nothing much. It's been a long day."

Brigid reached into the truck and pulled a piece of straw out from the hair near his hat and held it up. "I guess it involved a horse?"

"It usually does." He took off his hat and ran his fingers through his hair, pulling out a few more pieces of straw, which he shook onto the floor of the truck. "Let me know if you need anything. I'll be in the house cleaning up."

Brigid moved away from the truck and he continued up the driveway. At the sound of the truck door slamming, she turned and watched him slowly limp up the steps to the house. He had his arm around his stomach and it looked like an extremely painful ascent. Maybe she should see if he was okay. She looked down at Judge. "What do you think? Should I check on him or is that overstepping my bounds here?"

Judge wagged his tail, but didn't offer any other guidance. Brigid smiled. "You're a big help. Okay, let's finish up and I'll give you some dinner. If he's really hurt, I'd feel terrible if I didn't do something. I'm just going to have to risk being a busybody."

Brigid fed Judge, got him settled in for the evening, and then walked to the house and up the steps. Scout was lying outside on the porch. He stood up and wagged his tail at her. "Hi Scout." She knocked on the door, peered through the glass, and waited, but there was no answer, just silence. Looking down at the dog, she stroked his fur and considered the possibilities. One, Clay was inside but too far away from the door to hear her knock. Two, he was out in a barn or somewhere else on the property. Three, he was lying in a heap somewhere, dying of some internal injury.

She looked at the dog's dark-brown eyes and knocked again. No answer. "Okay Scout, what am I supposed to do?" Like Judge, Scout wasn't offering up any suggestions. She turned the handle, opened the door, and Scout ran inside, across the living room, through the kitchen, and disappeared down the hall around a corner.

A few seconds later, Scout ran back into the kitchen followed by Clay, who was rubbing a towel on his wet hair, looking down at the dog. "Hey buddy, I thought you were outside with your cats."

Brigid put her hand to her mouth and uttered a tiny squeak of mortification. Clay looked over at her, raised his eyebrows, and wrapped the towel around his waist with a grin. "Oops. I didn't know you were here."

"I...sorry! I just wanted to see if you were okay. It seemed like you might be hurt." Brigid's cheeks were so warm it felt like they were on fire. They had to be a fantastic shade of crimson by now. Underneath those grubby jeans and t-shirts,

Clay was incredibly well-built. Wow. No wonder he didn't get tired—those were some serious muscles. Riding horses all the time had benefits she hadn't considered before.

"I didn't mean to scare you." Clay gestured toward the table. "Jeez, you look like you're going to have a stroke or something. Sit down."

Brigid scuttled to the table. "I'm so sorry. I shouldn't have just barged into your house like this. I did knock."

"Yeah, I was in the shower. I know it's not the prettiest sight, but I'm assuming you've seen a naked man before since you were married and all."

She looked at him more closely as he sat down across from her. Along with quite a few scars, he had what looked to be recent abrasions. "Did something happen today? You were limping."

"Just a horse problem." He put his elbows on the table and leaned forward with a groan. "Well, not really. It was more like a people problem. Horses are fine. It's their owners that are stupid half the time."

"What happened?"

"It's the same horse I went to see yesterday. He's a beautiful thoroughbred. Just a gorgeous horse. But the guy who owns him is a dolt." Clay rubbed at the back of his hand, which was bleeding again. "I suppose it's one problem of living in a small town. He was a friend of my brother's so I felt like I had to help him out."

"That was nice of you."

"Well, I won't be going back. Fool me twice, and I'm done." He glanced at the window. "Actually, it's more than twice, now that I think about it. You'd think I'd learn."

"Was this the horse with the bad feet?"

"Yeah. Lots of thoroughbreds are kinda tender-footed. And sometimes they can be high-strung. You have to be careful, but usually everything is fine. No problem. But you combine a horse like that with a stupid owner and you can get into something that's not safe. No farrier in his right mind would go out there again."

Brigid pointed at his hand. "What did you cut yourself on?"

"I'm not sure. I was getting out of the way after the horse started kicking. Then the next thing you know, he's galloping off into nowhere." He shrugged. "I got up, gave the guy a piece of my mind, and left. I was too blind angry about what happened to think much. I didn't even know my hand was bleeding until I was halfway back here."

"Are you okay?"

"I feel better now that I took a shower. But I should probably get dressed." He stumbled to get up from the chair and grabbed at the towel around his waist. "Do you want something to eat? It's getting late."

Brigid got up, went over to him, and looked up at his face. "You're not okay. I can tell. Where does it hurt?"

"Everywhere." He smiled. "I'm getting way too old for this. Used to be I could just roll away from that kind of thing, get back up, and keep going. Now that I've got more miles on me, it doesn't work like that anymore."

"Are you seriously hurt? Do you need to go to a hospital? I should take you to a doctor."

"Brigid, don't give me that mother hen look. I'm just banged up a little. Let me get dressed and we can have something to eat." He put his hand on her shoulder and gave it a gentle rub. "You can tell me about your day. It's got to have been better than mine."

He turned and disappeared down the hallway. Brigid looked down at Scout, who was lying on the floor. The dog raised his head expectantly and gave her a quizzical look. "I don't know either, Scout. But if you don't mind, I think I'll stay for a little longer, just in case he's really hurt and doing some dumb macho cowboy thing. You know how men can be." Scout wagged his tail in agreement.

～

While Clay was off presumably putting on some clothes, Brigid peeked in the refrigerator to see if there was anything resembling food in there. During her marriage, John had never cooked anything. When she wasn't around, his idea of cooking had been pressing buttons on a microwave.

During her quick investigation, she was pleased to discover actual vegetables in the crisper drawer. The lettuce wasn't brown and the carrots weren't dried out and desiccated. That was promising. A quick rummage through the freezer revealed bags of frozen veggies and fruit and some mysterious things in plastic containers. Maybe leftovers.

Having completed her food snooping, she sat down at the table to wait, suddenly overwhelmingly tired from the events of the day. All the running around and the stressful trip to the vet had caught up with her. She slumped down in the chair, stretched out her legs, and closed her eyes. Resting her arms on the table in front of her, she could practically feel the adrenaline drain from her system.

At the sound of Clay's footsteps walking back into the room, she opened her eyes and put her hands in her lap.

His eyebrows drew together and he squinted at her. "What happened to you?"

"I guess I'm a little tired."

"You were going to tell me about your day." He went to the refrigerator and pulled out some of the vegetables. "How do you feel about soup and salad?"

She pushed herself back from the table and walked over to the counter next to him. "That sounds wonderful. But you don't have to do this. I can go home and get out of your way."

"I swear, you have to be the most fretful woman I have ever met." He pulled lettuce out of a bag and thumped it on the counter. "I wouldn't have asked you if you wanted something to eat if I were trying to get rid of you."

"Well, okay. Thank you. I do want to stay for a little while and make sure you're okay. I can help cut that up if you want."

He handed her the head of lettuce. "Go for it."

Brigid took a chef's knife from the block, pulled out a cutting board, and began chopping. One of her many jobs had been doing food prep for a salad bar place, so she had some wicked knife-wielding skills.

Clay looked at the pile of chopped lettuce on the board. "That's a little frightening to witness."

She grinned at him. "I've done some time in commercial kitchens."

"I'll say. Have at the carrots." He passed her the bag. "So what did you do today?"

While she quickly julienned the carrots, she told him about her trip to the library and the dog with puppies. "I asked Tracy to make a list of the people Dr. Cassidy thinks might be willing to help out. I can't take care of newborn puppies and all these dogs myself."

"You're right. You can't."

"It's like I have to do everything all at once. I need to form a nonprofit, recruit volunteers, take care of dogs, put up flyers, and a dozen other things. This is turning into way more than I expected. I made a huge list, and then when I looked at it, after I got over the urge to cry, I couldn't figure out what to do first."

Clay dumped the contents of one of the mystery containers from the freezer into a pot on the stove. "What's most important?"

"Finding foster homes for the dogs. Or permanent ones would be even better."

"What gets you there the quickest?"

"I suppose finding volunteers. Putting up flyers maybe? Having the dogs actually returned to the people who lost them would be best of all."

"Okay. Do that first."

"I can't make flyers. I need a computer, but I haven't had a chance to look into that yet." She turned and reached for a bag of red peppers that Clay had placed on the counter. "I've been busy."

"Well, you could borrow mine I suppose."

"*You* have a computer?"

He waved the spoon at her. "Hey, you don't have to look so surprised. Mostly I use it for email and accounting stuff, but it came with a bunch of other programs. You could probably find something you could use for flyers on the thing."

Brigid put down the knife. "Really? Are you sure?"

"You're going to be here all the time anyway for the dogs. And most of the time it's just sitting there being an expensive paperweight."

"I don't know what to say. That's incredibly generous of you."

"If you do this nonprofit thing, you need to get used to the idea that people are going to do nice things because they support what you're doing to help the dogs." He stopped stirring and paused to taste the soup. "Hey, not bad. That froze better than I thought it would."

"I guess you're right. It's all about the dogs, not me."

Clay poured the soup into bowls. "Well, yes and no. It helps if people like you. If you were mean and nasty, I wouldn't let you near my computer. But here you are, making sure that I'm not about to die, which is thoughtful and kind-hearted."

"Well you *are* feeding me, which I appreciate." Brigid set the salad bowl on the table and set out some plates. "Thanks for helping me think this through. I have felt like my brain has been tied up in knots all day."

Clay sat down and moaned as he reached for the salad. "Look at the bright side. At least you didn't spend your day rolling in horse manure to avoid getting kicked in the head like I did."

Brigid laughed as she sat down next to him. "The worst part is that I know you mean that literally." She reached over and tentatively touched the back of his hand. "Are you sure you're okay? I'm still worried about you."

He turned his hand upward to clasp hers. "That's sweet, but I'll be fine. I'm still fast enough to get out of the way."

"You're not just saying that are you?"

"No, I'm not. But I think I may hang up my anvil. Shoeing is something I can do, but it feels like it's time for me to be done with it. Just because you *can* do something doesn't mean you *have* to. I like training better, and I have more control over the environment."

"That does sound safer anyway. Either that or you need to hire your own stunt man." Brigid looked into his eyes and gave his hand a squeeze. "You're not indestructible, you know."

"Actually, I break more easily than you might think." He pulled her hand to his chest, drawing her closer to him, the clean scent of whatever shampoo or soap he used drifting in the air between them.

Brigid's eyes widened and her heart beat faster. The golden flecks in his eyes sparkled in the lamp light with an unmistakable look. She knew what that look meant and part of her wanted to jump out of the chair and run screaming from the room. But as he slowly and tenderly moved toward her, she focused instead on his kindness and set her fears aside. Closing her eyes, she let him kiss her. All the tension in her body evaporated and she let herself enjoy the feel of his warm lips and the slow caress of his hand as he moved to put his arm around her.

He released his hold, looked into her eyes, and whispered, "You're okay, right?"

Brigid traced the scar on his chin with her fingertip. "Yes, I am. Thanks for asking."

"Just checking. Because I might want to do that again."

"Okay. I might like that."

~

They sat holding hands and quietly ate their soup. Although eating one-handed was a little tricky, Brigid hadn't held anyone's hand in a long time, and the warmth of Clay's hand in hers was comforting. The skin on his palm was rough and calloused, but the contact was calming, as if he could sense how nervous she was. He glanced at her, "You haven't run away yet, so that's promising."

She put down her spoon. How did he do that? Were her thoughts that obvious? "This soup is delicious. Do you have the recipe?"

"Nope. I made it up. It was one of those clean-out-the-refrigerator soups. I have no idea what I did." He pointed the spoon toward the bowl. "It's unique like a snowflake."

"A melted one."

"Very funny." He let go of her hand and winced as he got up to carry his dishes over to the sink.

Brigid quickly gobbled down her last few bites of salad and got up to help. "I can clean up."

"Since I feel like I've been run over, I'm not going to argue that point. Just chuck it all in the dishwasher. It's nowhere near full. I'll run it sooner or later."

Brigid put her bowl in the sink and turned to face him. "If you won't see a doctor, you should at least go lie down and get some rest."

"I hate to admit it, but that sounds like a fine idea." He moved closer to her, so they were practically touching. "You know how I warned you that I might want to kiss you again?"

She looked up into his eyes. "Yes."

"I'm thinking I might want to do that now."

"Okay."

Clay wrapped her in his arms and bent his head to kiss her as Brigid stood on her tip toes and put her arms around his neck. Unlike the first soft tender kiss, this time his lips were hungry and passionate on hers.

As the kiss became more intense, Brigid was suffused with sensations she hadn't experienced in an extremely long time, which was both electrifying and alarming. Crazed hormones took over and it was like her body had completely disconnected from her brain. Hadn't she just vowed to be done with men? What was she doing?

She pushed Clay away from her and took a deep breath trying to slow the hammering of her heart in her chest. "Wow. Um. That was…just…wow."

"I hope that's good." He scanned her face, his brow furrowed in concern. "You're not upset are you? Please don't be."

"No. I just haven't. I mean, well, it's been a while and I guess I forgot how that, well…that was just a lot of feelings all at once."

"The feelings aren't bad, are they?"

"No. Well, yes sometimes. I guess I got scared."

Clay put his hand on her neck and caressed her cheek with his thumb. "I don't know exactly what happened to you before, but I want you to know I won't ever hurt you. I promise. Just tell me if what I'm doing upsets you, okay?"

"Okay. I'm afraid you might be finding out more about me than you ever wanted to know."

"Hey, I like finding out because I like *you*." He took her hand in his and grinned. "And don't talk to me about wanting, honey. You might have noticed I'm sorely attracted to you.

Kissing those luscious lips of yours only made it worse. But I'm a patient man and I understand that everyone has a past."

"Sorry I'm a little messed up."

"We're all messed up in our own ways. Heaven knows I am." He wrapped his arms around her again and gave her a gentle heart-melting kiss. "I'm gonna go to bed now. I'll see you in the morning. You drive safe, okay?"

After he left, Brigid cleaned up the kitchen, slowly and methodically hand-washing the dishes while she tried to sort out her tangled emotions. On the one hand, she could easily see herself falling hard for Clay. He was compassionate and funny, and the attraction definitely wasn't one-sided. She couldn't deny it anymore. He was utterly sexy, and the fact that he obviously found her attractive made him even more enticing. Part of her wanted to forget about everything and everyone else, jump into bed with him, and find out exactly how good it would be. If the way he kissed her was any indication, the answer was likely *very, very* good. But she'd been down that road before and it ended in disaster.

Following her heart, or more accurately, her raging hormones, had certainly not served Brigid well in the past. What happened with John was ample evidence of that. When they were first married, no one could have convinced Brigid that she wouldn't enjoy the adventure of military life. She was head-over-heels in love and wanted excitement—traveling and seeing new parts of the country and the world.

When they had first met, John had taken her to a military gala and as he swirled her around the dance floor, Brigid's long formal gown had flown out around her. She felt like Ginger Rogers, beautiful and glamorous. And of course, Richard Gere in *An Officer and a Gentleman* had nothing on John in uniform. He was the most gorgeous man she'd ever met, and when he took her to watch ships pull into port, with sailors standing at attention around the perimeter, Brigid's heart had swelled with patriotism and love for her country. Then when she'd attended John's best friend's military wedding, she'd cried like everyone else. With all the pomp and ceremony, there wasn't a dry eye in the church.

But no one ever talked about what happened to Deborah Winger after Richard Gere carried her out of the dreary factory at the end of the movie. In the beginning of Brigid's marriage, she spent a lot of time trying to keep her sense of humor and making the best of everything. Determined to be the best Army wife in the history of the military, she made every effort to look like she had everything under control. But her stress level increased when she couldn't reach John for weeks. It wasn't very romantic to be stuck in some town in the middle of nowhere all alone during a blizzard. There had been many lonely and depressing experiences like that one. And then when she finally did see John, all he wanted to do was "let off some steam." Over time, his drinking increased to the point that he started blacking out. Half the time he didn't even remember the fights they had. How were you supposed to work out marital issues when your spouse didn't remember what you were arguing about?

The stupidest part was that almost right up to the end, they kept trying to make the marriage work. Both of them were nothing if not stubborn. Neither one of them would concede defeat. Even with all their problems, they'd been determined to stick it out because they believed that tired old quote from Vince Lombardi that "winners never quit." They'd doggedly argued their way through basic training, deployments, countless moves, new jobs, and just plain starting over again and again. Unfortunately, a marriage wasn't a football game and the process of setting up a new life in a new location and trying to make new friends repeatedly wore them both down.

Then John went and got himself killed. Of course, John didn't die before writing a vicious letter filled with words that would live in infamy. That awful "Dear Jane" letter crossed in the mail with her own "Dear John" letter. When she was writing it, scrawling all those furious epithets, she'd grimaced at the irony that his name was actually John. Then after he died, the letter she'd written was returned.

Although John never got the letter, in the end, it didn't really matter anyway. Ultimately, the stress and distance was just too much for their marriage to handle. Before he died, John apparently had enough time to change the beneficiary on his military life insurance policy back to his mother, so in a way, he got the last word, after all.

Brigid also had gained a complete understanding of exactly how angry she could get at another human being. She had never experienced such intense fury with anyone else. And she absolutely *never* wanted to go through that again for any reason.

Brigid shook her head in exasperation. She was such an idiot. The whole reason she was in Alpine Grove was to start over. Had she learned absolutely nothing from her marriage? Getting involved with Clay was doomed to disaster. She should never have let him kiss her. Why on earth was she doing this? And yet, she couldn't seem to resist his quiet, oddly peaceful way of looking at the world. For a guy who had spent his time doing idiotic death-defying stunts and working with huge, potentially dangerous animals, he was strangely introspective. Against her better judgment, she found him intriguing and easy to talk to. For reasons she didn't understand, she was constantly blurting out things that she'd never said to anyone else. Why did she feel compelled to confide in him?

She looked around the cozy old kitchen. It didn't help that she was coming out here every day. If she could find some foster homes, she could move the dogs away from here. It would be better for them to stay in homes with their own families, and maybe she'd make some new friends in the bargain. The last thing she needed was to complicate her life with another difficult man who would end up making a whole lot of demands on her time. She had more than enough to do. Too much, in fact. Tomorrow, she'd work on calling volunteers. And finally make those flyers.

If Clay happened to be around, she needed to try to avoid letting herself revert into a lust-obsessed fool again, and tell him to back off. She had far too many other things to deal with right now. They'd be far better off as friends than as lovers. He already knew that she'd completely botched her marriage. If he were smart, he'd understand that it would be much better for both of them if they didn't cross the line from being friends into any type of physical relationship again.

Brigid dried and put away the last dish and carefully placed the spoons in the silverware drawer, straightening it up a little so the forks, knives, and spoons were organized into tidy stacks with the handles all lined up precisely.

Satisfied that she'd cleaned up as much as she could, she walked through the house and out the door, closing it behind her. Time to go home. Gypsy was probably wondering where her dinner was by now. Good thing dogs were a lot more forgiving than people.

Chapter 5

Nugget & the Arabian

The next morning, Brigid went through the routine of feeding Gypsy, walking Nugget at the police station, and heading out to the ranch to tend to Judge. This was Nugget's last day at the station, since no one had come looking for him. It was looking like he'd be going with her to the ranch the next day. Brigid was upset about the pretty greyhound, who was clearly sad and confused. He probably wondered where his people had gone. The only good news was that no more dogs had come in overnight.

Brigid called Tracy at the vet clinic and was happy to learn that the sheltie and her five new puppies were all doing fine. They'd named the sheltie Shelby after a friend of Tracy's who lived in Los Angeles, but they hadn't named the puppies yet, since they were tiny and almost impossible to tell apart.

While she had Tracy on the phone, Brigid also made an appointment for Judge to get another dip, since she didn't see a way to do it at the ranch. With everything else that had happened, she'd forgotten to ask Clay about that and also about bringing Gypsy with her to the ranch. She had put a notebook in her bag so she could write down all the things she needed to remember to do, so she wouldn't forget something important.

When she arrived at the ranch, everything was quiet and she went into the barn and got Judge ready for his walk.

As usual, he was delighted to see her and thrilled about his outing. What a sweet dog. Some family was going to be very lucky when they adopted him.

She and Judge slowly meandered along the driveway, enjoying the pretty weather. A storm front was supposed to move in, but for the moment, it was a gorgeous day. The horses were out grazing in their pasture and the grasses were bending gracefully in the light breeze. Occasionally a horse would swish its tail or a bird would swoop by, but nothing else disturbed the tranquility of the scene. Brigid took a deep breath and gazed out over the meadow while Judge fixated on a particularly exciting aroma below. Even though it was kind of a pain to drive out to the ranch every day, it was easy to enjoy being here once she arrived.

They returned to the barn and Brigid put Judge back in his kennel. He hopped up on his platform bed and wagged his tail a few times before settling in on his blanket. Brigid walked back out into the sunlight as a red minivan cruised up the driveway, kicking up a plume of dust behind it. The woman behind the wheel was wearing sunglasses, and her long thick light-brown hair flew around her as she zoomed by and parked up near the house next to Brigid's car. Apparently Clay had company. Maybe Brigid wasn't the only woman visiting the ranch. She felt a little stupid realizing that the thought had never even occurred to her that other women might stop by to see Clay. Duh. He'd lived here forever and as she well knew, he certainly wasn't unattractive. The guy probably had no shortage of female companionship.

Brigid wasn't sure what to do. This could be awkward. She stepped back next to the barn as the woman got out and started up the steps. With the boots she was wearing, the woman was probably seven or eight inches taller than Brigid, with the type of willowy build short women could only dream about. Women like that never had problems finding jeans that actually fit. And hers certainly did.

Clay opened the front door wearing a tattered white terrycloth bathrobe and clutching a cup of coffee. His feet were bare and he grinned at the woman who stopped in front of him. She took off her sunglasses, grabbed his shoulders, and gave him a shake before wrapping her arms around him in a massive hug. He held out the coffee in an effort to avoid dumping it all over her and returned the hug, obviously glad to see her.

Brigid wasn't sure what to make of this little reunion. She had planned to go inside to use the computer, but that was before she discovered she'd be interrupting Clay's rendezvous with Ms. Tall Huggy Woman. Fine. Brigid could just go home and figure out how to buy a computer of her own. Maybe she could set that eager librarian on a new research project to find a super-cheap computer that wouldn't skyrocket her credit card over its limit.

As Brigid walked up the driveway toward her car, Clay noticed her and waved. "Hey Brigid. Come on inside."

The tall woman turned to look at Brigid and smiled. She seemed somewhat familiar. Maybe she'd been at the bar. Was she one of the waitresses?

As Brigid approached, she realized that although the woman had fantastic hair, it might be a really good dye job because she was a lot older than Brigid had thought initially. The tiny wrinkles around her eyes indicated that like many women over a certain age, she hadn't embraced the virtues of sunscreen until later in life.

Clay said, "Brigid, this is my sister Tamara Joanne Hadley Lindquist."

Brigid walked up the steps and the woman stretched out her hand. "Please call me TJ."

"If you call her Tammy Jo, she'll hit you," Clay said with a smirk.

Proving the point, TJ whacked him on the upper arm. "Shut up, baby brother."

Brigid shook her hand. "It's nice to meet you." Upon closer inspection, although she had much more delicate features, TJ's eyes were almost identical to Clay's. They were the same warm brown with lighter flecks. The family resemblance was unmistakable.

TJ waved both hands vertically in front of Clay's bathrobe. "Are you planning on getting dressed any time soon? They're going to be here in a few minutes."

"It's been kind of a slow morning." He turned to go inside. "I took some more of those pain killers and fell asleep again."

"You are such a bonehead." TJ followed him and turned her head to watch as Scout shot through the door. "Hi Scout. 'Bye Scout."

"You probably want to catch up," Brigid said. "I was just going to use the computer, if you could show me where it is."

Clay said, "Yeah, uh, okay. I forgot. Hold on. Let me put on some clothes and I'll get it going for you. Have some coffee." He shuffled off down the hallway.

TJ grabbed two mugs and poured coffee from the half-empty pot. She handed one to Brigid and leaned against the counter. "So how do you know Clay?"

Brigid took a sip of coffee. That was the polite way of asking, "Who are you and what are you doing here?" The answer was more complicated than Brigid wanted to admit, so she said simply, "Clay agreed to put a kennel in the barn for a dog. Or more than one, I guess. They're for stray dogs that need homes because their time is up at the police station."

"You mean in the cattle barn?"

Brigid gestured toward the door, "The tall red one over there. I'm trying to find the dogs foster placements or people to adopt them and Clay set up a couple of temporary kennels for the time being."

"That's interesting." TJ took a sip of coffee. "I thought he was going to use the old barn for an indoor arena."

"He mentioned that, but this is only temporary. I'm trying to start a nonprofit and find foster families to take the dogs until they are adopted."

"That's ambitious."

"It's more work than I expected it would be. But there's no animal shelter here. I guess the dogs get shipped off somewhere."

"I know. There's a regional animal-control facility in the southern part of the county, not too far from where I live. Cedar County is huge, so as I understand it, the place is always full."

"Really? So you know about this?"

She nodded. "It's good what you're trying to do. Alpine Grove needs to do a better job of handling animal issues now that so many more people live here. The whole stray dog problem has been shoved aside for too long."

"It sounds like it."

Clay shuffled into the room and put his coffee cup on the counter. He looked less rumpled, but still tired. His pupils were dilated which made his eyes seem extra dark. Brigid raised her eyebrows at him. "Those must be some serious pain-killers."

"Yeah, I had some lying around from last time."

TJ crossed her arms. "You know you aren't supposed to take old medication like that."

"If I were a horse, I'd have given myself some bute and called it good. But I'm not, and people aren't supposed to take horse drugs, so you'd yell at me for that too. Last night I felt like dirt and a couple of aspirin wasn't going to cut it." He wrapped an arm around TJ's shoulders and gave her a squeeze. "Thanks for coming up and helping me out. These pills make me kind of fuzzy and stupid."

"You knew I would." TJ shrugged away from him and put her mug on the counter. "But I can only stay one night. I need to get back to Jim and the kids."

"I know." Clay smiled at her. "But I'll let you ride Hank. You know you want to."

TJ turned toward the window. "I saw him out there. He's looking good. You must be pleased."

"Yeah, he's coming along nicely. I could set up some barrels for you so you can put him through his paces." He looked at Brigid, who had been standing quietly, feeling like a non-equestrian third wheel. He gestured toward the hallway. "Oh yeah, the computer. I forgot again. This way."

They walked past the stairs that went up to the second floor, and she followed Clay into a small bedroom that had been converted into an office. A computer sat on a desk, surrounded by mountains of papers. Clay reached around, turned on the computer and monitor, and then tapped some keys to log in. He pointed toward the chair. "All yours. I need to go deal with this horse. They're supposed to arrive in about fifteen minutes, assuming they didn't get lost."

Brigid sat down in the chair. "Is that why TJ is here?"

"Yeah. She's the best horsewoman you'll ever meet. I called her last night and asked her to help out with this… uh, what do you call it? Um…oh yeah…*Arabian*! He looks to be a beautiful animal and they're bringing him all the way from Nevada, so it was too late to cancel." He put his hand on her shoulder. "This horse is one of the ones you want to stay away from, okay?"

"No problem. I'll just figure out how to make some flyers and go."

He tucked a strand of hair behind her ear. "You'll be back later though, right?"

"Yes, I have to walk Judge." She moved her head away from his hand. "I, ah, was thinking that it might be a good idea to not do…well…I think we should be friends."

Clay pulled his hand away and took a step back from the chair. "Is something wrong?"

"No. I just think we both have a lot going on, and it's probably best not to get involved. I promise I'll work really hard to get these dogs out of your barn as soon as possible, so you can turn it into an arena like you want."

"Are you worried about that? Because I'm not. I've been talking about turning it into an arena for ages and didn't do anything about it. There's no rush."

TJ yelled from the other room, "Clay, what are you *doing*? They're here."

He glanced at the doorway and then at Brigid. "I've got to go and deal with this, but I'd like to finish this conversation later."

"Be careful." She turned to the computer and stared at the icons for a moment. The confused look on Clay's face probably wasn't just from the drugs. Oh well. He'd just have to deal with it. With a small shake of her head, she clicked an icon and got to work.

~

By the time Brigid had figured out the computer enough to create flyers, she probably had sprouted a few new gray hairs. But in the end, she had prevailed against the vagaries of technology. She carefully shut down the computer and left the office with her printouts clutched to her chest. Since she didn't have photographs of the dogs, she was hoping "Found: black greyhound" would be descriptive enough.

Closing the door to the house behind her, she got into her car. Clay and TJ didn't seem to be around anywhere. Maybe they were out in the horse barn. Presumably, the people who dropped off the creature had left by now.

On her way home, she stopped by the Kmart and got an answering machine, more paper for Clay's printer, and a few other odds and ends just to give her credit card a little more exercise. Then she stopped by the vet clinic, picked up the list of potential volunteers from Tracy, and took a peek at the puppies. They were so tiny! Who wouldn't want to adopt something so adorable? While she was processing Brigid's credit card to pay for more puppy care, Tracy assured her that both the momma dog and her babies were doing well.

Once Brigid was finally back at home, she curled up with Gypsy on the sofa and pulled out her long to-do list. She stroked the little dog's head. "Oh Gypsy, I forgot *again* to ask Clay about taking you out there with me. He was all doped up from pain-killers and his sister was there. I don't know her and it was uncomfortable and awkward. But you're probably getting tired of me disappearing on you all the time. I promise things will settle down soon. There's no reason you couldn't have hung out with me while I was fighting with the computer today. I could have really used the moral support."

Gypsy wagged her tail and gave Brigid's hand a lick as a show of solidarity. Before returning to her tasks, Brigid gave the little dog a hug. "You are such a good girl."

Later she went back to the station to walk Nugget. On her way out, she stopped by Jake's office, where he was chowing down on junk food again. He wiped a glob of ketchup from his mouth with a napkin. "Hi Brigid. How's it going?"

"Great! No new dogs, right?"

"Nothing on my radar today. You taking the skinny one tomorrow?"

"I'll pick up Nugget tomorrow morning. I put up some flyers and I'm hoping someone will call."

"Yeah, good luck. You were right. That's a pretty dog. I'm kinda surprised no one came by looking for it."

"I know. It breaks my heart to see how lonely and confused he is. See you tomorrow."

Brigid stopped by her house to feed Gypsy an early dinner and then got back in the Honda for the evening trip out to the ranch. She wasn't looking forward to continuing the "just friends" conversation with Clay. Finishing that discussion was probably going to involve saying things that were better left unsaid, particularly in front of his sister.

At the ranch, Brigid took Judge out for his walk, again enjoying the peaceful late afternoon scene. The scent of warm grasses and wildflowers wafted on the breeze. Spring was certainly beautiful here. As they slowly meandered back up the driveway, she noticed a few lights had been turned on in the house. Clay and TJ were both inside, their movements visible through the glass door and the windows along the wrap-around porch.

She settled Judge in his kennel and closed the gate with a sigh. "I guess I have to do this now. Tomorrow, you'll get to meet your new barn-mate, Nugget." The dog wagged his tail, circled a few times on his platform bed and laid down. "Be good, Judgie."

Brigid walked to the house, up the steps, and knocked on the door. Clay and TJ were sitting at the table and Clay waved at her to come inside. As she walked across the living room toward the kitchen, Clay stood up and gestured toward the table. "Want something to eat? TJ was just telling me how she was about to make dinner."

"No I wasn't," TJ said, and took a long pull from the beer bottle in front of her.

Brigid shook her head. "I can't stay. But you said you wanted to talk to me."

Clay reached into a cabinet and grabbed a bag of tortilla chips. "I do, but I'm hungry. Why don't you sit down for a minute? Do you want something to drink? TJ brought beer."

"Which Clay isn't having until he stops taking those pills," TJ said, glaring at him.

"No thank you. I'm fine," Brigid said.

"I'm drug-free now, so you can just calm yourself down." Clay thumped bowls of chips and salsa on the table and turned back to the refrigerator. "I'm having a beer."

Brigid sat down. Clay's eyes didn't look strange anymore and he seemed significantly more alert. She wasn't sure what to say. Maybe she'd walked into the middle of a family dispute. Oh perfect. After a few more seconds of uncomfortable silence, she volunteered, "Did the horse arrive okay?"

"Yes, he's fine." TJ said. "But he was definitely ready to get out of that trailer."

"He's a little reactive, but with some desensitization work he'll be a good horse, I think." Clay picked up a tortilla chip and sat down next to TJ. "The guy who owns him seems willing to let me invest the time in the training the horse needs."

"You said he brought the horse here from Nevada?" Brigid said.

"The horse world is a lot smaller than you might think. Word gets around," TJ said. She shoved at Clay, who was busily munching more chips. "He's famous."

Clay rolled his eyes melodramatically. "Ugh, spare me."

"You are. Believe me, no one finds that more surprising than I do." TJ said.

"I don't think the guy was terribly impressed this morning, since I probably sounded like I was half stoned." He grinned at Brigid and said in a surfer dude voice, "Wow, man, it's like…a *horse. Cool!*"

Brigid laughed. "I doubt it was that bad."

"Good thing you let me do the talking for all the hard questions. Wise move, Gumby," TJ said.

Brigid raised her eyebrows. "Gumby?"

"Shut up, Tammy Jo," Clay said.

TJ whacked him on the arm. "You shut up. And I hope now that your brain is back on straight, you'll stay away from that Yearwood horse."

"I'm not going back there. I told Brigid that last night after I got home." He gestured at her across the table. "Hey, back me up here."

Brigid nodded. "It's true. He did say that."

TJ looked unconvinced. "I can't believe you went out there in the first place. Are you nuts? You know Randy Yearwood is as dumb as a box of rocks."

"That's not the horse's fault. And Randy was a friend of Cole's so I felt obligated." Clay crunched on a tortilla chip. "It turns out the horse might be a little skittish."

"Gee, you think so? When we talked last night, I believe the technical term you used was *fruitcake*," TJ said.

Clay held a tortilla chip in front of him and gazed at it thoughtfully. "Brigid, is that greyhound showing up tomorrow?"

"I'm afraid so. He was still there when I left. I put up flyers though. I hope he won't be here long," Brigid said.

"What is the name of your organization?" TJ asked.

Brigid reached for a chip. "I don't have one yet."

TJ got up and went to the refrigerator. "You probably should talk to a lawyer. There's a guy in town here. His parents own the hardware store. Or they used to anyway."

"Yeah, Larry Lowell is still here, I think," Clay said. "TJ knows about this stuff since she's on the board of the Education Alliance. They raise money for school programs and needed a smarty-pants accountant."

TJ handed Clay another beer and sat down. "You could have been a smarty-pants accountant too, if you wanted. You were supposed to be getting a business degree."

"I don't recommend working ten horses a day until all hours of the morning while you're in school. It cuts into your study time." Clay waved a chip at TJ. "Why are you still ragging on this after all this time?"

"Because you could have been killed yesterday, you bonehead." TJ sighed. "I still think you would have stayed in school if you hadn't met that woman."

Brigid could tell by the irritated expression on Clay's face that he probably would rather she not hear this conversation. She dipped a chip into the salsa and tried to look nonchalant like she wasn't interested, even though she was closely monitoring every word.

"Do you really have to go there right now, Tammy Jo?" Clay said.

TJ thumped his arm. "I'm just saying your brief, ill-fated marriage didn't help matters. After Cole died, you were a mess, and then you go and hook up with her. When that falls apart after ten minutes, the next thing I know you're traveling all over the country taking unbelievably stupid risks. Mom and Dad were terrified you were actually *trying* to kill yourself."

"I talked to Dad the other day and he sounded good. They're in New Mexico somewhere. I guess they found some great RV park where they've been for a few weeks." Clay took a sip from his beer. "We've made our peace."

TJ leaned forward, resting her elbows on the table. "I know. It's just that you really scared me when you called yesterday, Clay. I already lost one brother. I don't want to lose you too."

He put his arm around TJ's shoulder and hugged her. "Don't worry about me. That's not going to happen if I have any say in it."

∿

After getting upset at Clay, TJ seemed to run out of energy, and she excused herself to go upstairs and call her husband. Brigid stood up. "I should go."

Clay slowly pushed himself up from the table. "I'll walk you out."

"You look tired. I think I can make it down the steps to my car all by myself."

"You're right. I am tired. And I haven't had enough beer to cover up the fact that everything hurts again. But I want to talk to you."

Brigid turned to leave and Clay followed her out to her car. He leaned against the driver's side door, effectively blocking her access to it. Sneaky. He raised a palm toward the darkening sky. "So, could you please tell me what happened between yesterday and today?"

"Nothing. I just think it's a bad idea to start anything right now. We barely know each other and as you've already figured out, I'm not exactly good at relationships. I think it's better for both of us to just remain friends."

He crossed his arms. "That's quite a speech."

"Well, it's true." She'd practiced it in her head a hundred times and thought it was pretty good actually.

"That all sounds very logical. But you didn't really say anything about how you feel." He reached out to take her hand. "And I'd like to know."

"I feel fine."

"You know that's not what I mean." He interlaced his fingers with hers. "I know how I feel about you, but I'd like to know how you feel about me. Maybe it's been a while, but the last time I checked, most women don't generally kiss someone like you kissed me last night without feeling *anything*."

"Well, of course I like you. You've been very nice to me and helped with the dogs."

"I like you too." He pulled her toward him, so she stepped forward close enough to sense the halo of heat from his body warming the cool evening air. "And I'm glad you think I'm nice. That's not a word often used to describe me."

"Well, I do think you're a nice person. But like I said, my history…my marriage…well I don't need to go into it, since you obviously already *know,* but it was a disaster. I'm just trying not to make another mistake. It's better this way."

"Or maybe it's time to let the past be in the past." He scanned her face as he slowly pulled her into his embrace and pressed his lips to hers. Shivers went down her spine and her pulse began to race. Maybe he had a point. Clay didn't look, sound, smell, taste, or behave like John, so why did she keep expecting him to? Finally, she just gave in to the sensations, letting herself feel whatever she was going to feel, grabbing at his shirt, and running her hands underneath the cloth, trying to get closer and touch more of that warm, intoxicating skin.

By the time they released each other, they were both breathing heavily. He cupped her jaw in his palm and smiled. "I gotta tell you, I don't think that's a mistake."

She leaned her head against his hand and closed her eyes, enjoying the caress of his fingers threading through her hair. "You might be right. *Nice* might not be the best word to describe you."

He ran a fingertip around the edge of her ear. "So how do you feel?"

She opened her eyes again. "Good. Too good. Way, way too good."

"So does that mean we're more than just friends?"

"I don't know that I can come out here and see you every day and *not* think about kissing you." At the look in his eyes, she put her hand against his chest. "But if we do this, we need to go really slowly."

"As slow as you want. I'm like a turtle."

Brigid giggled. "I thought you were Gumby."

"I'm going to kill Tammy Jo for saying that."

She tapped his chest playfully with her fingertips. "Hey, don't call her Tammy Jo."

Brigid drove home in a daze. After giving Gypsy some affection, she grabbed a sandwich and then went up to bed. She stared at the ceiling unable to sleep, reliving the feel of Clay's body wrapped around hers. One kiss and she'd completely caved. Okay sure, it was a mind-blowing kiss, but what were the odds that she wouldn't mess this up? He was going to regret ever meeting her. With a sigh, she rolled over and squeezed her eyes shut in an effort to empty her mind. Some things were better not to think about.

~

The next morning, Brigid went to the station to pick up Nugget. The flyers had netted zero interest so far, and he was still there waiting for the owners he'd probably never see again. Brigid continued to hold out a tiny hope that she'd get a message on her new answering machine one day from a family desperate to have him returned to them. But until then or until he found a new home, Nugget would be a guest of the V Bar H ranch.

At the station, she waved to Jake and went out to the kennels. In addition to Nugget, a new dog was dancing around frantically in a kennel. It was a young dog that looked like some type of schnauzer. She'd checked her answering machine. When had this dog shown up? It appeared Nugget's excursion was going to have to wait a few minutes.

The new dog was yapping like crazy, which Nugget did not seem to appreciate. He was curled up in the corner of his cage looking sad. "Sorry sweetie. Let me walk this wild thing, then I'll take you out to the ranch. Judge is kind of a goof, but at least he's usually quieter than this dog."

When Brigid walked the schnauzer, it became apparent that the dog had not spent much time on a leash before. The dog zigged and zagged attempting to drag Brigid every which way. When she brought the little dog back to the cage, she discovered to her dismay that the space needed to be cleaned. Although the fact that the dog was cute was a big point in her favor, the fact that she wasn't housebroken was not going help her get adopted.

Brigid sighed and put the dog in different kennel, then busied herself cleaning the first one. As she got down on her knees, she was reminded of an Eric Clapton song. She glanced over at the dog's inquisitive expression. "What do you think of Layla?" The dog jumped around looking pleased and Brigid sat back on her heels. "Okay. If it works for you, it works for me." Brigid laughed as Layla ran around in a happy circle, seemingly thrilled with her new moniker.

Brigid leashed up Nugget, who in his quiet way seemed to understand that he was leaving the yappy schnauzer behind. They walked through the station and Brigid stopped at Jake's office. "I'm taking Nugget. Do you have the forms for me to sign?"

Jake rummaged through the piles of folders on his desk and yanked one out. "Here you go."

Nugget stood quietly next to Brigid while she signed her name. She looked up at Jake. "When did the schnauzer show up?"

"Early this morning we got a call. It was chasing a cat in town. The dog treed the cat and was barking its head off, waking up half the neighborhood. No one could catch it, so they called us. Officer Davidson is pretty cranky about the whole thing."

"I'll be back later to walk her. Unfortunately, she doesn't seem to be housebroken, so if you see her looking anxious, please take her out."

"Now that you're coming by, I don't go back there."

Brigid clenched the leash in her hand more tightly. "Maybe you could check just this once? I'll be back later, as usual."

"All right. I guess I can."

Brigid walked Nugget through the building and out to her car. She opened the back door of the Honda and the dog gave her a disconsolate look, as if he didn't know what to do. Brigid said, "Come on, get in. Load up. Let's go!" in a happy, perky voice as she gestured toward the car. Nugget stood motionless, staring at her as if she'd lost her mind.

Brigid's shoulders slumped. "Really? You've never ridden in a car before? How did they get you here?" The dog was skinny, but tall. She tried wrapping her arms around Nugget's torso and putting his front paws on the floor of the back of the car. Nugget stood motionless and turned his head to gaze at her incredulously. "Oh come on, Nugget. The back feet too." She lifted the dog's hind end into the car. With a small grunt, Nugget scuttled forward and she closed the door.

Brigid got into the driver's seat and found Nugget's long nose next to her ear. She pushed it gently. "Nugget, you need to back up." He turned and hopped up on the back-seat. Brigid looked in the rear-view mirror and saw nothing except an expanse of black fur.

Using her side mirrors, she backed out of the parking space and headed north toward the ranch. Nugget perched on the back seat, wobbling precariously every time she slowed down. Naturally, the one traffic light in Alpine Grove was red, and he fell off the seat onto the floor when she stopped. She turned to look over her shoulder at him. "Sorry." Nugget glared at her and hopped back up onto the seat. "This would all be so much better if you would just lie down, you know." Nugget wasn't buying into the idea and continued his precarious vigil.

By the time they reached the highway, Nugget was drooling profusely. Brigid opened a back window for him, but all it seemed to do was cause dog slobber to fly around the car. She wiped a slimy glob off her cheek and rubbed her hand on her jeans.

At the turn to the ranch, Nugget lost his balance again and fell off the seat. He then made some ghastly retching sounds before spewing the contents of his stomach all over the back of the Honda.

Brigid turned to looked over her shoulder and found Nugget's nose next to her head again. He heaved up the last of his breakfast onto her shoulder, shirt, and pants. It was quite a performance in projectile vomiting. "Gross, Nugget! What is in that food you have been eating at the station? That is the worst smell, ever. Ugh."

Brigid pulled up next to the barn, where Judge was barking gleefully within. She looked around to see who was here. Clay was in the arena with a shiny black horse doing something, although it was impossible to tell what. Outside the fence, TJ was sitting on Hank, leaning forward, and resting her elbows on the saddle, watching him.

Brigid turned back to the car and saw that Nugget had spewed used dog food all over the back of the front seat as well as the floor of the car. Nice. A piece of well-digested kibble caught her eye and she brushed it off her shoulder. She probably smelled like the interior of Nugget's stomach now. Yuck.

After gathering the leash from the front seat, she unloaded Nugget from the car. Unlike getting into the car, getting out was no problem for the dog. But now he was disgusting and reeked of vomit. As did she. There was no way she could put him in the cage like this. She needed to hose him off, but the tiny laundry sink near the tack room wasn't going to cut it. A hose had to be around somewhere, since they wouldn't use that sink to fill the huge horse troughs, much less to wash horses.

She walked with the dog around to the side of the barn and the arena came into view. Nugget let out a sharp bark, followed by a spate of hysterical howling, growling, whining, and shrieky err-howling, rrring, rowling and other bizarre alien barking noises that were totally uncharacteristic and alarming. Startled, Brigid struggled to hold the whirling dog, dragging him back around the building toward the entrance.

Up until this point, Nugget had never uttered a peep in Brigid's presence. Once he was back in front of the building, he calmed down and Brigid let out the breath she didn't realize she'd been holding.

TJ walked around the side of the barn and gestured toward the arena. "What in heaven's name are you doing with that dog? Didn't you see the Arabian over there?"

"Maybe Nugget doesn't like horses. I've never seen him behave this way. I've never even heard him make a sound before."

"Well, clearly he knows how. You need to deal with this dog and keep him away from the horses—especially the Arabian."

"Do you know if there's a hose somewhere around here?"

TJ gestured toward the other side of the building. "On the outside. Over there." She stomped back around the barn, grumbling under her breath.

Brigid flicked a piece of well-masticated dog food off Nugget's back. "I don't think she's your biggest fan." Nugget just stared at her with his big round dark-brown eyes. "It's okay, sweetie. I don't think she likes me much either."

~

Brigid walked around the other side of the barn and found an old green hose with the end dangling into a large galvanized metal water trough. She readjusted her hold on the leash and bent down to turn the water on. Nugget barked sharply in her ear and she leaped away from the spigot.

The dog had turned to face Clay, who was leaning casually on the building. She glared at him and twisted the leash in her hands. "I think I'm deaf in one ear now."

He raised his eyebrows and said in a voice that was almost a whisper. "You're not looking or smelling your best either. Is that dog food on your shirt?"

Brigid looked down. Yuck. "Nugget got carsick. I'm not sure my Honda will ever be the same."

"You might want to lower your voice. It's clear you've had a rough morning, but the dog is picking up the fact you're mad about it. You're upsetting him, and I think he's upset enough just being here as it is."

Nugget was standing motionless looking at them, his eyes wide. Brigid said, "He likes me, but I'm not so sure he likes you. Jake said he's not fond of men. And I really don't think he likes horses *at all*. He lost his marbles when he saw that black horse."

"I know. My darling big sister is all over my case again. That woman has a nasty tongue on her and the last thing I need is another lecture." He moved away from the wall putting his hands behind his back and stepping slowly around Brigid. She turned her head because she could barely hear him. The words he was saying didn't match how he was saying them. He had to be just as furious with her as TJ was, but he said softly, "I told you about that Arabian, Brigid. He's reactive and just about as green as a horse can be. You need to be careful."

"I didn't get near him! We were way over here. I can't help it if Nugget barked."

"Look at him." Clay inclined his head slightly toward Nugget. "His pupils are so big, his eyes are practically black, and his tail is glued underneath his legs touching his belly."

"Well, at least he's being quiet now, even though you're still here. Maybe Jake was wrong about his attitude toward men."

"But, look at him. He's not happy. Not happy at all. He's afraid and uncertain because of all the new smells everywhere. And he's probably got a sore tummy, but he's still hungry too, since his breakfast is all over your car. And you."

Clay had moved slowly so that he was now standing alongside Nugget, who sniffed at him a few times but was otherwise unconcerned. Somehow, Clay had made himself seem smaller. Brigid couldn't tell what he'd done. Maybe he was hunching his shoulders.

He was so quiet that Brigid wasn't sure when Clay first touched the dog, but now he was doing something with his fingertips on Nugget's back. The dog pulled his lips back as if he were going to snarl, but no sound came out. Brigid clenched her hands, tightening up on the leash, and both Clay and Nugget looked at her at the same time.

Clay continued what he was doing and said, "Stop messing with the leash. He can feel that."

"Look at him. He's showing his teeth. Be careful! I think he's about to bite you."

"No he's not." Clay put his other hand on the dog, his fingers running down Nugget's back in long strokes, and Brigid realized he was doing some type of dog massage.

He glanced up at her. "When I was on the road, I met a guy with a couple Borzois. I think we were in Omaha at the time. Have you ever seen those dogs? Russian wolfhounds? They're huge and if you're not paying attention, they can vacuum food off a kitchen counter in thirty seconds flat without even having to stretch. But they're the sweetest dogs you'll ever meet. Greyhounds and Borzois are both sight hounds. I found out that these dogs don't just run like the wind. They smile too. It's a sign of submission, not aggression."

Brigid looked more closely at Nugget. His pupils had returned to normal and his head and tail had both dropped. The dog's body language did seem to indicate that he was more relaxed. "I had no idea."

With one hand still on the dog, Clay reached into a back pocket and pulled out a red bandanna, which he held out to Nugget. He whispered something to the dog, who looked concerned about the cloth, but took a few tentative sniffs.

"What are you doing?" Brigid said.

"Letting him get to know what that Arabian smells like. They aren't going to get near each other, but he's going to smell that horse living here, so he needs to get used to it."

"What did you do? Rub that all over the horse?"

Clay straightened slightly and handed the bandanna to Brigid. "I'll have you know that this isn't just any bandanna. This is a very scary horse-eating bandanna."

Brigid laughed. "There certainly are a lot of horse-eating things around here."

"Horse-eating things could be anywhere. You just never know." Clay started rubbing Nugget in a slightly different way. He nodded at Brigid. "Why don't you dunk that in the trough and clean him up a little. The water in the trough isn't as cold. If you point that hose at him, I promise you, he won't appreciate the temperature of what comes up from the well."

Brigid wiped down the dog as best she could while Clay whispered to Nugget about the bed he'd made for him and how he had a friendly but kind of dopey roommate to keep him company. Brigid felt like a little piece of her heart melted as Clay continued to massage the dog while she cleaned him. Clay was literally whispering sweet nothings in the greyhound's ear and Nugget seemed to enjoy all the endearments and attention.

When Brigid was done, Clay stood up straight and stretched his arms out in front of him. "My thrashed-out back is likely to let me know about this tonight."

They walked Nugget around the barn area to help him acclimate a little more. TJ must have put the Arabian away somewhere and the horses grazing off on the other end of the field didn't seem to worry Nugget. Finally, they walked back to the barn, where Judge barked a few times to express his excitement about the canine visitor. Brigid reassured him that his walk was next on the agenda.

Nugget strolled inside his new enclosure and immediately went to the platform bed in the back, which sported an old blanket much like the one in Judge's kennel. Nugget moaned in satisfaction and grunted a few times as he curled up and settled in.

Brigid put her hand on Clay's arm. "After you were hurt, you still made another dog bed. Look at how Nugget loves it. Thank you."

"Well, I wasn't so doped-up and stupid that I couldn't still use a hammer."

Brigid went to Judge's kennel and put on his leash for his walk. Clay stood quietly and followed them out of the barn. They walked together down the driveway while Judge busied himself with his morning routine. Brigid leaned on the pasture fence waiting for Judge. "So were you massaging Nugget?"

"Sort of, but it's a little different than a regular massage. It's a horse thing called TTouch. The woman who invented it is one of the nicest ladies you ever want to meet, and I talked to her at a couple horse clinics. The idea with TTouch is that it helps calm animals that are experiencing stress."

"Interesting. Whatever you did certainly seemed to work on Nugget."

With a sly half-smile, he said, "Maybe I'll try it on you sometime."

Chapter 6

Stinks & Storms

Driving home in the Honda was unpleasant, even with all the windows down. While Nugget was getting his massage, the residue of the dog's digestive disturbance had ample time to seep deep into the car upholstery and carpet. Having the smell on her clothes as well just increased the overpowering and incredibly noxious aroma swirling around as Brigid drove back to town.

She walked into her house feeling windblown and stinky. After a largely futile attempt to clean the Honda and a quick shower, she set to work calling potential volunteers on the list she'd gotten from Tracy at the vet clinic. She spent far too much time talking to answering machines, which was frustrating. Didn't anyone ever pick up the phone? Clearly, it was time to reassess the plan of attack. If she was going to have to leave messages, maybe the easiest thing would be to invite everyone to a meeting at her house. It probably would be a good idea to create an invitation and put it at the vet clinic and other places around town as well.

During the cold-calling festival, Brigid did manage to get through to a couple of women who sounded interested and said they would come. One woman named Judith was on the board of some other nonprofit. She seemed a little bossy, but basically nice. Another woman named Sonia had retired in Alpine Grove and admitted she was looking for something to do. She was extremely cordial and polite, but didn't want to chat. Little did the woman know how very *many* things Brigid could give her to do.

Later, Brigid decided to go to the station before heading back out to the ranch, since she could walk the several blocks to get there instead of driving. The less time she spent in her Honda, the better. After her effort to de-stink the car, she'd left the windows down in the hope that someone would steal it. Maybe someone out there was dumb enough to rip off a car that smelled like dog barf. Probably not, but a girl could dream.

She got to the station and discovered to her dismay that Layla's kennel needed cleaning once again. She took the dog for a long walk, cleaned the kennel, and fed the dog her dinner. Brigid wrote a reminder to herself in her little notebook to make flyers about the schnauzer. Maybe she had been an outdoor dog.

Some people had dogs like Scout that never left the yard. Layla wasn't like that and it was hard to imagine Layla staying put, much less being focused on anything like Scout was. That dog was so fixated on tending to his cats, he'd never leave the ranch. Even though Brigid had never actually seen the cats, it was encouraging to know that he'd apparently adjusted to the lack of cattle to herd. Dogs could be so adaptable.

Brigid smiled at the thought of Scout as she made herself a quickie sandwich and fed Gypsy an early dinner. Bracing herself against the smell, she got back in the Honda for the journey northward. Horses were stinky. Maybe Clay had recommendations for different cleaning chemicals she could try on the interior of her car. Although having seen his truck, maybe not.

At the ranch, she parked the car in front of the barn and went to let out Nugget and Judge. The both stood up, barking and wagging expectantly at her. "Hello boys. Are you ready to go out?" After refreshing their water dishes, she decided to take Nugget out first to see if she could determine if his mood had improved after an afternoon of rest. "Sorry Judgie. I need to see how he's doing first."

Nugget pressed his head into her thigh and she stroked his smooth fur. "Aww, you must be feeling better. You're doing the snuggle thing again." After Brigid attached his leash, they went out the door. She was a little apprehensive about taking him out, but she hadn't seen the Arabian anywhere, so she hoped everything would be okay.

They had a mercifully uneventful walk down the driveway and back. Nugget seemed to be back to his typical quiet self, happily trotting along and delicately poking and sniffing at the grass with his long snout. When he was done, she returned him to his kennel and repeated the process with Judge. After feeding them dinner, she went up to the house to use the computer. Clay wasn't outside and she was afraid to barge into the house again. She knocked as loudly as possible on the door, but got nothing except silence in response.

She turned and leaned on the porch railing, looking out across the pastures, unsure what to do. The horses were contentedly grazing in the late afternoon twilight as usual. It was quiet and peaceful, until all four horses suddenly raised their heads simultaneously.

Across the road in the distance, a black horse leaped out from the opening in the trees, dirt flying up from his hooves. Clay was riding the horse bareback, his body pressed against the horse's neck as the horse galloped across the meadow toward the road. Brigid watched as he eased the horse out of the gallop to a trot, then to a walk. He turned the horse away from the house and went down the road toward the highway. Brigid wondered where they were going. A few minutes later, they appeared out of a copse of aspens, walking up the road toward the house. The gleaming ebony horse practically pranced up the driveway having obviously enjoyed the circuitous route through the trees.

They took another detour around the barns and arena and then continued up to the house, stopping in front of Brigid on the porch. The horse seemed somewhat concerned about having someone standing there, but Clay did something and the horse just snorted and stood quietly.

A little afraid to move, Brigid smiled slightly. "So this is the scary horse?"

"Aw, he's not so scary. Just young. Meet Aziz. He's got some longer, fancier name, but I can never remember it."

"He's gorgeous. I don't think I've ever seen such a pretty horse up close."

"Yeah, he knows it too." Clay slid off and took the reins. "Want to walk with us while he cools down some more?"

"Are you sure I won't cause a problem?"

"He's fine. It's good for him to meet new people."

Brigid walked down the stairs, keeping a close eye on the horse's movements as she stepped over next to Clay. "All right, but keep him away from dog food bags. If he freaks out, I'm running away as fast as I can."

"See, you're learning from my mistakes."

"I'll leave you to get stepped on and abraded. I'm way too big of a chicken to gallop some gigantic horse across a field, particularly with no saddle."

"We were working on paying attention to speed and direction. Going fast and slow over different terrain. Sometimes a saddle can get in the way of communication. It depends on the horse. You convey a lot with your body, so not having anything between you and the horse can be helpful in certain situations. It can help with bonding."

"Sure."

"It's also kind of fun."

"Your sister might be right about you being a little nuts."

"Probably."

～

After Aziz was cooled down, Clay turned him out into a pasture and the sleek Arabian ambled off into the expanse of grass. Brigid leaned on the fence watching him as Clay closed the gate.

They started back to the house and Brigid said, "Would it be okay if I use your computer again? I need to make another flyer for a dog and one about a meeting I'm having at my house."

"Sure. I'm not doing anything with it."

"I'll try not to stay too late."

Clay stopped and turned to her. "I told you, it's no big deal. Do what you need to do."

"I'm just worried you might want your privacy."

"There used to be people crawling all over this property." He gestured toward a small building that was set away from the house. "That's why that bunk-house is there. It's got five sets of old wooden bunk beds that were full of ranch hands at certain times of year."

"That must have been interesting."

"It had its moments. Privacy is not something I'm particularly concerned about and I like having you here. Pretend you're a ranch hand if it helps."

Brigid laughed. "I don't think anyone will confuse me with a ranch hand."

"Well, you're a lot prettier and you smell better than most of them. Except maybe earlier today."

"I took a shower."

He grinned and bent to sniff at her. "Yeah, I noticed. That's quite an improvement."

They went back to the house and Clay turned on the computer for Brigid. As she settled into the office chair, he picked up a stack of papers and put them on the floor with a thump. "Sorry about the mess in here. You want something to eat?"

"No thank you. You don't have to feed me all the time."

"All right." He crouched down next to the pile of paper and started riffling through it. "I know my filing system isn't the greatest, but I need to grab a phone number out of here."

"I didn't know that was a filing system."

"I take the archaeological approach. Older stuff is at the bottom. You have to dig for it." He stood up, holding a small yellow sticky note. "See! I knew just where it was."

"Impressive. You have many talents."

Clay placed his hands on the back of the chair and leaned over to whisper in her ear, "You don't know the half of it. Let me know if you need anything."

He left the room and Brigid got to work creating her flyers. Good thing she'd had so many secretarial jobs and knew how to touch-type. And that Clay had moved some of the junk off the desk. Last time she was here, she kept bumping into piles of papers, but she'd been afraid to touch anything. Years of office work had taught her to never mess with stuff on someone else's desk without asking first.

With a yawn, she leaned her elbow on the desk, resting her head on her palm as she slowly pecked at characters on the keyboard with one finger. After the long day of being thrown-up on, cleaning, and driving in her disgusting car, maybe she was a little tired.

She jolted awake just as the chair rolled out from under her. At the sensation of falling, her heart skittered in her chest, and then suddenly Clay's hands grabbed her under the armpits. Setting her back on the chair, he moved back so she could resettle herself. He was wearing nothing except boxer shorts, which revealed the fact that the many bruises on his body had become quite a colorful rainbow of hurt. He scratched his chin absently. "Sorry. I didn't mean to startle you. I saw the light on and came downstairs to turn it off."

Brigid looked at the screen which no longer displayed her document. It was black with stars shooting by, so it was like she was flying through an episode of *Star Trek*. "What time is it?"

"About two-thirty."

"In the morning?"

"Uh yeah, what do you think? It's dark outside."

Brigid glanced at the window, which indicated that he was right. It was pitch-black out there and the rain had finally arrived. She tapped the space bar and her document reappeared. She had managed to type three words. How pathetic. "I guess I fell asleep. I need to finish this and get home."

"Why don't you just sleep here and finish it in the morning?"

"I told you, I'm not ready for that."

"Not with *me*." Clay sighed and rubbed his face with his hands, then gestured toward the door. "I didn't mean it like that. This is a four-bedroom house. Just pick a room that doesn't have me in it and go to sleep. I think sheets are on the beds. I'm sure the one TJ stayed in has them anyway. She gets all hysterical about that kind of thing."

"I can't do that. I have to get home. Gypsy is there all by herself."

"I'm sure she'll be fine. But you shouldn't drive in the middle of the night when you're this tired and there's a storm."

"I guess it was kind of a long day." Brigid slumped in the chair. "I didn't realize how exhausted I was."

Clay leaned against the desk. "You're not going to be able to keep up all this running around forever."

"I know. For one thing, I'm going to have to get a job before I bankrupt myself. My savings aren't going to last much longer, particularly if I keep handing my credit card over to the Alpine Grove Veterinary Clinic."

"I'm sure you'll figure something out. You're doing great so far."

"I don't know about that. And I'm not sure what I'm going to do about my car either. At this point, I'm thinking I should just drive into the lake. I think it's the only thing that will kill the odor."

Clay smiled. "That is a pretty rank smell you've got there."

"I also had to clean up after a new dog at the station. I think after today my nostrils may never be the same."

"Well, honey, I'm afraid you've set out on a hard road. Take it from me, caring for animals is a full-time job. I don't care what kind they are—cows, horses, dogs—they always need tending. And the more animals you have, the more people it takes."

"Today, I called the names on a list of possible volunteers. I couldn't get through to most of them, but I'm setting up a meeting. I'm sure everything will be better when I have some help."

"That sounds like a good start." He reached out a hand to her. "I'm tired, I hurt, and I want to go back to bed. Let's find you a room, okay? I promise I'll get you up early and make you coffee, so you can finish this up."

Brigid took his hand and stood up. "I found out the other day that the coffee you have here *is* really good."

Before leading her out of the room, he bent to give her a quick kiss. "Thanks for noticing."

That wasn't all she'd noticed, but she resisted the urge to touch all that enticing exposed skin. Her fingertips were practically begging to traverse those stomach muscles, bruised or not. Brigid was reminded of those signs in antique shops, "Look, but don't touch." Touching could lead to breaking and she was already broken enough.

∼

Brigid sat bolt upright in bed, the sound of her heartbeat thundering in her ears. A light flashed, briefly illuminating the room. Where was she? She covered her face with her hands, squeezing her eyes shut. Her cheeks were wet, and the screams continued to run through her mind like a continuous audio loop that wouldn't stop. Not again. It was the dream. The one she hoped she'd never have again. It was back.

Something nudged her and she screamed again, lashing out with her arms. "Get away from me. Stop it! Don't touch me!"

"Brigid, honey, open your eyes. It's me."

She peeked through her lashes and Clay was sitting on the edge of bed with his hands on her wrists, holding her still. Shaking her arms free, she wrapped them around herself. A thunderclap broke the silence and Brigid hunched down, put her hands over her ears, and shut her eyes tightly again, trying to make the lingering images from the dream stop. It needed to get out of her mind.

Clay touched her hand and she looked at him. Another lightning flash lit up his face, and she finally fully returned to the present, remembering where she was and why. He said in a soft voice, "You were screaming."

"I'm sorry. I had a nightmare."

"I'll say. Scout is hiding under my bed." He wiped the tears off her cheeks with a fingertip and smiled. "He's not much of a guard dog anymore."

Brigid tried to return the smile. "I'll say."

"Do you want to tell me about it?"

"You shouldn't have to deal with this. I thought the nightmares were gone. It's not your problem."

A sharp thunderclap ripped through the air and Brigid cringed, hunching down toward the bed. Clay took her hand between both of his. "How about this? I'll crawl in here and hold you until you fall back asleep. If you want to talk, you can. If not, well, I'll probably fall asleep because I'm tired. So you might get to find out if I snore."

"Do you really snore?"

"How should I know? I'm asleep. You'll have to drag Scout out from under my bed and ask him."

Brigid flipped the bed covers back. "Okay. But if you do snore I reserve the right to throw you out."

"It's a deal. Move over." Clay crawled in and put his arms around her. Brigid nestled into his embrace, laid her head on his chest, and closed her eyes. He stroked her hair and whispered, "Everything will be okay, honey. Just go to sleep."

Brigid put her palm flat on Clay's chest so she could feel the beating of his heart. "It's a recurring dream…nightmare really…it hasn't happened in a long time. I thought, or well, I hoped it wouldn't happen again. In the dream, I'm in a room, and it's like my old apartment, but not exactly. It's dark and the windows are all boarded up. I'm trapped."

"What happens?"

Brigid rubbed at her eye with her hand. "My husband or ex-husband or dead husband or whatever you want to call him—John is there. And he's yelling at me."

"That doesn't sound good."

"It wasn't. I mean, we yelled a lot, so that part isn't that different from when I was awake. But this dream is sort of like our last fight, which was worse. It was the last argument we had before he went back to Iraq the last time."

"What was it about?"

"Silverware."

Clay paused his hand movement, resting his palm on her hair. "You mean like forks and spoons?"

"Exactly. We had fights about the most stupid things. It was too embarrassing to ever talk about with anyone. Part of me can't believe I'm telling you this now. But John was a neat-freak and the silverware was one thing he was really picky about. He didn't like it when the silverware wasn't stacked perfectly into orderly piles in the silverware drawer. Spoons and forks had to be nested just right."

"I'm not sure I've ever seen that. Well, except I just noticed the spoons were kind of tidy here. I figured TJ got on some new organizational kick or something."

"No, that was me. During that last fight, John went off about how I was too stupid to even wash dishes right. He yanked out the silverware drawer and dumped it, so everything clattered all over the floor. Then, well, he said much worse things and started destroying our apartment, pushing over furniture and punching holes in the wall. It was like he just finally went over the edge. All those smashing noises—it was so loud—I just kept screaming for him to stop."

"I'm sorry."

"Maybe the thunder and being in a strange place made me dream about it again."

"That's possible."

"Like I said, we fought all the time. He'd gotten angry at me lots of times, but it hadn't been as scary. Before he came home on leave, something bad happened in Iraq that he wouldn't talk about. I guess it was classified."

"So you don't know what happened?"

"No and I never will, but that's okay. I've read enough about PTSD now to know that probably was what was going on."

"Did he hurt you?"

"Yes."

"More than once?"

"Yes. Which I hate telling you because now you're going to wonder what was wrong with me, staying in a situation like that for so long. Everyone says, 'why don't you just leave?' but I kept thinking I couldn't just leave him. How could I do that when he was defending our country? Marriage is a commitment. He was away a lot of the time and I kept thinking we'd be able to work it out if he were home. I felt like I couldn't abandon him while he was in Iraq. I refused to admit how unhappy I was and I was too stubborn to give up. Army wives are supposed to be tough and support their husbands through thick and thin. I kept thinking it would get better, but it just kept getting worse instead."

"You didn't call anyone? Like a counselor? Or a doctor?"

"No. A lot of it was threats, so mostly I was scared when John was home. Over time, there were so many things that set him off, it was like I was tip-toeing around my own house. After that last fight, he disappeared. I don't know where he slept that night, but the next day he got on a plane back to Iraq. I cleaned up the apartment and then wrote a Dear John letter that he never got. After he died, it came back to me, along with his own letter saying more or less the same thing."

Clay readjusted himself, slumping down on the bed so he could look at her face. Pushing a lock of hair behind her ear, he said. "I don't know what to say other than I'm sorry and

I wish there were something I could do to help beyond just sitting here and listening."

"That's enough. You're very easy to talk to."

He grinned. "I don't think most people would agree with you. Usually, they use words like distant, irritable, or other terms you might not say in polite company."

"I don't understand that at all. Maybe it helps that I know you were married before and it didn't work out."

"My sister does have a big mouth."

"Maybe, but it's so obvious TJ loves you. She'd do anything for you. I envy that. My sister and I are estranged, I guess you'd say."

"That doesn't have to be permanent. I didn't talk to my parents for a long time, or to TJ, for that matter. We had to work out some stuff."

"I got that impression." Brigid ran her hand down his arm to take his hand in hers. "I'm sorry about your brother. How old was he when he died?"

"Nineteen. He was in-between me and TJ. Following in those footsteps wasn't easy. He was the football hero and prom king and all that stuff. And of course, TJ was the smart one."

"How did he die?"

Clay sighed. "It was one of those farm accidents you read about sometimes. A tractor rolled on him. I felt guilty about it for years."

"We're you driving the tractor?"

"No, he was. But I felt like it was my fault. TJ was home from college and Dad made us go pick up some hay in the front pasture."

"You mean the field out near the highway?"

"Yeah. You've probably seen those huge machines that pick up the bales, but they never used them in the part near the highway because it has some uneven and rocky areas. We had to pick up those by hand ourselves using a tractor pulling a flatbed trailer."

"That sounds like a lot of work."

"Yeah and we all hated it. That's why it wasn't done. It was supposed to rain and Dad said we needed to get it in so the hay wouldn't get spoiled. So we were all bent out of shape about having to go out there. But when you have that many cattle, you need all the hay you can get to make it through winter."

"I never really thought much about that. No wonder the barn is so big."

"Tell me about it. So that day, TJ called dibs on shoving the bales around on the trailer. Then my brother Cole and I were fighting about who was going to have to throw the bales up to the trailer versus who would drive the tractor."

"TJ wanted to move bales of hay? I think I'd rather drive the tractor."

"She hated that tractor with a fierce passion. Half the time it stalled out on her, and I think that's how she learned to cuss like a sailor. She had some complicated system she'd figured out where she could lay all the bales in rows so she minimized how many she had to lift."

"So I guess you were the one who had to throw them?"

"Yeah, I lost the argument. For years, that ate me up—that Cole would still be alive if I'd been the one driving that crummy old tractor."

"What happened?"

"Cole was going too fast, partly I think to make me work harder because he was pissed at me, and partly to get the job over with more quickly. He had a date and he wanted to get to town. I guess he wasn't paying attention and he hit a boulder that we'd all known was there for years. But the whole thing, tractor, trailer just flipped."

"What happened to TJ?"

"She got thrown off and broke her ankle. But Cole was trapped and crushed. I was holding a bale and it was like I watched the whole thing in slow motion, but then woke up and realized what had just happened. I ran down to the highway waving my arms and screaming to get someone to stop. The next few days half of Alpine Grove was out here at the ranch."

"That must have been horrible. I think that would give me nightmares too."

"Not as much as you might think. I found different ways to torture myself I guess." Clay caressed her cheek. "I think it just takes time to work through these things and learn to live with what happened."

Brigid hugged him and laid her cheek back on his chest. "I tell myself that all the time."

"It will be okay." Clay moved to put his arm around her again. "He can't hurt you anymore. Now it's just memories."

"I know. I keep hoping the memories will fade, but it's taking so long." Brigid let out a long breath. Clay was touching her back lightly and it felt unbelievably good. "Are you doing that horse massage thing?"

"Maybe a little."

"I think I see why Nugget liked it so much."

"I told you horses never lie. That goes for dogs too."

Brigid murmured an assent and her last conscious thought before she fell asleep was that it was entirely possible this was the most relaxed she'd been in almost a decade.

~

At the sound of a dog bark, Brigid sat up and looked around the room. A clock radio was blaring somewhere. Clay rolled over, leaped out of bed, and ran out the bedroom door. Early morning sunlight streamed in through the window. The alarm was summarily silenced and Brigid heard Clay say something to the dog.

He walked back into the bedroom and stood in the doorway. "Sorry. Forgot to turn off the alarm. You wanted to get up early." He ran his fingers through his tousled hair. "Coffee."

Turning on his heel, he left, undoubtedly on a mission for caffeine. Brigid stretched her arms above her head and got up to make the bed. She'd slept incredibly soundly.

Downstairs, she found Clay in the kitchen leaning against the counter, holding a mug of coffee like his life depended on it. He turned and reached into a cabinet to get her a mug. She took the mug from him. "You're not much of a morning person, are you?"

"I'm grateful that coffee exists."

Brigid poured herself some coffee. "I'm going to work on the flyers and walk the dogs as fast as I can. I have to get back home. I'm being a terrible dog-mom to Gypsy."

"I think she'll be okay. From the sounds of it, she thinks you're her heroine."

She put down her mug and stood in front of him. "Thank you for letting me stay and talking to me. Last night meant a lot to me."

"I think it's good to talk these things out sometimes. I haven't told anyone about Cole in a long time either." He took a sip of coffee and gave her a mock-lascivious leer over the edge of the mug. "And hey, any time you want to stay over and sleep with me again is fine by me."

Brigid giggled. "No doubt." She put her arms around his waist and looked up into his eyes. "Thanks for also, um, well, just letting me sleep. You don't snore, by the way."

"Good." He gave her kiss on the forehead. "You do. But it's kind of cute."

Brigid got home later than she'd wanted, hurriedly fed Gypsy, and then ran to the police station to deal with Layla. After finally taking a shower, she drove around town putting up flyers. She also dropped off information at the vet clinic about her meeting for potential volunteers.

Tracy reached over the desk, took the paper, and looked at it. "Cool. I can come if you want. By the way, we need to know when you can take Shelby and the puppies."

"Can you keep them here a little while longer? They're still so tiny. I'm hoping that someone at the meeting will be able to foster them. I talked to one lady who is retired and looking for something to do."

"Five puppies give you a whole lot to do."

"I know. Maybe you could help me make taking care of them and cleaning up puppy poo sound really, really fun."

"I'll do my best. Come take a look, and that will help you sell the deal. Puppies this cute should be illegal."

Brigid laughed and followed Tracy back to the cages. The five tiny puppies were asleep, but Tracy was right. They were absolutely adorable little bundles of brown fur curled up next to Shelby, who was also enjoying a nap.

Brigid whispered, "You weren't kidding. I certainly don't think they'll have any trouble getting adopted."

"Who could resist those little faces?"

"Don't let me stay too long or my resolve will weaken."

Tracy smiled. "I know. I keep warning my doxie that she could end up with a baby brother or sister if she doesn't behave herself. Roxy is not amused."

After repeating the process of feeding and walking Layla, Brigid went back home to pick up Gypsy. As she loaded the little dog into the car, she said, "Clay said you could come visit with me while I use the computer. I have so much stuff to do before this meeting. But a trip out to the country will be fun. It's a big house and you can meet Scout. You'll see." Gypsy seemed up for anything and wagged her tail as she sniffed at the back seat a few times.

When Brigid arrived at the ranch, Clay was doing something with Aziz in the arena, so she drove up to the house and let Gypsy wander around in the grassy area near the porch before carrying her inside. Scout shot out the door, ignoring both of them. "'Bye Scout."

She put Gypsy down in the living room and the small dog wandered around with her nose to the floor sniffing furiously. Brigid smiled. "See, I told you it would be interesting."

Gypsy followed her back to the office and curled up on a dog bed in the corner while Brigid turned on the computer. She couldn't believe how lucky she was to have such a sweet, easygoing dog. After her initial adjustment, Gypsy seemed completely content to hang out at the house in town or with Brigid. Layla the hyperactive schnauzer needed to take a few lessons from Gypsy.

Much later, Gypsy stood up and barked ferociously, startling Brigid from the form she was creating. Clay crouched down and then sat on the floor in the doorway with his legs out in front of him. "Hey, little dog. You must be Gypsy."

Gypsy offered him a tentative wag and sat back down, keeping a close eye to make sure he didn't make any false moves. Brigid said, "It's okay, Gypsy."

Clay wiggled his fingers slightly. "If you sit next to me, she'll probably come over and check me out."

"Okay." Brigid walked across the room and sat down next to him. "You probably smell like horse though. I hope she doesn't hate horses like Nugget does."

"To a dog, this whole house probably smells like fifty years of horses, cows, and who knows what else. If she hasn't freaked out yet, I'm sure she'll be fine."

Gypsy walked over to Brigid and wagged her tail slightly as she sniffed at Clay's leg. She continued to snuffle at him until she reached his sock, which was particularly fascinating. Her nostrils quivered as she savored the fragrance.

Brigid nudged his shoulder. "Those must be some really stinky socks."

"Believe me, they're better than the boots. I leave them outside."

After Clay passed the sniff test, Gypsy curled up in Brigid's lap and she began petting the soft fur on the dog's back. "I guess you meet with her approval, after all."

"I'm glad." He touched Brigid's arm. "So do you want something to eat?"

"No thanks. I should really walk the boys and then get home. I was hoping to be here for just a little while, but I have a ton of documents I need to create for this meeting on Monday, and it's taking a while. One kind of silly problem I'm running into is that I still have no name for this organization. I need to create all these forms for the volunteers I'm hoping to sign up, but I don't know what name to use."

"Brigid's Dogs doesn't work, huh?"

"Very funny. Alpine Grove something or other? It's not an animal shelter. It's just to adopt the dogs. But someday it could take cats too, I guess. Alpine Grove Animals? Adoptions? Animal Care? Animal Rescue? Is it a society like a Humane Society?"

"I don't know." He pulled his leg up and wrapped an arm around it. "To me that sort of implies an animal shelter with a building. Just make sure the acronym doesn't spell anything dirty. Or dumb. There was one group called AGOG, which although kinda dopey, still wasn't as bad as AGAG."

Brigid giggled. "Well, animal adoptions would be A-G-A-A. Aga? That's a stove isn't it?"

"Maybe. Even if it is, it probably isn't spelled with two *As* at the end. A-G-A-C? A-G-A-R? A-G-H-S?"

"I think AGAA works well enough, at least for these forms. When I do all the nonprofit incorporation stuff, I have to have a board of directors. Then we can vote on something official."

Clay gathered his feet under him and stood up. "That sounds like a plan."

Gypsy woke up and stretched as Clay held out his hand to Brigid to help her up. She gave him a hug. "Thanks for helping me think this through. I'm really nervous about this meeting."

"I'm sure you'll do fine. Anyone who attends is bound to care about animals, so you've got some common ground to start."

"I'm worried they'll think I'm an outsider trying to meddle."

"Well, the fact they don't know you has advantages. In a small town, stories tend to run wild. No one has any stories about you yet. Be thankful for that."

Brigid wondered at the unusually hard tone in his voice. Maybe he was speaking from personal experience. In any case, he probably did have a point.

~

The next morning, Brigid tended to Layla at the station. Tuesday was the dog's last day there and as usual, no owner had come forward. It was depressing. Brigid was desperately hoping that someone at the meeting would take the little schnauzer into foster care. Alternatively, if someone took Nugget, it would free up a kennel at the ranch. She hated the idea of asking Clay to set up yet *another* enclosure. Eventually, he'd reach a point when he'd stop being so obliging about adding canine residents. No matter how much he said he liked her and what she was trying to do, it wasn't a good idea to strain their friendship and find out what that point might be.

The Honda was still stinky, but Brigid was trying to get used to it. Gypsy liked driving around with the back windows open anyway. Before the big storm, when Clay had gone out to tend to the horses, he had rolled up her car windows.

She had forgotten about them, so it was a good thing he remembered. Remoisturizing the vomit probably wouldn't have improved matters.

While Brigid drove north toward the ranch, she mentally ticked off all the items she needed to do before the meeting the next day. It was possible quite a few people could show up. She was going to have to play hostess, which meant a trip to the grocery store for food. Not to mention cleaning the house. All this running around hadn't left much time for housekeeping and Gypsy seemed to be embarking on a spring shedding extravaganza. The fur situation was getting a little out of hand. John would have had a heart attack if he saw the state of her floors. And the silverware drawer was a disgrace. A shrink would have a field day with this post-mortem passive-aggressive sloppiness she'd been working on.

When she arrived at the ranch, four saddled horses were standing next to one another, looking sleepy. They were tied to a metal bar in front of the horse barn, swishing their tails. It looked like they were ready for a ride or a nap. Brigid looked over her shoulder at Gypsy, who was standing up looking expectant. "I'll be right back. Let me see what they're up to over there." The dog wagged and sat back down.

Brigid walked over to the horse barn and went inside. Clay came out of the tack room, examining some bridles in his hands. He looked up and stopped short, catching one of the leather straps before he dropped it. "Hey there, you startled me. You don't usually come over to this barn. You might encounter a horse here, you know."

"I saw all the horses lined up and I wanted to find out what you're doing. I don't want to take out Nugget until you're done."

"I gave the dogs a walk before I saddled up the horses. I've got a mom and her kids coming out for a ride."

"Thank you, but you didn't have to do that. I could have come out earlier if I'd known."

"It doesn't matter. I was here, and we had an enjoyable walk. They're good dogs. And you're going to have to get used to not doing everything yourself here real soon now if you get all those volunteers on board."

Brigid smiled. "Cross your fingers! After I finish up these documents today, I have to go to the store. I think feeding people might improve the mood of the room."

"Food is always a good idea."

"I do feel bad that you had to do my job though. Except now that I said that, I need to ask you a favor. Because of the meeting, I can't come out here tomorrow night. Could you deal with the dogs?"

"Sure. I gave the boys some treats to encourage them to behave like gentlemen, and now they think I walk on water."

Brigid laughed. "That's great. Well, I'll get out of your way now. It looks like you have a lot to do."

He shook the bridles in his hand to straighten out a strap, and flipped the reins over his shoulder. "I'm pretty sure I've put a bridle on a horse before."

"Have fun." Brigid turned to leave the barn. "Gypsy and I will be inside."

"Brigid?"

She turned around and Clay was right there in front of her. The man moved like a cat. His ability to move silently was a little disarming. She looked up at his face. "Yes."

Clay cupped her cheek with his hand and kissed her in a way that made the to-do list in her head vaporize into the ether. He stroked her cheek with his thumb. "I'm glad to see you."

"I, ah, am glad to see you too."

"Just making sure we're still more than friends."

Brigid nodded. "Yes…yes, definitely."

"Good. Because I was thinking I liked it when you stayed over here."

"I did too."

"You think that might happen again sometime?"

"Not until after this meeting and things settle down a little. You're a turtle, remember?"

"Even turtles like to know they're getting *somewhere*."

Brigid threw her arms around his waist and laid her head against his chest, hugging him hard. "You are. I promise."

"I'm glad." He kissed the top of her head. "I hear a car. It's probably filled with a couple of horse-crazy little girls that I need to corral before they get to petting poor old Willy to within an inch of his life. We can talk more later."

They walked outside back into the sun and Brigid started up the driveway to the house. She turned to look back behind her as two little brunette girls rushed out of the car toward the barn, their long braids bouncing as they ran.

Clay intercepted them before they got to the horses, crouching down so they could hug him. One climbed on his back and a woman who was obviously the mother waved to Clay and made an "oops, sorry" face.

He put down the smaller girl and showed the taller one how to carry the bridles, so she wouldn't drag the reins on the ground. Brigid thought about her first horseback ride in junior high school. If she'd had someone like Clay teaching her about horses, she probably would have enjoyed it. She'd never met a more patient person. He'd be a great father someday.

An unfamiliar ache of sadness reminded Brigid that she would never be a mother. She hadn't thought about that fact much since she'd arrived in Alpine Grove, pushing it out of her mind to focus on other things. But most people, including men, wanted kids. For all his complaining about being old, Clay wasn't *that* old. It was far from too late for fatherhood, if that was something he wanted.

Why on earth was he still interested in her, after all the things she'd told him? The guy must be a glutton for punishment. She was an emotional disaster area. Nobody was *that* patient, and eventually, he'd probably figure out that being with her was just too much work and say forget it. But at least they'd never have to have an uncomfortable conversation about her permanently child-free status.

With a sigh, she opened the door of the Honda and picked up Gypsy. "You're my baby, right Gypsy? Let's go finish up my documents so we can go home and start getting ready for our big party tomorrow." The little dog wagged her tail as Brigid carried her up the stairs to the house.

Chapter 7

Meetings

The next day, Brigid rushed through her dog-tending duties at the station and the ranch so she could get home and prepare munchies for the meeting later in the afternoon.

Clay had been out in the arena with Aziz, and she waved at him in passing, being sure to walk Nugget the other way up toward the house, so he couldn't see the horse. Judge, as usual, didn't care one way or another, happily continuing on his walk oblivious to everything except the exciting scents along the ground.

When she returned home, Brigid moved into power cooking mode. While Gypsy supervised, she created mini-spanakopitas, stuffed jalapeños, eggplant crostini, three types of dip, and chopped up countless veggies. She hadn't done much cooking in a long time, since making meals for herself wasn't particularly interesting. As she sampled her creations, she remembered how much fun she used to have cooking for her family when she was growing up. Mom had been thrilled when Brigid asked to make dinner once a week, so she could experiment with some of the recipes in her mother's huge collection of cookbooks. One thing was certain: no one would be leaving this meeting hungry.

While Brigid was out giving Layla her afternoon walk, Clay left a message wishing her luck and letting her know that the dogs were fine. He also said that TJ was driving up to attend the meeting, which surprised Brigid. The last time she'd seen the woman, TJ had been furious with her. But TJ obviously knew a lot about nonprofits, which could be extremely helpful in the long run. Maybe Clay had talked her into it. In his low-key way, he could be absurdly persuasive.

The doorbell rang and Gypsy started barking vigorously. Brigid picked her up and answered the door. Tracy stood outside with her veterinary smock draped over her forearm. She saw Gypsy and held out her hands to caress the dog. "Gypsy! Look at you. The cushy life definitely agrees with you."

Brigid waved her hand toward the living room. "Come on in."

Tracy walked into the house and turned her head to look at the dining room table, which was covered with an array of platters and bowls. "You made food! I think I love you. Sorry, I'm a little early. I came here on my way home, since I had to work late again and I didn't have time to run home first. I'm starving."

"Help yourself." Brigid put Gypsy back down on the floor and the dog followed Tracy toward the table. "I hope everything is okay at the clinic."

Tracy popped a chip into her mouth. "It is now. And before you ask, the puppies are fine too."

The doorbell rang again and Brigid said, "Could you keep an eye on Gypsy?"

"Sure." Tracy crouched down and offered the dog a corner of a corn chip.

Brigid opened the door and greeted Kat, Joel, and a number of women Brigid didn't recognize. Although she'd seen everyone's name on the list, she had no idea what most of the meeting attendees looked like. The women introduced themselves and everyone made a beeline for the food table. Tracy gave Kat a hug and picked up Gypsy so they could pet and coo at her.

More people turned up, including a tall woman with sandy hair who chatted with Joel and Kat. It was clear they knew each other well. TJ was the last to arrive. Brigid thanked her for coming and pointed her toward the crowd around the food. Everyone seemed to know someone. It was like Alpine Grove old-home week right here in her dining room.

Once everyone had a plate of goodies and something to drink, Brigid clinked a fork on her glass. "Thank you all for coming. Could you take a seat in the living room so we can get started? I have a lot of information to give you and I'm sure you all want to get home."

Everyone milled around selecting seating and Brigid was amused to see that Gypsy settled herself in Kat's lap. The dog knew an easy mark when she saw one. Kat was holding Joel's hand, but released it long enough to give the dog a little piece of crostini crust. TJ was staring at Kat for some reason. Did they know each other? Brigid shook her head, trying to ignore the various allegiances and friendships that pervaded the room. Now was not the time to figure out small-town social dynamics. She had way too many other problems to deal with at the moment.

Brigid handed out papers for people to pass around. "Some of this was mentioned on the flyer, but here are the things I would like to talk about this evening. The first thing is the dogs that are in foster care right now. There are a mother dog and her five puppies, a greyhound, a schnauzer, and a Lab mix with a skin condition."

A woman raised her hand. "I talked to you about the puppies the other day. Remember me?" She peered around at the others. "I'm Leslie and my kids and I talked about fostering the mom and puppies. I'm home all day and the rug rats have been begging me for a dog for ages. I want them to understand that pets take work. If they live up to their promises and help me care for the dogs, we might adopt one of the pups too…permanently, I mean."

"That's wonderful. And thank you for introducing yourself. I'm not sure how many of you know each other, so maybe you could say your name. Plus, even though I think I talked to most of you, I'm new in town, so it will help me put names with faces." Brigid set more papers on the table and sat down. "There are forms I'll need you to fill out if you want to foster a dog. And there's a document with information about how the program works and your responsibilities. All dogs will need to be fixed before they are adopted, so I've set up an account with the veterinarian. Foster parents will need to set up the appointments and take care of the dog while it recuperates from the surgery."

A sleek, well-dressed woman with shoulder-length chestnut hair said, "As I'm sure most of you know, I'm Judith Alistair. And I, for one, would like to know more about what you've been doing up until now before I commit to anything. Where are the dogs staying now?"

"The puppies are at the vet because they're still really small. Tracy says they are ready to go to a foster home though."

"In fact, we'd *like* them to go," Tracy volunteered. "They're starting to get more active, so they need more room."

"Layla is the schnauzer. She's at the station now, but her time there is up tomorrow." Brigid took a sip of water. She hadn't talked this much in years. "The greyhound is named Nugget and the Lab is named Judge. They are out at the V Bar H ranch off the highway. I don't know if you're familiar with it, but there was an empty barn and Clay Hadley set up kennels for me to use temporarily."

"Well, that's not acceptable." Judith said.

Another woman piped up, "Oh my goodness, you have dogs out there? Aren't you worried?"

Judith waved off the comment, "Debbie, I agree, but right now I'd like to know what the greyhound is like. I think they are lovely aristocratic-looking dogs, but I'd like to know more about this one's history."

"Nugget is a sweetie." Brigid smiled. "He puts his forehead on you to snuggle. It's so cute. He's quiet and I think he'd probably prefer to spend his days being a couch potato."

"He doesn't like horses though," TJ said. "So it would be good if he can stay somewhere else."

Judith looked over at the people on the sofa. "Tamara, I didn't see you there. I assume you would know about the current arrangement, wouldn't you?"

"Yes, I would, *Judy*," TJ said.

Brigid mentally cringed. Clearly, there was no love lost between these women. "Judith, if you're interested in taking Nugget, that would be great. That leaves room for another dog to be able to go out to the ranch. I should mention that Layla, the schnauzer, needs a little work on housebreaking, which I know makes her more challenging to foster."

A bald man wearing glasses with heavy black frames said, "I'm sure she just needs a little structure. I've housebroken dozens of dogs over the years. Sometimes using a crate can be very effective. Or a doggie door. There are many approaches. Oh, my name is Ed, by the way."

Brigid handed him a form. "As you saw on the flyer, another thing I was hoping to do is find people who are willing to walk dogs while they are being housed at the station. I've been walking and feeding them twice a day, morning and evening."

A blonde woman with a pixie haircut raised her hand. "My name is Maren. That's what I'm interested in doing. I work at the clerk's office and I just need to get away sometimes. I kept thinking about your flyer and the poor dogs there. Thinking about them just made me want to cry."

"I have a sign-up form with time slots." Brigid quickly handed Maren the paper, hoping she wouldn't start sobbing. The shape of Maren's eyebrows made her look perpetually on the brink of tears. "Please pass it around."

A woman with long stringy black hair sitting next to Maren hunched over writing her name. That was two people anyway. Brigid marveled at the idea that she might not have to go to the police station every single day anymore.

By the end of the meeting, Brigid felt like a great weight had been lifted from her shoulders. The puppies, Nugget, and Layla had foster homes. Maren, her shy friend Maddie, and a woman named Cindy—who as it turned out was Joel's sister—had agreed to walk dogs. Kat and Joel offered to help with computer-related tasks like flyers and forms. Brigid wanted to jump for joy that she wouldn't have to stay up all night fighting with Clay's computer anymore. TJ said she'd work with Brigid on getting the nonprofit set up.

After all the papers had been filled out and discussed, Brigid suggested that they get some more munchies, and finalize arrangements with one another. Leslie huddled with Tracy about the puppies and Brigid was busy dealing with Judith and Ed about their foster dogs. The dog-walkers left and Kat and Joel ended up talking with TJ over near the window. Maybe they were discussing geeky stuff. In-between Judith's pet-care pontifications, Brigid glanced at them from the corner of her eye. Whatever they were talking about, it seemed serious and Kat had a death grip on Joel's hand.

Debbie came up next to Judith and Brigid and announced, "I'm so happy you're taking the dog, Judith."

"I'm sure I can provide a better environment than that," Judith said.

Brigid smiled at Debbie. "You still could take Judge if you're that worried about him staying in a kennel in the barn."

Debbie scrunched her shoulders like a turtle retreating into its shell. "What you said about his fur—it sounds so icky. I can't handle that. Judith has years of experience with dogs. She showed miniature poodles, you know."

"She told me about her experience showing and caring for dogs. It's very impressive. And I understand about Judge. I know we'll find him a home. To be honest, he's such a happy-go-lucky dog, he's the one I'm least worried about. I have a vet appointment to get him dipped again this week. It's hard to tell, but I do think it's helping," Brigid said.

A look passed between Debbie and Judith, and the two women seemed to tacitly agree on something.

"I'd like to talk to you privately about this *arrangement* you have at the ranch," Judith said.

"That's fine. You have my phone number," Brigid said. "Please feel free to call.

"I will." Judith turned to Debbie. "Are you ready? We should get going."

The two women said their farewells and Brigid breathed a small sigh of relief. TJ, Kat, and Joel came up and thanked her for the food and Brigid gave Kat a hug. "Thank you for taking over the computing things. I was tearing my hair out."

Kat said, "Just send me an email. I'm using my computer all the time anyway and it would be a welcome diversion from writer's block."

"Okay, I might need to call you until I figure out how I can get an email account. Maybe I should just bite the bullet and get my own computer," Brigid said.

"Realistically, the nonprofit should have one." TJ said. "I think the next thing we need to talk about is raising money. You're footing the bill for everything, aren't you?"

"I am. I wish I were independently wealthy, but I'm not. My widow's pension only takes me so far," Brigid said.

TJ put her hand on Brigid's shoulder. "Are you coming out to the ranch tomorrow? I'll be there in the morning before I head home."

"Yes, I need to get Nugget ready to go to Judith's house," Brigid said.

"Okay, we'll talk then."

Once everyone had left, Brigid thought she might collapse from exhaustion and the interpersonal stresses of so many guests in her house. She wasn't used to dealing with multiple people at once and her nerves were shot.

Gypsy was contentedly snoring on the sofa and Brigid sat down next to her. "I think you've got the right idea. I'm going to set an alarm and clean up this mess tomorrow."

Gypsy just raised her head and wagged her tail a few times, which was enough encouragement for Brigid. She picked up the dog and went upstairs to lose herself in some escapist fiction that had nothing to do with homeless dogs or small towns.

～

The sweet scent of lilacs wafted through the open window as Joel and Kat drove though the leafy residential side streets of Alpine Grove and out of town after the meeting at Brigid's house. Fruit trees were blooming and gardens were starting to explode with color.

Joel shifted gears and put his hand on Kat's leg. "You're okay, right?"

"I'm fine. I guess it never occurred to me that I'd meet someone who knew my mother… I mean my *birth* mother." She covered his hand with hers. "But that's stupid, when you stop and think about it. Obviously, people would have known my mother before she died. It's like I didn't consider the fact that Alpine Grove existed before I got here."

"I guess you look a lot like her."

Kat released his hand so he could shift gears. "I suppose. I saw a few pictures of her when she was little, but not very many. Louise probably has a lot more."

"It sounds like your mom and TJ were really good friends."

"I think so. She knew all about Kelly's pregnancy…well, me, I guess…and then Louise shipping me off to be adopted after Kelly died. It was kind of weird to hear a different perspective on the whole story. Like it became more real. When Louise told me I was adopted, it really wasn't a big surprise in some ways, since, well, you've met my mom. Or my adoptive mom. The way TJ described Kelly, she wasn't just someone from a long time ago that I never got to meet. She was a person with faults, a weird sense of humor, hopes, and dreams. Someone I would have probably liked. TJ still really misses her."

"I know. Seeing you seemed to upset her, since she had no idea you lived here."

"When I found out I was adopted, some people thought I should freak out or be upset by the whole thing. Maria, for example. She thought I took it too well." Kat turned to him and gestured in frustration. "What does that even *mean*? What was I supposed to do? Run around the house screaming and crying? So, I was adopted. *So what*? Nothing changed. I'm still me."

He glanced at her. "Well, I for one, am glad you didn't run around screaming, particularly since I live in that house."

"Thanks for coming with me to this meeting. You know how I hate social scenes with a bunch of people I don't know."

"No problem. I was surprised Cindy showed up."

"I called her. She is your sister after all, and she walks dogs for a living."

"I suppose." Joel scowled. "She could probably stand some karma points after almost losing my dog too."

"Well, I didn't put it quite that way, but yes."

Joel turned onto a back road, headed north, and put his hand back on Kat's leg. "That was nice of you to help Brigid."

"I'm impressed she's trying to do this. What a lot of work." Kat squeezed his hand. "In addition to all the dog walking, forms, papers, blah, blah, just dealing with that meeting and cooking all those appetizers? It makes me tired just thinking about it. And those little spinach turnover things made me swoon. I tried to control myself, but I could have eaten fifty of them."

Joel chuckled. "Yeah, you were camped out next to that tray."

"Okay, maybe I wasn't being as discreet as I thought. I always hate introducing myself and you in situations like that. There needs to be a word other than *boyfriend* to describe someone you live with. It sounds like we're twelve-year olds on the playground."

"Well, *roommates* makes it sound like we barely know each other and just shake hands in passing."

"True. But *lovers* makes it sound like we never get out of bed. Or like we're part of the cast of *Days of Our Lives*. I'm sorry, but I just can't introduce you as, 'my lover' with a straight face."

Joel smiled. "I don't think I can either. You'd give me a funny look and then we'd both start laughing."

"That would be embarrassing. I'm enough of a social mutant as it is."

They turned and went down the driveway toward the house and Joel parked the truck under a large cedar tree. Kat got out and looked up at the towering evergreens and the starry sky beyond. "It always smells so good here. It's one of those things I notice almost every time I come home."

"Me too." Joel took her hand and swung it between them. "You know, we should get married."

"Okay, sure." Kat jerked her head to look at him. "What? Wait. Was that you proposing? It was, right?"

"Yes, it was. I guess that wasn't particularly romantic, was it?" He stopped and turned to grin at her. "I've just been thinking about it for a while."

"And you came to a logical conclusion?"

"You know me so well. I love you and I want to spend the rest of my life with you, so I think we should get married." He wrapped his arms around her. "Assuming you agree, that is."

Kat ran her fingertips along the side of his neck. "Yes. I definitely agree. But at the risk of sounding mercenary, I'd like a ring. After all the confusion with Ned, I want to make sure this actually happened and it wasn't just a really, really good dream."

"It did happen. I promise." He took her hand again and pulled her toward the house. "I have an idea."

They went inside and were greeted by an uproar of vociferous barking. Kat turned on the light and looked down the stairs at the canine faces behind the gate. "Hi guys. Hold on for a couple minutes."

She followed Joel into the bedroom. "What are you up to?"

Joel was rummaging around in a drawer in his dresser. "I'm looking for something."

"Well, if it's socks, I think you've found them."

"Nope." He pulled a long black box from the drawer and handed it to her.

Kat looked down at the leather case, which was obviously designed for jewelry. Her heart was pounding in her chest as she sat down on the edge of the bed. She opened the lid and several pieces of jewelry sparkled in the dim lamplight. "Wow. What is all this?"

Joel sat next to her on the bed and pulled a ring from the box. "I'm not sure if this is something you would like. If you don't, it's fine, we can get something else. But all of these were my mother's. When my parents died, Cindy got most of Mom's jewelry, but I took a few things." He held out a ring with a glittering square-cut diamond. "Including this."

Kat held out her left hand, which was shaking. "Oh my God, it's beautiful."

He put the ring on her finger and slid it around. "Okay, it might be a little big."

"I'm guessing your mom was a zillion feet tall like you and Cindy." Kat looked down at the ring on her finger, holding it in place with her other hand. "I can get it resized."

He pulled some other jewelry from the box. "You could have the jeweler add some other stones to it if you like. Make it your own."

Kat looked through the pieces, some of which were obviously very old. She looked into his eyes. "I don't know what to say. These are antiques. I couldn't take them apart."

"Why not?" He held up a bracelet. "You never wear bracelets. This one is sort of funny-looking, which is why Cindy didn't want it. But the rubies are nice."

"Well, they're *yours*, for one thing."

"I don't wear bracelets either."

"You know what I mean."

"One aspect of getting married is that what's mine is yours." He handed the bracelet to her. "I hope you'll be wearing the ring for a long time, so you should like it."

Kat looked down at the bracelet, then back at Joel. "You're sure?"

"Very. I love you."

She fisted her hand so the ring wouldn't fall off, put her arms around his neck, and kissed him. "I love you back. I guess now I need to call you my fiancé."

"I guess you do. Until you call me your husband."

"I like the sound of that."

"Me too."

~

The next day, Brigid left later than usual for her excursion out to the ranch. Cleaning up the kitchen disaster took longer than she expected and then Jake called from the police station to check and make sure Ed was really allowed to take Layla.

After reassuring Jake that all was well, she hugged Gypsy, ran out of the house, and jumped into the stinky Honda. The stench had faded enough that if she rolled down the windows, it wasn't too horrible. Or maybe she was getting used to it.

So much had happened since the last time she'd talked to Clay, and she couldn't wait to tell him about the success of the meeting. It would be so much fun to get his take on it, since he probably knew some of these people far better than she did.

As she turned into the driveway to the ranch, the panoramic view ahead of her was like a palette of every possible shade of green. It had rained lightly overnight and in the morning light, the glittering moisture seemed to add a crisp clarity to the lush colors of sprouting vegetation. The meadows were a deep emerald and the evergreen trees beyond were a dark hunter green. In between, the shrubs and forbs ranged from a mossy to an almost teal hue. Brigid wished she were an artist so she could capture it.

Exiting the trees, she drove up past the barns to the house. Her heart sank when she discovered that another car was parked in the driveway next to the barn. She wasn't *that* late. Judith wasn't supposed to show up for another half hour. Pulling up in front of the house, she got out of the car and looked up at the sound of the front door closing. Clay was walking down the porch steps toward her, holding a cup of coffee.

Thrilled to see him, she practically skipped toward the house with a grin on her face. He smiled, but put out his hand in front of him to stop the impending hug. "You sure look happy."

"I am. I have so many things to tell you."

He took a sip of coffee and motioned toward the barn with the mug. "I know, but maybe you could deal with that woman first."

"I'm sorry I'm late, but Judith wasn't supposed to show up for another half hour. I thought I'd have plenty of time to walk Nugget."

Clay shrugged. "I politely suggested that she might not want to feed him, but she didn't want to hear it, so I went inside and got another cup of coffee. Judge was barking his head off. It sounds like he finally shut up anyway."

"Uh oh. Did she feed Nugget?"

"I don't know. I do know she's not much for suggestions. I'd take it as a personal favor if you could get her off my land as soon as possible."

Brigid was taken aback at his words, but managed to stammer, "Okay." What had Judith said? Clay was gripping the handle of the mug so tightly, his hand was practically shaking. Was he angry? It was hard to tell.

"I'll be in the barn having a conversation with Aziz if you need anything."

Brigid smiled. "Did he find more horse-eating things to be scared of?"

"No, it's not that kind of conversation." Clay took another sip of coffee. "I'll see you later."

"Wait! Is TJ still here? She said maybe we could talk this morning."

Clay gestured toward the house dismissively as he turned to go, "She's inside packing."

Brigid stood for a moment watching him stride toward the horse barn, and then turned to go deal with the dogs and Judith.

At the sight of Brigid, Judge began barking sharply, working himself up into an exuberant howl. She bent down and shushed him. "Judge, enough!" With a final yip to punctuate his excitement, the dog stood and wagged expectantly.

Judith was standing next to Nugget's cage, frowning at the greyhound. She strode toward Brigid. "This dog is dreadfully thin! Haven't you been feeding it? This poor animal looks like he is starving."

Brigid stood up. "Greyhounds are naturally thin. It's just what they look like."

"My experience is with poodles. I'll need to talk to my colleagues who know this breed. In any case, I gave him some food, which seemed to improve his disposition."

"That might not have been a good idea. I told you last night—he gets car sick."

"I'm sure it will be fine. I bought a crate with a pillow to put in the back of my vehicle, which is much safer and more comfortable for the animal. I will need to be reimbursed for those expenses. Do you have a form?"

"When we talked about foster responsibilities, I mentioned that reimbursements need to be approved. And that I still need to create the request form. Everything needs to be tracked."

"Well, wouldn't you have approved it?"

"Probably, but maybe not right now. I need to work out some money…well, I need to talk with everyone about doing some fundraising."

Judith waved off the comment. "Fine. Give me the form when you get it. I want to get out of here and get the dog settled. I've set up one of the guest bedrooms for him."

"Okay." She opened the cage door and Nugget did his snuggling move with his head. Brigid looked over to grin at Judith. "See! Isn't this the cutest thing?"

"That's very nice. Let me go open up the car." Judith turned and walked out of the barn.

Brigid crouched down next to Nugget and rubbed his ears. "It will be okay, sweetie. No more loud roommate. Judith knows a lot about dogs, and it sounds like you even get your *own* room. But I'm going to miss you." She clipped on the leash and led him out.

After a short walk around the yard, Brigid loaded Nugget into the crate in the back of Judith's rather opulent-looking, brand-new Land Rover. The dog didn't look too excited about another car ride, but Brigid knew that staying in a home would be better for him. From the sounds of it, Judith had everything all ready, and she was obviously eager to get him home.

Brigid waved goodbye as Judith turned the car around and left the ranch. She turned at the sound of the front door closing. TJ was walking down the steps with a small duffel bag over her shoulder. She was leaving *already*? What was with everybody this morning?

Hustling up the driveway toward the house, she met TJ at her car. "Hi, I was hoping we could talk for a minute."

TJ looked down at the ground, "I really should get home."

"Thank you so much for coming last night. I was hoping we could talk a little about fundraising this morning, but Judith showed up early for Nugget."

"I know."

At the expression on TJ's face, Brigid had to ask. "What is going on? Is there a problem with Judith I don't know about?"

"Just ancient history."

"I'm sorry if she upset you. She does seem very committed to helping Nugget though. She has lots of connections in the dog show world and said she has a friend who loves greyhounds. The woman might come to Alpine Grove to visit Nugget and maybe even adopt him. I really want him to find a home where someone will appreciate what a wonderful dog he is."

"I hope so too. Don't worry about Judith. She's not a bad person and I know she loves dogs. It's just there's some bad blood between our families. And she has a special dislike for Clay, which bugs me."

Brigid shook her head. "I don't understand that. He's been great with the dogs and so generous about everything."

"So…about that." TJ readjusted her bag on her shoulder. "I, well, don't know what's going on with you and Clay, but I want you to know that he is the most tender-hearted person you will ever meet. I know he acts like a bonehead sometimes and he'll never tell you, but he's had some hurt heaped onto him and he takes it hard."

"Okay." Brigid smiled weakly, not sure exactly how to respond. "I guess right now he's having a conversation with a horse."

"Yeah, he does that when he's upset." TJ opened the door to her car, then turned back to Brigid. "We can talk about fundraising ideas on the phone if you want. Just give me a call."

"I will."

Brigid watched as the minivan slowly cruised away. The mood of the morning had gone from exaltation to bewilderment all in the span of about a half hour. It was strange, and Brigid had no idea what happened. She really wanted to talk to Clay, particularly if he was upset. But she still needed to walk Judge. As she started back down the driveway, Clay emerged from the horse barn mounted on Aziz.

The horse's black coat looked particularly shiny in the morning light. Maybe Clay had brushed him. Were there hair products for horses? She had no clue, but the rippling equine muscles practically shimmered in the sunlight. He was absolutely stunning, even to someone who knew next to nothing about horses.

Brigid waved at Clay, who turned Aziz to walk up the driveway to meet her. The grim expression on his face combined with his perch astride the enormous animal made Clay seem unusually imposing. In a lame attempt at conversation, she said, "I guess you're going for a ride?"

"I don't have any responsibilities today, so I'm going to the falls."

"There's a waterfall around here? I had no idea."

"It's back in the national forest land. About a half-day ride each way. I might be back late."

"I was thinking that when I come back this afternoon to walk Judge, I could bring you the leftovers from the meeting. You fed me, and I thought I might return the favor as a thank you for your help with the dogs. The spanikopita is gone, but I still have lots of other yummy stuff I made."

"I'd like that." He moved the reins to start turning Aziz around.

"Wait!"

He turned the horse back and looked down at her expectantly. "Okay."

Brigid reached up and put her hand on his thigh. "Please promise me you won't do horse yoga on *this* horse."

"All right." He put his hand on hers and gave it a squeeze. "If I get an overpowering urge to do yoga out there in the forest, I'll do it on the ground."

Brigid reluctantly let go of Clay's leg. "Thank you. Please be careful."

～

When Brigid got back to her house, the light on her answering machine was flashing frantically. She picked up Gypsy and put her in her lap as she wrote down phone numbers and notes about the messages.

Jake had called to let her know that two women he'd never seen before stopped by about walking dogs.

Maren called to complain that Jake was mean to her and Maddie. Ed called to let her know that he had picked up Layla and that she wasn't housebroken. Brigid put her palm over her face and groaned. Judith called to tell her that Nugget had vomited all over the crate and she wanted to be reimbursed for getting the dog pillow dry-cleaned.

Brigid stopped petting Gypsy. "Dry-cleaned? Who buys a dog bed that needs to be dry-cleaned?" Gypsy looked up at Brigid. "Sorry Gypsy, but *really*. Is she kidding me?"

The only message with good news was from Leslie, who said the puppies were adorable and the kids were fighting over who got to take care of them. She also volunteered that Dr. Cassidy thought the puppies might be sheltie mixed with pug.

"Pug, huh? Well, who knows? The last time I saw them they just looked brown and furry." Gypsy wagged her tail. "I'm sure Shelby isn't about to kiss and tell either."

Brigid spent most of the rest of the day returning phone calls and placating volunteers. She also set up a date to have coffee with Sonia, who had expressed interest in helping raise money. At the end of the meeting at Brigid's house, the woman had pulled her aside and explained that because she was retired she finally had time to travel, so she couldn't commit to a hands-on role tending to dogs or fostering, but she did want to help.

By the time she was done with the calls, Brigid was desperate to go anyplace where her telephone was not. She packed up all the leftovers from the meeting into a brown paper grocery bag and put on Gypsy's leash. They went out to the Honda with the goodies, and on the way stopped at the mailbox. Brigid pulled out her credit-card bill, took a look, and jammed it into her purse. Perfect. That would be some fun reading. Maybe Sonia or TJ had ideas for making money extremely quickly because she was going to need it.

The ranch was quiet when she arrived. Horses were grazing in the pasture and bees were buzzing around the flowers, but other than that, everything was almost completely still. Clay was apparently still out in the forest somewhere with Aziz.

Brigid carried Gypsy and the bag of food up the steps and pounded on the door. Scout walked around from the other side of the wrap-around porch and wagged at her. She put Gypsy down and the smaller dog and Scout sniffed their greetings.

Brigid said, "So, is your dad home or not?" Scout wagged noncommittally and stared at the door, so Brigid opened it to let him inside. Because she'd lived for years in cities, it was odd to her that Clay didn't seem to worry about leaving his house unlocked all the time.

Scout settled into his dog bed in the living room, ready to resume his nap indoors while Brigid put the leftovers into the refrigerator. Since Clay wasn't home yet, maybe she could make that reimbursement request form before Judith bankrupted her. Gypsy padded into the office behind Brigid and curled up in the dog bed in the corner. Brigid smiled. This was a very dog-friendly home with dog beds located in almost every room. Scout had many options for quality sleep time.

The front door opened right after Brigid had uttered a very unladylike word at the computer. With a tiny squeak of excitement, she jumped out of the chair, walked out of the office, and found Clay in the kitchen. He was standing at the sink getting a drink of water, which was somewhat ironic because he was soaked and completely covered in mud. He turned around. "Hey there."

"What on earth happened to *you?*"

"Well, it turns out that waterfalls might be one of those horse-eating things. If I'd put more thought into it, I would have considered the fact that there aren't many waterfalls in the desert."

"You look like you've been mud-wrestling."

"Aren't mud-wrestlers supposed to be women?" He looked down and grinned, his teeth looking extra white against the dirt coating his face. "I don't think I'm built for that particular sport."

"I think men mud-wrestle too." She waved off the comment. "But that doesn't matter. Are you okay? You didn't get hurt, did you?"

"No, I'm fine. I was just standing there explaining to Aziz that he didn't need to be afraid of the noise and we didn't have to go through the mud all the way to the waterfall because it was too slippery."

"You slipped, didn't you?"

"Not exactly. I was leaning over looking at this weird spotted mushroom and Aziz nudged me with his big old nose so I lost my balance. I'm glad nobody saw it. I had a little trouble getting back up. I swear that horse was laughing at me."

Brigid smiled. "I brought the food. Are you hungry?"

"Starving. I'll go take a shower."

Brigid went out to walk and feed Judge, then busied herself in the kitchen heating up food. Even though Clay was filthy, his mood seemed far better than it had been earlier. Maybe there was something to be said for taking a horseback ride. For one thing, there were no phones out on the trail. She probably should call and check for messages on her machine, but she couldn't face it. The world was just going to have to live without her this evening.

Clay returned to the kitchen looking scrubbed and laundered. His bare feet were quiet on the old wood floor as he walked around surveying the array of plates scattered across the counter. He grabbed a crostini, took a bite, and made a theatrical expression of scrumptious pleasure. "Wow. TJ told me the food was good, but this is amazing."

"I haven't cooked anything in ages. It was fun. You missed out on some of the best stuff though."

"If you make food like this, next time I promise I'll show up."

Brigid put her hand on his forearm before he could snarf up another crostini. "I really appreciate you taking care of Judge last night."

"No big deal. We're buddies now."

"So I want to ask you about some things." She handed him a plate. "Maybe we could sit down instead of standing here inhaling food off the counter."

He took the plate and started loading items on it. "Did I mention I'm hungry?"

"You did. You're very focused."

Turning to the refrigerator, he pulled out a bottle of beer. "Want one?"

"No, I have to drive home later."

"Suit yourself." Clay settled into a chair with his beer and food. He paused in his consumption to look at Brigid across the table. "So okay, I think I'm not going to faint dead away now. Tell me about the meeting. TJ said you did great. I knew you would after all the work you did preparing for it."

Brigid grinned, happy to finally have his attention. "It went really well. All the dogs except for Judge have foster homes. And there are people who want to walk the dogs at the station while they are there. I couldn't believe it."

"So no more chats with Jake, huh?"

"No, except on the phone. That's plenty. Oh, and Leslie, the woman who took the puppies, picked them up from the vet today too. I guess Dr. C thinks the puppies might be mixed with pug."

"They're little pug-sheltie mixes? So you're saying people get to adopt a pugly?"

Brigid burst out laughing. "Yes! I never thought of that, but you're right. The pups are a bunch of little puglies. I love it! That's even fun to say."

"You've definitely got yourself a marketing gimmick there."

"True. Advertising them could be fun too. It doesn't hurt that they're adorable. But that reminds me. Kat and Joel are going to help me with all the horrible computer stuff! So you can have your computer back."

Clay popped a chip in his mouth. "That's a relief because you know how I was just clamoring to go do some accounting."

She laughed. "I noticed. I practically had to beat you off with a stick."

"Well, you might have to do that, but I can promise you it won't be because of accounting." He reached across the table and clasped her hand. "It's great to see you so happy, honey."

"I finally feel like I accomplished something...*real*. It's been such a long time. Even though it's been a lot of work, I know these dogs will find homes now. I just know it. And I'm so grateful for your help."

"I didn't do much, except provide an old, dirty barn."

"That's not true and you know it."

"Hey, all the real work was your doing. I think you're pretty amazing, in fact."

Brigid got up and went around the table to sit next to him. She took both his hands in hers and looked into his eyes. "Maybe, but you have been the best friend...more than friend...anyone could ever ask for."

"I'm glad you feel that way because I've been having more-than-friend thoughts again."

Brigid put her hand on the scruffy stubble on his cheek. "I have too, but I have to get home tonight."

"Okay." He wiggled his eyebrows suggestively. "But you'll let me know when you want to have another sleepover, right?"

"I will. Gypsy seems to like it here, so I could bring her, and then I wouldn't have to leave early. Thanks to all these new volunteers, the only dog I have to deal with is Judge and he's already here."

"I'm liking the sounds of this. You're quite a planner."

She gestured toward the plate. "Have some more food. I thought you were hungry."

As he bent his head to kiss her, he said, "I am, but not for food."

~

Clay helped Brigid put away the food and then kissed her goodnight. She drove home reluctantly. It was getting more and more difficult to leave. The night of the thunderstorm, being curled up with Clay in his embrace had made her feel so warm and safe. She often found herself daydreaming about it.

Brigid fell into a comfortable routine over the subsequent few weeks. At last, she didn't feel like she was constantly driving all over Alpine Grove like a mad woman. Although she still went out to the ranch twice a day to tend to Judge, the rest of the time she was free to work on other things.

Many days she talked with Sonia on the phone or in person about fundraising and administrative issues. They were getting the nonprofit set up and considering a few ideas for events and PR opportunities.

Brigid discovered to her delight that Sonia had a background in event planning. She had worked for a large professional association and planned conferences, so the older woman was a wealth of information. Although Sonia had seemed stand-offish at first, she'd warmed and now had a habit of calling Brigid "dearie" which Brigid had initially found condescending. But Sonia had explained that the word was a British term of endearment. Although Sonia had grown up in the United States, her mother was British and had moved back to the UK to retire, so Sonia visited her frequently. From Sonia's description, even at ninety-three, *mum* sounded like quite the force to be reckoned with.

Sonia had one thing in common with Brigid. They were both widows, a fact that seemed to surprise them both, given their age difference. Sonia and her husband had moved to Alpine Grove to build their dream house on the lake, but he'd had a heart attack a week before they were scheduled to move in. For different reasons, neither spoke about their husbands. It seemed better for their tenuous friendship that way.

After her husband died, Sonia had opted to stay in their rental apartment and listed the gorgeous new house for sale. Brigid had seen the photographs and couldn't understand why it had been on the market for so long. Many of Sonia's comments about her proposed travels were prefaced by, "When the house finally sells...."

On Brigid's morning trips out to the ranch, she almost never talked to Clay because he was usually out in the arena doing what Brigid thought of as "horse stuff." But on the afternoon run, she'd bring food or he'd invent something for dinner. Almost every evening, they ended up sitting around the old kitchen table talking about the day.

One morning when she arrived, it was unusually quiet. She walked Judge and put him back in his kennel. All of the horses were accounted for so maybe Clay was inside the house. When she'd seen him the night before, he hadn't said anything about going anywhere. She smiled at the sound of the door opening and said, "Hi Scout" as the dog shot out toward the horse barn.

Clay walked down the steps and waved. She ran up to him and gave him a hug. "I wondered where you were."

"On the phone. Aziz is heading back to Nevada soon."

"Really? You mean he's trained?"

"As much as he's going be for the time being." Clay gestured toward the barn. "I can't keep him forever. That horse is worth more than this ranch."

"You're kidding."

"Nope. He's got some mighty spendy bloodlines." Clay took her hand and interlaced his fingers with hers. "So what are you doing now?"

"I was about to head back home."

"Want to go for a ride instead?"

Brigid let go of his hand. "I don't think so. You know I'm not really good at that."

"Nobody is good when they first start out. You've been so busy working, you could use a break. Riding might help clear your head."

"I'm fine. Things are much better now that I have other people to help me."

"I'm glad to hear that, but you'd be doing me a favor. It would be great to take Aziz on a slow trail ride with someone else."

"Well, okay, I guess so."

"Hey, you might even enjoy it." Clay smiled and gave her a kiss. "Let's go get Willy."

After grooming and saddling the horses, Brigid got on Willy. Being on horseback didn't feel quite as foreign and scary this time, although she once again encouraged the horse to be gentle with her.

They rode down the driveway and Clay looked over at her. "Everything okay?"

"I'm okay and glad Willy is a slowpoke."

As Aziz did a small sideways two-step, Clay reined him in. "That's the idea. Aziz needs more experience with extreme-slow as a speed."

Brigid squeaked, "Don't let him get so close!"

"Aziz is just letting me know he'd rather go faster. I'm encouraging him not to. It's fine."

"What if he hits me? Willy could jump up or run off and dump me on the ground."

"That's unlikely, but I'll give you more space if you want." He hung off the side of Aziz and reached over to pet Willy's withers.

Brigid glanced at his hand, looked over at where he was, and clutched at the reins. "What are you *doing*?"

"Just showing you that Willy doesn't startle easily."

"Get back in the saddle before you kill yourself! Half of you is not even *on* the horse!"

Clay rearranged himself and patted Aziz's neck. "He's being so good, pretending like he's a trick-riding horse. We should reward him with a trot."

"I don't want to trot. I thought the whole point was to go slowly."

"When you train dogs, don't you give them a reward when they do what you ask?"

"Yes. But this is different."

"Not really."

"You're just bored. I'd rather not be on one of your more exciting rides where you gallop around and fall in the mud."

"Hey, he pushed me." Clay stroked the horse's shiny neck. "That wasn't my fault."

Brigid laughed. "I bet it was funny though."

"Aziz thought so." Clay turned Aziz up toward the forest trail and Willy fell in line behind them as they went into the trees. They rode for a while in silence, listening to the trilling of birds and the breeze whispering through the tree canopy above them. When the trail flattened and widened out, Clay waved to encourage Brigid to ride up next to him.

Brigid gave Willy a little kick and was more prepared this time for him to lurch into a speed-walking motion. A little thrill of excitement passed through her. The horse did what she asked and she didn't panic. She grinned at Clay. "Look, I didn't fall off."

"Of course you didn't." He smiled. "Aziz still deserves a trot, you know. He's being *reaaally* good here. You can do it. Just give Willy the word and he'll move out."

"He won't go faster than a trot will he?"

"Not unless you tell him to. You remember what I told you before about slowing down, right? Just pull back on the reins."

Brigid took a deep breath, kicked Willy, and told him to trot. As instructed, the horse increased his speed to a remarkably uncomfortable trot. Brigid clutched at the saddle horn and bumped along for a few minutes before pulling back on the reins and returning Willy to a walk.

She had been so focused on Willy, she had no idea what Clay was up to. She looked behind her and he grinned and waved before launching Aziz up next to her.

As he rode up alongside her, he said, "That was great! Way to go. I had Aziz wait, so you wouldn't get distracted."

"Thank you. I have to say trotting was unpleasant. Is it supposed to hurt?"

"Well, posting helps. It's easier on the butt. I can show you how if you like."

"Maybe later. My heart rate is finally starting to return to normal." Brigid patted Willy's neck. "He trotted though, and I didn't fall off. What a good boy."

"He is. I figure that he likes anything better than dealing with cows."

"Was he really a ranch horse?"

"Yeah, in his youth he was. He's related to another horse I had. They're both from a great line of quarter horses. We had a bunch over the years."

"I guess you must become attached to your horses, like I do with dogs."

"Absolutely. To this day, I still miss Pokey. I think about him all the time. He was the best horse I ever had."

"Oh no, are you telling me Gumby had a horse named Pokey?"

"Yup. That's where it came from."

Brigid burst out laughing. "I'm not sure I can ever look at you the same way."

"Hey, it's not easy being green."

Chapter 8

Moods & News

A few weeks after the meeting, Brigid finally got the news she'd been waiting to hear. Instead of yet another complaint or long-winded monologue about dog training, Ed called to say that Layla had been adopted. He dropped off the schnauzer's paperwork at Brigid's house and she gave him a hug. The gruff man said he was going to miss the little dog, but went on and on about how fantastic the dog's new family was.

Brigid was bursting with such joy that even another call from Jake couldn't ruin her mood. She loaded up Gypsy and some food into the car to head out to the ranch.

She knocked on the front door and peered through the window. Clay waved from within, and she went inside. Gypsy ran across the living room into the kitchen to sit next to Scout and closely monitor whatever Clay was up to.

Brigid walked up to the counter, put down the grocery bag, and threw her arms around Clay's neck. She stood on her tiptoes so she could give him a passionate kiss.

He stepped back and grinned at her. "You're sure in a good mood."

"Layla got adopted! It's our first real adoption. I can't believe it!"

He handed her a plate with cheese and crackers on it. "Have a seat."

Brigid took the plate and settled in at the table to snack. "Ed came by. I guess it all went really well. It's a wonderful home. Even talking to Jake didn't bring me down."

"What did he want? Did another dog come in?"

"Not today. I think he likes to call and whine at me. Remember I told you about a couple of volunteers who are walking dogs at the station—Maren and her friend Maddie? At the meeting, Maren looked like she was going to cry the whole time. I should have thought of it as foreshadowing, since apparently looks are not deceiving. Jake keeps calling me because Maren finds something to cry about almost every day and it's stressing him out. I'm a little afraid Maren might be kind of nuts. She has this edge to her voice."

Clay sat down next to her at the table. "What about the other M—what's her name—Maddie?"

"I don't know. She doesn't seem to speak at all."

"So, what you're saying is you've got plain and peanut M&Ms?"

Brigid covered her mouth to stifle a laugh. "You have got to stop making me laugh while I'm eating."

"Hey, I just call them like I see them." He pointed down at Gypsy, who was eying the cracker in his hand. "I see you brought your cohort. Did she want a field trip or something?"

"No. I was hoping we could stay over."

Clay put down the cracker and looked at her. "Are you saying what I *think* you're saying?"

"Yes, I am. If that's okay with you."

He grabbed the plate and took it to the sink, where it landed with a clatter. "Very much so."

Clay led her upstairs to the master bedroom. It was easily twice the size of the bedroom she'd stayed in the night of the thunderstorm, with high cathedral ceilings that gave it an open, airy feel. There were windows on three sides and Brigid walked across the room to the largest picture window, which had a panoramic view of the barns and pastures. She smiled at Clay. "This is like being in a tree house."

"The sunrises are pretty spectacular if you happen to be awake, which I try not to be anymore."

Brigid looked down at the long dresser in front of the window, which was covered with little horse figurines. She picked one up. "You collect horses?"

"No. They're my mom's. They used to be all over the house." He gestured around the room. The other flat surfaces were covered with herds of tiny horses as well. "They wouldn't fit in the RV, and she couldn't bear to give them up, so I told her I'd keep them here for her. Whenever she shows up, I have to go on a dusting rampage. What a gigantic pain those things are. She'd have a fit if she knew how grubby they are ninety-nine percent of the time."

Brigid laughed, "I won't reveal your dirty little secret."

"You have to make a few concessions when you buy the house you grew up in."

"Which room was yours?"

Clay sat down on the end of the bed. "The one you slept in before, across the hall. TJ's room was the office and Cole's was the other one up here, next to mine. I got rid of most of the bedroom furniture though. It was too...I don't know...

full of memories, I guess. And sleeping in your parents' bed is too weird."

Brigid turned away from the window, walked back to the bed, and stood in front of him. "There must have been a lot of adjustments after so much time away."

"Yeah. Mostly in my head. I probably spent too much time alone though."

"Really? But you must know half of Alpine Grove."

"Knowing people isn't the same as spending time with them. It's been good having you here, getting me out of my head."

Brigid wasn't quite sure what to say. "I've enjoyed being here too."

He put his hands on her upper arms and rubbed them slightly. "You sure about this?"

"Yes." Brigid put her hands on his shoulders and smiled. "I'm surprised you can't tell. For a while, I thought you could read my mind—it was like you could see into me. To be honest, it was a little creepy. I thought maybe you really *are* some kind of magic horse whisperer. But if that were the case, I don't think you'd fall off so much."

"If you ride as many horses as I have for as many years as I have, you're bound to fall off occasionally. But I don't think real magicians have bruises like I do. There's no magic to it." He ran his hands up her arms to her neck and cupped her jaw in his hands, caressing her cheeks with his fingertips. "It's just paying attention."

Brigid curled her fingers in the soft hair at the back of his neck. "You must have some amazing powers of observation then."

"Usually it's the eyes that tell you." He gazed up at her face intently. "People lie all the time with words. But if you look at someone's eyes, oftentimes you can see the true emotion— whether it's fear, love, hate, desperation, or whatever they're really thinking. It probably doesn't work with serial killers I guess, but with most people, if their eyes tell you something, you should believe it."

"That's how you knew I was afraid. And not telling the truth."

"I was drawn by your eyes from the moment I met you." He moved his arms around her back to pull her closer. "They are extremely expressive."

"They're just boring old hazel. I always wished I had green eyes. I was convinced that would have counteracted the Pippi effect."

"I think you're more *Anne of Green Gables* than Pippi."

Brigid leaned back on his hands to smile down at his face. "You're kidding. That's such a girl's book."

"I stole them from TJ's room. The whole series, one at a time, so she wouldn't notice. Anne was funny and smart and worked really hard, which reminds me of you."

"I don't know about that. I'm still working on it. Maybe by the time I'm eighty or ninety, I'll have it all figured out."

"I think you're doing just fine." He pulled her down into his lap so he could kiss her and murmured, "Better than fine, in fact."

The thrilling sensation of his lips on hers again swirled through her and she fumbled with the buttons on his shirt, wanting to feel the warmth of his skin. He captured her hand and lolled back on the bed, bringing her up next to him.

Brigid opened her eyes and Clay pushed her hair back from her face. "Don't be nervous, honey."

"I know. It's not like I haven't done…I mean I know how this works, but…well, this is so embarrassing. I've just been told I'm not very good at it."

"I'm not expecting you to swing from a trapeze or something, if that's what you're thinking."

Brigid laughed in spite of herself. "Well thank goodness for that. Just so you know, I'm not very good at yoga either."

"That's okay. If you let me take you riding again, I'll teach you some of my wicked yoga moves."

"I'd like that as long as it's on the ground." She looked into his eyes. "So what do you see in my eyes now?"

"Desire."

Moving closer to kiss him again, she said, "I think you're onto something here."

Much later, Brigid was enveloped in Clay's arms drifting in and out of sleep, listening to the relaxing sound of his even breathing. He started awake at a thump on the end of the bed, lifted his head, and grumbled, "Scout, we've had conversations about this." The dog stood staring down at them, wagging his long feathery tail. Clay sighed. "C'mon, dog. Would you either just lie down or go away?"

Brigid rolled over to face Clay. "Does he need to go out?"

"No. If you're wondering why I have a king-size bed, this is it. He's like Goldilocks all night. First, he sleeps on one bed, then another, and eventually, he ends up in here and wakes me up before he lies down, just to make sure I know he's there. As if I couldn't tell that a fifty-pound animal just jumped on my bed."

"You could block him out of the room. Close the door?"

"Nah, I don't bother. It's no big deal and it's just him and me here anyway." He moved his hand out from under the covers to trace the outline of her lips. "Well, usually, that is. If you want me to throw him out, I will."

"No, that's okay. He's all curled up now, keeping my feet warm."

"He thinks I don't know he sleeps on all the beds, but the dog hair is a giveaway. It's not like he doesn't have a dozen dog beds on the floor scattered through every room of this place."

"You are such a softie. TJ told me that too."

"My sister has a big mouth."

"I've been meaning to ask you something about TJ. The day after the meeting, she left here before I could ask, but I was wondering how she knows Kat. They seemed to have a lot to talk about."

"As I understand it, they never met before that night. It turns out that Kat is related to someone TJ used to know."

"I guess it really is a small town. It's going to take me forever to figure out all these relationships."

As he curled up closer to nuzzle her neck, he whispered, "Not as long as you might think."

～

The next morning, Brigid squinted at the light streaming through the windows. Clay wasn't kidding about the sunrise. He'd pulled the sheet over his head. Following suit, she yanked the sheet up to cover her eyes, which caused Scout to stand up and jump off the bed. Clay rolled over, stretched his arms over his head, and yawned.

She sidled up next to him and put her palms on his chest. "Good morning. Have you considered curtains?"

Wrapping his arms around her, he gave her a lingering kiss. "It *is* a good morning. The best one I can remember in a long time. There were curtains in here. They were lacy frilly things and I couldn't stand them, so I took them down."

She sat up and wrapped her arms around her knees, considering the slashes of pink and orange that blazed across the sky outside the window. "Maybe this is why people get up so early in the country."

"Because we're too lazy to hang curtains?" He sat up. "Maybe. All I know is that at this hour, I need coffee in a serious way."

"I should get home. I need to take Judge to the vet this afternoon for another dip."

"Well, then you don't have to rush off, do you?" He turned and leaned across her body so he could kiss her again.

"I should go home and take a shower."

"It may be out in the country, but we do have indoor plumbing, you know."

Brigid slumped down on the bed and pulled Clay down on top of her. "You're right. I don't have to rush off. If last night was any indication, this could go from a good morning to an even better morning."

"I think so."

Much later, Brigid was standing in the kitchen wearing a gigantic maroon t-shirt of Clay's that practically came down to her knees. It was from the Wall Drug Store in South Dakota, and the t-shirt proudly proclaimed the store was established in 1931. She wrapped her arms around Clay's waist and peered around his arm at the pan of eggs frying on the stove. "Are they done yet? I'm starving."

"Some things are worth waiting for." Clay took a sip of coffee. The phone rang and he handed her the mug and the spatula. "Take over for a minute."

Brigid stirred the eggs and smiled down at Gypsy, who was watching intently in case anything might leap out of the pan into her mouth. "Don't give me those sad eyes. You had your breakfast. And some of Scout's too."

Gypsy wagged her tail, looking pleased that she'd managed to score some of Scout's food while he wasn't paying attention.

Clay walked back into the kitchen and gestured toward the office. "It's for you."

"Me? No one knows I'm here."

"Well, someone figured it out."

She handed the spatula back to him. "Sorry about this."

In the office, she sat down at the desk and picked up the receiver. "This is Brigid."

There was a sniff and a tiny cough. "Bbbrigid! This is Maren. I'm at the police station and I need to talk to you about this dog. I'm *so* worried about him. It's a little beagle, but he's not friendly like the other beagles I've met before. I named him Lewis. He's a little nervous and overweight. It's like he's never been walked before. Jake said that when Lewis was picked up he acted aggressive, but I don't believe that. He's not like that with me at all. Just scared. You have to do something. I'm afraid they won't give him to you, and Maddie and I want to take him home right now." Maren dissolved into weeping and she could hear Jake in the background say,

"Hey, that's my phone. Get that dog out of my office. They aren't allowed to stay in here."

Brigid sat up straighter. "Maren? Maren, please calm down. I'll be there in a little while. Put the beagle back in the cage. His stray holding period is not up. We aren't allowed to take him yet. Do *not* take him home with you."

Maren snuffled a few times. "Why are you even out there? Everyone knows about Clay Hadley. We need to get the dogs adopted and away from there. I'm so worried about Judge too. The poor thing."

"Judge is fine, Maren. I want you to put the beagle back in his cage. *Right now!*"

Maren apparently got herself under control enough to cover the mouthpiece and say something to Jake, which Brigid could only partially hear, but it sounded like "I'm almost done." Returning to Brigid, she said, "All right. I'll go put the dog back. But you need to *do* something."

"I will. Please put the dog away now and let me talk to Jake."

"Fine." There were a few muffled noises and Jake said, "Hello? Brigid, uh, it would be good if you could come by here. I mean, we have rules, you know."

"I know. I'll be there a little later, okay? For now, I just want to apologize to you."

"Yeah, okay. I'll see ya."

Brigid hung up, leaned her elbows on the desk, and put her forehead on her palms. This Maren woman was going to drive her to drink. And what was this animosity toward Clay about? People kept making weird sideways comments. Ugh. She stood up and shook her head. Time for breakfast.

When she returned to the kitchen, Clay raised his eyebrows at her. "What was that all about?"

"It's Maren again. In between bouts of weeping, she let me know she's upset about a dog at the station. It sounds like she and Maddie are not big on following rules and now Jake is irritated with me. I hope they aren't going to mess up the arrangement I've set up there."

He handed her a plate. "Food might help."

"I think Maren may drive me insane. *Everything* is a crisis with her."

He pointed his fork toward the door. "So I suppose you have to go smooth things over with the cops?"

"I'm afraid so. I wish I could stay. I've got to go talk to them and take Judge to the vet for his dip." She paused, holding a fork full of eggs in the air. "I forgot to check my answering machine! There are probably twenty-five weepy calls from Maren before she thought to call here. Who knows who else might have called?"

"You're quite popular."

"I think you're confusing popularity with something else. Notoriety maybe? I feel like everyone hates me."

Clay pushed his plate forward and put his elbows on the table. "I don't hate you. Quite the opposite, actually. I could get used to waking up next to you every morning."

Brigid jerked her head to look at him. He wasn't kidding around. "What are you saying? I already told you, I'm not good at relationships."

"I think we had this conversation a while ago. After last night, you can't possibly think we're just friends, can you?"

"Obviously, it's more than that. But when you say *every morning*, it sounds like you're talking about something more serious."

"Just because you had a bad marriage that doesn't mean you can't be with anyone else ever again." He scratched at his ear and gazed out the window. "As my loudmouth sister mentioned, I've been married before too."

"That was a long time ago."

"True. And it flamed out in a bad way. But that doesn't mean that I can't recognize that the connection we have is special. Not to mention the chemistry."

Brigid put her palm to her cheek. It was warm and probably a spectacular shade of crimson by now. "Well yes, last night was incredible. But that's just sex."

"Which you also said you aren't *good* at. I think we proved beyond a shadow of a doubt multiple times that's certainly not true. So okay, maybe that's what you thought last night was about—just sex. Or maybe that's all you want to believe. But we've spent quite a bit of time together now and I know how I feel." He paused. "And I can see by the look on your face that's not something you want to hear about."

"It just feels so sudden."

"You say that even though you've been coming out here for weeks. How many times have we sat around in the kitchen eating together?"

"But we hardly know each other."

"What exactly do you need to know about me that you don't already know?" He crossed his arms across his chest. "You know where I live, you know what I do, and thanks to my sister and folks around town, you probably know what I've been up to just about my entire life. What else is there?"

"I don't know." Brigid threw up her hands in exasperation. "I just…this isn't what I wanted. It's not what I planned."

"Well, what do you want? Because I'd like to know." Clay looked out the window again. "I'll admit I'm no prize in a lot of ways. Maybe I've been wrong and you really don't care about me at all. And if that's the case, I'll finally take the hint and leave you alone."

Brigid's eyes widened and she reached over to take his hand, pulling it away from his chest. "No! That's not what I mean. Not at all."

"Then what *do* you mean?"

"You shouldn't care about me. No one should, but especially not you. You know better than anyone what a mess I am. Everything will just end in disaster and I don't want to hurt you."

"Unless you happen to be psychic, I don't know how you know that's what's going to happen." He took her other hand and faced her. "I think you're letting the opinions of one person—technically, one ghost—affect your life. You aren't responsible for how I feel, only how *you* feel."

"I suppose." She stared down at their hands. "I'm just so afraid of repeating the past."

"Maybe it's rash and impulsive or maybe I've just been lonely for too long, but I'm falling in love with you. And if you don't ever see yourself feeling the same way, it would be good to know that now, rather than later."

Brigid looked back up into his face. She knew every crease and scar and exactly how the little lines around his eyes crinkled when he laughed. Last night, she had memorized every contour of his jaw while he lay sleeping next to her in the moonlight.

"I feel so many things. It's like my heart woke up after being asleep for a long time." She leaned closer so they were almost touching and ran her fingers along the scar on his chin and down his throat to his collarbone. "I've been trying to deny it, but I can't say I don't care about you, because I do. I just hope you don't end up regretting that fact."

"No matter what, I won't regret the time we've spent together." Taking her hand again, he leaned to kiss her. "I suppose I may have engaged in some risky behavior in the past."

Brigid raised her eyebrows. "Gee, you think so?"

"Yeah, okay, don't give me that look. I know. This isn't like that. Being with you is not a risk to me. And even if it is, it's one I'm willing to take."

~

After calling her answering machine and listening to many messages, Brigid decided it would be easier to take Gypsy home and deal with all the volunteer issues first, and then come back to the ranch and pick up Judge for his trip to the vet clinic.

Once she got home, she methodically returned all the calls, leaving messages and answering questions. Sonia wanted to change the time for their coffee meeting the next day. She'd also said the librarian had found a book with a lot of fundraising ideas and that she'd bring it with her.

After getting caught up with the phone calls, she reluctantly walked over to the police station. She was dreading hearing what Jake had to say. It would be even worse if he'd shared his complaints with the chief.

She walked into the building and peered into Jake's office. Since he wasn't around at the moment, Brigid figured she'd take the opportunity to meet the new beagle. Continuing out toward the back, she exited the building. The beagle started baying at the sight of Brigid. He certainly didn't seem aggressive, just loud.

She crouched down in front of the cage, which seemed to confuse the dog. They evaluated each other for a moment and then Brigid went to get a leash, figuring that since she was here, she could at least give him a walk around the yard. He seemed friendly enough and Brigid walked around the area, letting him sniff happily. She sat down on a stack of cinder blocks that had been dropped off for some municipal project. The dog sat in front of her wagging his tail in the dust, and she bent to pet the smooth fur on his head. "You don't seem like much of a killer, Lewis. If your family doesn't come pick you up, you might get to go out and visit the ranch and meet Judge. What do you think?" He panted and looked pleased with the idea and Brigid stood up again. "Okay, that sounds like a plan. Let me get this all sorted out for you."

After putting Lewis back in his kennel, Brigid looked around for Jake again. She peeked into Chief Russell's office and he looked up from a pile of papers. Before she could get away, he said, "Brigid! I need to talk to you."

"Okay." Drat. The chief was the last person she wanted to see. Slowly walking into his office, she smiled and held out her hand as he stood up. "It's good to see you again."

After shaking her hand, he gestured to the chair. "We need to talk about those *people* that are walking dogs now."

"I know. I spoke with Jake briefly this morning and that's why I'm here. I stopped by to talk to him."

"He's out getting lunch. He wanted to have me talk to you anyway."

"Oh. Okay, I was afraid of that."

"This is a police station and we can't have people constantly crying in the hallways. It can be stressful enough here as it is without that."

"I know. I talked to Maren. I'd really like to have more than just me walking dogs."

"While I agree that finding help can be difficult, you need to do something about that woman before Jake throttles her. There's an old saying in management: 'hire slowly and fire quickly.' That goes double for volunteers."

Brigid shook her head. "But she loves dogs and seems so dedicated—she hasn't missed a shift. I'm asking people to do this out of the goodness of their heart. What if I never find anyone else?"

"There are plenty of dog-lovers in this community. You've just gotten started. Once you meet more people, they'll step up."

"I wish I shared your optimism." Brigid stood up. "But I'll tell her not to come back and I'll walk dogs myself if I have to until I get more people signed up. I appreciate your patience and apologize for the trouble she's caused. I'll try to do a better job of screening people in the future."

The chief stood up and put out his hand. "I'm sure you will."

Brigid looked at the dog-walking schedule hanging on the wall. It was a copy of the one she had at home. Maren was signed up for multiple slots. With a sigh, she grabbed a pen off the desk and crossed out Maren's name. Cindy was still doing some of the walks, but Maddie didn't seem to come here on her own, only with Maren.

Maybe Maddie was too shy. Brigid made a mental note to call and explain the situation to her too. Maybe Maddie would be willing to take some of Maren's shifts herself. Otherwise, Brigid was going to be spending a whole lot of time here again.

She walked home slowly, enjoying the sights and smells of the flowers blooming in the gardens throughout the residential neighborhoods. Spring in Alpine Grove certainly had been pretty and now it was practically summer. Something buzzed by her ear and she smacked at her neck with her palm. She pulled her hand away and saw a small smear of blood. Score one for Mr. Mosquito.

When she arrived at the ranch to collect Judge, Clay was riding Hank back from the arena. He waved and dismounted, leading the horse toward her. Brigid stopped and waited. Sometimes he looked like such a quintessential cowboy. No wonder they loved him in Hollywood.

He removed his hat and held it with the reins while he ran his fingers through his hair. "Hey there. What happened?"

"I'm picking up Judge, remember?"

"I know that. But you look a whole lot more pissed-off than you did when you left."

"I was in such a good mood this morning. I should have just stayed here."

Clay smiled as he put his hat back on. "You'll get no argument from me."

"I have to walk dogs again. The chief basically said to keep the nutty M away from the station."

"Sometimes you feel like a nut, sometimes you don't."

Brigid laughed. "That's the wrong candy and you know it."

He took her hand. "I'm just checking to see if you've lost your sense of humor."

"No." Brigid interlaced her fingers with his. "But I have to walk dogs at the station again, so I probably can't spend as much time out here with you as I was hoping."

"We'll figure it out. I'm not going anywhere."

She turned and stood on her toes to kiss Clay and Hank snorted loudly in her ear. Clay grinned. "Not in front of the horse, honey."

As usual, Judge was thrilled to see Brigid and he happily jumped into the car for the trip back to town. In addition to smelling like aging dog barf, the Honda also was starting to make an odd noise from somewhere deep underneath the car. Brigid was determined to ignore it, although if the car died, then she'd really need to get a job. She couldn't live off her credit cards forever. Companies had a tendency to get persnickety about the credit limits on their cards.

At the clinic, a woman Brigid had never met introduced herself as Gail and said Tracy was waiting for them in the back. By now, Brigid knew the way and she found Tracy at the big sink surrounded by the various soaps and concoctions they needed for the dip.

Tracy waved a gloved hand. "Are you ready to kill some mites?"

Brigid picked up a pair of gloves off the counter. "As ready as I'll ever be."

The two women got down to the task of washing and dipping Judge who once again took the process with a remarkable degree of calm. Maybe it was his partial water-dog heritage, but he didn't seem to mind the many baths much at all.

Tracy rubbed some soap on the dog's back and said, "So I know it's been a while, but belated thanks for the fantastic munchies at the meeting. It was memorable. I think that's the best food I've eaten since I went to Napa last fall."

"You're welcome. I'm glad you came."

"I didn't do much except eat. And talk about puppies."

"Well, it was great having you there. I was on cloud nine afterward with everyone volunteering. And since then, we've gotten some more dogs into foster homes and even one adopted! It was fantastic."

Tracy glanced at her. "I get the impression things aren't so fantastic now?"

"Well they were. But I think Judith is going to bankrupt me with her expensive tastes. And I'm afraid Maren needs professional psychiatric help."

"I don't know Maren well. I'm not sure how long she's lived here, but she hasn't been to the vet. Judith is just, well, pleased with her status in the community. In my head, I imagine her as a peacock strutting around."

Brigid giggled, "That's a nice way of putting it."

"She's like me in that she grew up here, so she knows everyone. But she married a guy who made a lot of money in construction, building fancy houses on the lake. That kind of changed her, I guess."

"Interesting. I will say, she certainly has a nice new car. I was jealous. Thanks to Nugget, my car smells like well-aged dog vomit. I can't get the smell out of it."

Tracy laughed, "Don't get me started on cars. I hate mine. My boyfriend keeps fixing the stupid thing, even though I keep asking him to drive it off a cliff to put it out of its misery."

"Well, that's nice he can fix it. In addition to smelling awful, I think my Honda may have a death rattle now. And even though I don't think Judith likes me, I know she's taking good care of Nugget. She was very upset that he was at the ranch."

"Well, I don't think she likes the Hadleys much."

Brigid turned to Tracy and raised a soapy glove in exasperation. "Yes! What's *with* that? I keep getting all these odd snide comments about Clay."

"The Hadleys had some problems in the past I guess. I don't really know much about it, since I was a little kid and living out at a commune. I've just heard second-hand stuff. Just rumors really."

"I've been spending a lot of time at the ranch and Clay has been nothing but kind to me."

"Oh, really?"

Brigid looked down at Judge and scrubbed more assiduously, avoiding Tracy's inquisitive gaze. "I just don't see what everyone's problem is with him."

"I don't know. When he's brought in Scout, I've found him kind of hard to relate to. He's so quiet and it's like he's watching you all the time, which makes me nervous. Then I try to be funny and he never laughs. Not even a smile. Everything is always so serious with him."

Brigid paused in her scrubbing. "That's interesting. When I'm around him, he makes me laugh all the time."

"Well, that's a good thing then. I wouldn't worry about other people. This town is chock full of rumors." Tracy poured the last of the dip on Judge's hind leg. "And this guy is just about ready to roll."

Brigid helped Tracy towel off Judge, considering the conversation. Maybe her own impressions of Clay were skewed. History had shown that she wasn't good at character assessment when her heart was involved. She'd thought John was perfect in every way back when she met him. What if her impressions of Clay were wrong too?

Brigid drove back to the ranch with Judge. The dog was standing up in the back seat, enjoying all the scents on the breezes flowing through the window. She glanced at his reflection in the mirror and smiled. All the baths and dips were working. New soft brown fur was growing in and he was actually starting to become a rather handsome young dog.

She parked in front of the house and walked Judge around the ranch before putting him back in his enclosure. As she stood waiting for him, she evaluated the best way to fire Maren. Should she call her, or try to intercept her at the station the next morning and do it in person? But there other people could be around and that might feel more public and make it even worse.

She gave Judge his dinner and he settled in on his dog bed to rest. The trip to the vet had worn them both out and Brigid walked slowly up to the house. Firing someone was not on the list of life experiences she wanted to have. All those self-help books didn't cover stuff like this.

Clay was in the kitchen snacking again. He waved a chip at her and stood up. "Hey, how was the vet?"

"Tiring. Judge is resting on his bed. Dr. C wasn't around this time, so Tracy and I did it."

"Half the time I see her, I have to do a double-take. Sometimes I forget she's an adult now. I still think of her as one of the little kids from the commune."

"She mentioned she grew up here. I think she's half scared of you."

"Yeah, right. I'm real scary." He popped the chip in his mouth and made a face.

Brigid laughed as she put her arms around his waist. "I know! I told her you make me laugh all the time. She said you never even crack a smile."

"When you're missing some teeth, you kind of get out of the habit. It tends to be a turn-off. Definitely not so good for your social life, particularly in Hollywood, where people are concerned about appearances."

"I suppose so. But you smile all the time now."

He put his hand on her cheek and bent to kiss her. "Being happier helps quite a bit too."

Brigid released him, walked to the table, and picked up a chip. "While I was driving out here, I was trying to figure out how to fire Maren. I know she's going to cry again and it makes me feel sick. I hate crying. I hardly ever cry."

"Some people cry more than others. Maybe for her it's like frowning."

"Or breathing." Brigid smiled. "Apparently, I need to be on horseback to cry."

"I prefer yoga, but to each her own."

After discussing the pros and cons of firing in person versus over the phone with Clay, Brigid helped him do dishes and got ready to leave. He put his palms on her shoulders. "I sure hope you find some more volunteers soon."

She stood on her tip toes and kissed him. "After last night, I'm motivated. I'd far rather spend the night with you than in my cold bed all alone. I'll see you tomorrow and let you know how it goes."

The next morning, Brigid got up early, fed Gypsy, and went to the station. She'd decided that the best thing to do would be to attend the morning dog walk and talk to Maren in person. Maybe she could reason with her and they could work something out. Brigid didn't want to lose Maren as a volunteer if she didn't have to. The yard where the kennels were located wasn't particularly public, so they could walk the dogs, then talk. That was the hope anyway.

When Brigid went out to the yard, Lewis bayed his joyous greeting. She went into the kennel, asked him to sit, and put a leash on him. Someone had taught the dog the sit command and he seemed proud of his ability to follow the instruction. She bent to ruffle his ears. "You're a good boy, aren't you?"

Maren and Maddie came out the door from the station, and Maren ran across the yard to the beagle. The dog looked somewhat taken aback at the woman's galumphing approach. She stood in front of the dog, slapping her knees. "It's me, it's meeee!" in a high-pitched screechy voice that made Brigid cringe. Maren bent down so her face was close to the beagle's. "Don't you want to give me a kiss?"

Brigid said, "What are you doing? I asked him to sit. He's being good. Don't encourage him to jump on you."

She straightened. "Dogs love me and they always want to say hi with hugs and kisses. It's so cute!"

"Could you lower your voice?" Brigid crouched down next to Lewis and rubbed his chest. "I think you're scaring him a little."

"No, dogs always love me! He's just shy. Probably he was abused."

Brigid turned to Maddie. "Hi Maddie, how are you?"

The woman's dark eyes widened and she bowed her head, her long stringy clumps of mahogany hair falling in front of her face. She mumbled, "Fine."

Brigid said, "I'd like to go on the walk with you today with Lewis. Then I need to talk to you."

"We like to walk by ourselves. I have to get to work, you know. I've told them that I'm coming in a half-hour late so I can volunteer here," Maren said.

"All right. If you don't have time, I'll walk Lewis after we talk. Maybe we could sit down over there?"

A tear slid out of Maren's eye. "Is something wrong? Lewis is going to be sent away isn't he? I knew it! I just knew it!"

Brigid put her hand on Maren's arm. "No, he's fine. Kat made flyers and Sonia is hanging more up today. If no one claims him, he'll stay at the ranch with Judge until he finds a new home. It's all fine and going according to plan."

"Noooo!" Maren sobbed. "He can't go out there. He *can't*! I'll take him home. I'll foster him."

Brigid took a deep breath. Clearly, there was no reasoning with this woman. "Maren, I think we need to find something else for you to do. This isn't working out. Taking care of these dogs can be an emotional roller coaster, and I understand that."

Maren gulped back a sob. "What are you saying?"

"I don't think you should come back here to the police station. It seems to be a little too much for you to handle," Brigid said evenly. "I'll take over here, but maybe there's something else you can help with."

"No. I like walking dogs. I knew it! You're just some type of control freak, aren't you?" Maren shook her index finger. "You don't even care about these dogs…taking them out to that horrible ranch and locking them in cages. It's cruel!"

"You haven't seen it, but there's a nice set-up out there. Judge is happy and he's looking so healthy now. His fur is coming in beautifully. I think we'll be able to put him up for adoption soon," Brigid said.

"That guy—what's his name who lives there—I heard he's a creep!" Maren waved her arms frantically. "You shouldn't have dogs there. Everyone knows he was arrested. And then there are stories about what he did when he was working on those movies too. I heard he even stole a horse once!"

Brigid's patience had officially come to an end. "Listen Maren, I'm sorry, but please don't come back tomorrow. I'll take over the dog walking from now on."

Maddie pushed her hair behind her ear. "You mean you're firing her?"

"Yes, I am, if you want to put it that way." Brigid gave Maddie an encouraging smile. "If you'd like to walk dogs alone, we can try that and see how it goes. But I think I'd like to go on a few walks with you first. We should work on doing a little training with these guys to help improve their chances for adoption."

Maddie stared at the ground and shook her head.

Maren started to bawl loudly, and between hysterical breaths managed to sputter, "I...can't....believe....this!" Turning to Maddie she said, "Let's...get...out...of...here!"

Brigid watched as the two women practically ran from the yard. She looked down at Lewis, who wagged his tail a few times. "I think it's just you and me now, kid."

After she got home, Brigid called Sonia to let her know what had happened. Her friend was sympathetic and said it was the right thing to do, but Brigid wasn't so sure.

Mostly she wanted a hug and to talk to Clay. Getting up at the crack of dawn and driving back to town in the morning would be worth it if she got to spend the night snuggled up with him again. Cindy Ross was scheduled to do Lewis's evening walk, so Brigid picked up Gypsy and carried her out to the Honda for the trip to the ranch.

～

Very early the next morning, Brigid was lying alongside Clay with her ear pressed to his chest and the covers pulled over her head to block out the sun. It was so relaxing lying next to him listening to his heart beat. She didn't want to get up and face the day yet. It was too early and he was so warm.

The phone next to the bed jangled and both of them bolted upright, disentangling their limbs so Clay could reach over to grab the handset. As he grumbled, "Hello," Brigid pulled the sheet back over her head.

From underneath, she heard him say, "Why in heaven's name are you calling so early?" After a pause, he said. "You know I don't get the paper. I don't *want* to be informed."

Brigid peeked out from under the sheet. Given the expression on his face, whatever Clay was hearing was not making him happy at all.

"Fine. I'll get a paper. Later. Right now, I'm going back to sleep." He hung up the phone and turned to wrap his arms around Brigid. "Good morning."

"What was that all about?"

"My sister had to report the morning news to me."

"Now? Does she do this kind of thing often?"

"No." He kissed her. "Apparently, you're famous."

"What are you talking about?"

"There's a less-than-flattering letter about you in the editorial section of the local newspaper."

"What does it say?"

"Well, TJ says I need to pick up a paper and read it for myself. But I guess the gist of it is that you're not looking out for the best interests of the homeless dogs of Alpine Grove."

"You've got to be kidding."

"Nope."

"How can that be?"

"Apparently, your association with me isn't helping, given the cruel conditions we've subjected Judge to and all."

Brigid put her face in her palms. "Maren wrote it, didn't she?"

He pulled her hands down and hugged her tightly. "'Fraid so, honey."

"How can you be so calm?" Brigid moved away so she could look at him. "Don't you see? This is terrible. Sonia and I were just about to start pulling together the fundraiser. She has everything all laid out. This will kill any hope of anyone ever wanting to attend, much less donate."

"It will be okay. These things always blow over. The paper doesn't really have much else to do, so things like this end up in print. But it will be replaced tomorrow with the next cranky letter from some curmudgeon all bent out of shape about something else. Tomorrow some old coot will be carping about how people are driving too fast to get to the espresso stand or something."

"That's not true. People never seem to forget *anything* around here." Brigid gestured toward the window. "I keep hearing about how there's something wrong with this ranch... and with *you*. I have no idea what they're talking about, but the impression I get is that it's all about stuff that happened years ago."

"Well, I told you that stories run rampant. And I've done some kind of stupid things. I think you already know about most of it though." He shrugged. "But if there's something you want to know, just ask."

"Maren said you were arrested for being a horse thief."

"More like a horse relocator. I wasn't charged with anything."

"I'm sorry. I don't know why I'm even bringing this up." Brigid hugged him. "I need to walk Judge then get back to town and deal with Lewis."

Brigid took Gypsy home, and as soon as she walked in the door, the phone was ringing. Sonia called to commiserate about the letter, and they agreed to meet later to talk about what the bad press meant to their upcoming plans. As soon as she hung up with Sonia, Judith called. She said, "I read

Maren's editorial in the paper this morning. I told you it's imperative to get those dogs away from that ranch."

Brigid wanted to tear her hair out. Judith might be a brilliant dog expert, but something about the woman's personality had a way of getting on Brigid's last nerve. "What on earth is your problem with Clay Hadley?"

"Well you know he was arrested, don't you?"

"He's not a horse thief, for heaven's sake. Why is everyone harping on this?"

"I certainly wouldn't put stealing a horse past him, but that's not what I meant. He was arrested for assault."

"Assault? You can't be serious."

"It's true. Perhaps you don't know him as well as you think you do."

"I don't believe you."

"Ask your friends at the police station then."

"Fine. I will."

"I wanted to let you know that my friend has agreed to adopt Nugget. She came to visit and fell in love with him. He will be moving to Lake Tahoe. They have a lovely home there. I'll give the paperwork to Sonia later today."

"Thank you. That's wonderful news."

"I may be able to foster another dog, but only if you agree to stop keeping dogs at the V Bar H ranch."

"Judge is still there while he's undergoing treatment. I don't suppose you'd like to foster a dog with mange, would you?"

"No, I would not. I told you before—you absolutely must get him away from there."

"Thank you for your input. I'll keep that in mind."

After Brigid hung up, she wanted to rip the phone out of the wall and heave it across the room. Fortunately, for her rental house, she had to go walk Lewis. Gypsy looked up at her with concern. "I'm sorry Gypsy, but that woman is such a know-it-all. She makes me crazy. Let me feed you so I can get out of here before the phone rings again."

Brigid went to the station, and walked Lewis, who really was a great little dog. Maybe Ed would be willing to foster him. She walked out though the station and Jake waved at her, "Boy, am I glad to see you!"

Brigid wasn't in the mood to talk to him, but she smiled politely. "You too. We had a couple of foster homes open up, so I hope one of them can take Lewis. In any case, he'll be out of here soon."

"That's great. But even better, thanks for getting rid of that crying chick. She was a total nut job."

"It turns out she's quite a good writer too."

"What do you mean?"

"I guess there's some terrible letter in the paper about me. Oh, and she hates Clay Hadley and the V Bar H ranch. It's all really depressing."

"I'm sorry Brigid. I guess there was some trouble out there years ago, but I don't know what that has to do with you."

"Nothing. I don't suppose you know if Clay Hadley was arrested, do you?"

"Well, not off-hand, but they hired a bunch of typists to load old records into our database, so we can look up more reports now. It goes way back. There aren't details…those are all in the paper files, but I can look up a name and see a one-sentence description. I've hardly used it yet. Wanna try it out?"

Brigid paused. She felt like she was violating some type of promise, but her curiosity got the better of her. "Sure, look up Clayton Hadley and see what you find."

Jake carefully pecked at the keys on the keyboard. His tongue stuck out of the corner of his mouth as he concentrated on the screen. "Hey, look at that! It works. That's so cool."

"What does it say?"

"He was arrested twice for assault. Once in 1975 and once in 1976. Like I said, it doesn't say what it was about though. Just an arrest."

A tightness gripped Brigid's chest and she felt almost dizzy. "That's fine. Thank you for looking it up. I need to go now."

Jake grinned at the computer. "I can't believe it worked. Gotta love technology."

Brigid nodded and backed out of the office. "I'll see you later."

She walked as quickly as she could through the residential streets back to her house, her mind ablaze with the information about Clay, swirling from one incendiary thought to the next. How could she possibly have been so stupid? Assault? That meant some type of physical attack. Probably violence related to anger. People weren't arrested for no reason, after all. And certainly not *twice*.

Clay had never gotten angry when she was around him. Maybe he became violent. He said she knew everything there was to know about him, but it wasn't true. She had no idea how he'd behave if he became completely furious about something. He was a physical person and it was only a matter of time before something set him off. Everyone got angry sooner or later and she was very sure she didn't want to find out what that would be like in his case.

Brigid was not going to jeopardize her physical and mental health again. That absolutely wasn't going to happen because she wouldn't let it. Judge's skin was healed enough now that she could probably foster him herself now that he wouldn't bleed all over the pretty furniture in her house. Given all the bad press, Clay would probably agree it was better this way. If they didn't see each other every day, things would cool off, and he'd forget about her.

She brushed a tear from her face as she opened the door to her house. Forgetting about Clay wasn't going to be so easy. It would be impossible, in fact. But she'd just have to get over it. Memories faded, after all.

Gypsy stood in the living room wagging her tail expectantly. Brigid took one look at the sweet furry brown dog and burst into tears. She picked up Gypsy and carried her to the sofa, hugging the dog's stubby body to her chest as she wept. "Oh Gypsy, what have I done?"

Chapter 9

Consequences

B rigid spent most of the afternoon crying, eating ice cream, and listening to her answering machine take calls. She did manage to leave a message with Sonia canceling their coffee date. The last thing Brigid wanted to do was talk about Maren's letter. She was probably the only person left in Alpine Grove who hadn't read the horrible missive, but she couldn't stand to think about it anymore.

By the time she needed to go walk Lewis again, she had pulled herself together enough to call Ed and ask about foster care. After his success with Layla, he seemed enthusiastic about the idea of taking Lewis, which was a relief. Now she just needed to get out to the ranch, talk to Clay, and take Judge home.

While Brigid was out walking Lewis, Sonia left a message. They'd planned to do a big event at the community hall, but it turned out the building was booked through the fall. Brigid was too tired to deal with anything else today. She had to go get Judge. After saying goodbye to Gypsy, she went out to the Honda. Time to get this over with.

When Brigid arrived at the ranch, everything looked the same, but *she* felt so different that it all seemed foreign and strange. She parked next to the barn, went inside, and put the leash Judge's collar. He wagged in delight, ready for his walk.

253

While Judge went through his evening routine, she slowly ambled down the driveway, trying not to think about the fact that she wouldn't be coming here again. She'd miss the quiet and the scent of warm grass, horses, and wildflowers that filled the air.

The door to the house opened and Clay walked down the steps from the porch. He glanced toward her car parked next to the barn and then waved at her and smiled. She raised her hand in greeting and started back toward the house with Judge.

As they got closer, he squinted at her. "What happened to you? Are you okay?"

"It's been a long day."

He moved to take her hand and the look of surprise on his face as she pulled away made Brigid feel a little sick. She said, "I really need to talk to you."

"Okay. Do you want to come inside? I was just about to snack on some chips and salsa while I figure out what's for dinner."

"No. It's about Judge. I'm going to take him with me back to my house tonight."

"Did you find him a home?" He grinned. "Maybe that stupid letter backfired. They say all publicity is good publicity, right?"

"I think it's best if Judge doesn't stay here."

"What? He's fine. Same as ever."

"I'll find other places for the dogs to stay from now on. You can have your barn back."

"Okay." He pressed his lips together and stared at her for a moment. "This *is* about that letter, isn't it?"

"I haven't read it, but Sonia gave me the highlights."

"Are you actually going to cave to the demands of that nutty crying woman? Really? I have the paper in the house. You should read what she said. She comes off like a bellyaching lunatic."

"I don't know about that, but I found out that it's true that you were arrested."

He crossed his arms across his chest. "I never said I wasn't."

"Yes, you did."

"No, I said I wasn't charged as a horse thief. And I wasn't."

"You were arrested for assault...*twice*! That means you attacked people."

"But not charged." Clay stepped closer and held out his arms toward her. "You got the whole story on all this, didn't you?"

"I asked Jake to look it up in some database. It has a sentence about each arrest." Brigid looked at the sky trying to will her eyes not to cry anymore. Today, she'd learned that being on horseback was definitely not a requirement for tears.

He dropped his arms. "One sentence. Really?"

Finally, she composed herself enough to say, "You *have* to know what the word assault means. And what it means to me. Why didn't you say something?"

"What do you want me to say? That I was arrested twenty years ago? Okay, I was. That's not the kind of thing you tend to bring up in conversation."

"Maybe you should have, given that you've *attacked* people."

"I didn't attack anyone. Obviously you didn't bother to find out what actually happened or you'd know that."

"Well then *tell* me!"

Clay started to speak, then stopped and looked into her eyes. "I can tell you, but I'm starting to think it won't make any difference. You're going to believe what you want to believe about me."

"What's that supposed to mean?"

He paused for a long moment and finally said in a low husky voice, "I'm not sure that anything I do or say is ever going to change your mind about who you think I am. If after all the time we've spent together, it helps you to believe that I beat up horses, women, children, and small animals, you can just go ahead and keep doing that. I give up."

"Clay, wait!"

"What?"

"I...I'm not sure. I just don't want you to hate me."

The grim expression on his face softened slightly. "I don't hate you, honey. You know that. But until you decide to trust me, at least a little, I think we're done here." He bent to give Judge a pat and glanced over at the horse barn. "I really have to leave now. Drive safely and take good care of this guy, okay? I'm going to miss him."

Brigid nodded. As he stalked away, she hurried over to collect Judge's things before she burst into tears again. What had she just done? The dog trotted along next to her, oblivious to her mood and ready for whatever was next. She put him in his kennel one last time while she picked up the bowls and leashes and carried them out to the car. It was getting late and it occurred to her to wonder where Clay was going.

She opened the back door of the Honda and turned at the sound of a horse whinnying. Clay had retrieved Hank from the pasture and was riding down the driveway. He urged the horse to a gallop, which kicked up a trailing plume of dust until they veered off into the trees.

Brigid stood motionless in the driveway as the dust settled back to the ground. How stupid was it to ride around in the dark? Horses didn't have headlights. What if Clay got hurt? Was he doing something incredibly dangerous here or was riding around at night the type of thing he did all the time? She had no idea. Should she do something? Maybe she should call someone. Or maybe that would make him even more angry with her. He wanted her to trust him? Fine. She'd just have to trust that he'd been riding around those woods since childhood and he actually wasn't going to kill himself.

As she loaded Judge into the car and drove away, she thought maybe she'd call TJ when she got home, just in case.

∼

When Brigid got home, Judge and Gypsy had a happy reunion and chased each other around the house for a while until they collapsed into two furry heaps, panting heavily.

Unable to think of an excuse to put it off any longer, Brigid looked up TJ's number and said a silent plea that she would get the answering machine. It was Friday night. With any luck, she'd be out with her family doing something fun.

As the automated voice suggested she leave a message after the beep, Brigid breathed a sigh of relief. But what should she say? After a small moment of panic, she blurted out, "TJ? Um, this is Brigid. I, uh, don't know…well, is it dangerous to ride a horse at night? When I left the ranch,

Clay rode off, and well, I don't know. I thought I should let you know. Okay, well, that's it. Talk to you later."

After hanging up the phone, Brigid covered her face with her hands. As if TJ didn't already think she was a complete moron. At least her conscience was clear now. Time to feed the dogs and herself.

Once she'd had dinner and copious amounts of ice cream for dessert, Brigid felt like she could face listening to the messages on her machine. The red light had been flashing at her like an irksome beacon since she got home.

The messages were a predictable lot. Sonia wanted to talk about the event and setting up the first board-of-director's meeting. Jake called to let her know a new dog had arrived at the station. She'd meet the new canine tomorrow when she went over there, but at the moment, Brigid couldn't face talking to another person. She was emotionally exhausted and everything she had been trying to do to help the dogs was starting to feel utterly futile.

No matter how much work she did, stray dogs would keep coming in. Some might be sick like Judge. Some might not even be savable, and that idea terrified her. There was just no end to it. Plus now, thanks to Maren, everyone in Alpine Grove thought she was a cruel dog hater. Worst of all, in the back of her mind she still was worried about Clay. She really wanted to talk to him, but couldn't. Although she'd always known she'd hurt him in the end, it was so much worse than she'd ever imagined it might be.

After confining Judge to the kitchen using a baby gate Ed had given her after Layla was adopted, Brigid went upstairs with Gypsy. Maybe tomorrow would be better. It couldn't be any worse.

The next few days were filled with dog-walking and meetings. Ed took Lewis home into foster care and Brigid met with Sonia a few times trying to figure out what to do about the fundraising problem. Sonia had done a huge amount of work getting everything figured out for an event, except for the venue. Calls all over town had been fruitless. Places that had space like the convention facilities at the Enchanted Moose were booked up for the entire summer.

They decided to set aside the event idea for a while and consider some smaller-scale fundraising options before Brigid's credit card reached its limit. They also spent lots of time working on the bylaws for the new nonprofit and talking to people about being on the board.

As she did with just about everyone she met, Brigid had mentioned her need for employment to Sonia. Although Sonia promised to put some thought into it, she hadn't really lived in Alpine Grove long, so she didn't know many more people than Brigid did. So far, no one seemed to have leads on any hiring going on anywhere in the vicinity. If Brigid didn't find a job soon, she'd have to leave and let someone else take over the whole nonprofit project. In some ways, that might not be so bad, after all.

As Clay had predicted, no one had mentioned Maren's letter, except for Judith who praised Brigid's good judgment for getting the dogs away from "that dreadful place." As an expression of goodwill, Judith also proudly proclaimed she was willing to take another foster dog.

Sonia had cut out Maren's letter from the paper, along with a follow-up "me too" editorial from Maddie. She gave them to Brigid to read one day over coffee.

Yes, she was biased, but to Brigid, Maren and Maddie sounded like a bunch of whiners. Their complaints seemed to have been widely ignored and oddly enough, since the letters had appeared, a few new people had called Brigid about volunteering to walk dogs at the station and to let her know they supported what she was trying to do. It was a welcome glimmer of hope after she'd felt so terrible about her role in the bad press for the nascent nonprofit.

A week after she'd brought Judge home with her, she returned from the vet with him after another dip and settled him into the kitchen behind the baby gate to dry off. He was so easygoing that the difference between her kitchen floor and the dog bed in the barn didn't seem to be of much consequence. His fur was looking good and she made a mental note to ask Kat to make an adoption flyer for him. He was just about ready for his forever home.

The thought of Judge curled up on his dog bed in the barn reminded her of Clay. Missing him was a constant ache she couldn't shake. It was like her heart actually physically hurt from wanting to see him again. But he'd made it clear they were done, and intellectually she knew it was for the best. Some people were lucky in love, but she wasn't one of them. Maybe she should try playing cards. Since she couldn't find a job, maybe she could become a professional gambler. Yeah, right.

Brigid was startled from her repetitive morose ruminations on her relationship and career failures by the sound of the phone ringing. Although she wanted to let the machine pick it up, she was tired of people complaining that they always had to talk to it instead of to her. Fine. She reached over, grabbed the receiver, and said, "Hello."

"Hi, it's TJ."

Brigid's stomach churned at the woman's stern businesslike voice. Of all the times to pick up the phone. She'd never heard back from TJ about Clay, so she'd assumed he was okay, but TJ was undoubtedly not a charter member of the Brigid fan club at this point. "Hi, ah, how are you?"

"I'm fine. I'm driving up to Alpine Grove this weekend and I'd like to meet with you."

"Okay."

"I'm meeting Kat at the diner and I was thinking after we're done talking, I could talk to you."

Brigid did a mental eye roll. TJ certainly was efficient. "That would be fine."

They set up a time to meet and Brigid marked it on her calendar. TJ had been helpful before, but Brigid doubted nonprofit organizations were what Clay's sister wanted to talk about.

~

That Saturday, Brigid walked down to the diner, which was one of the places she and Sonia often met for coffee. She waved to the woman behind the counter and looked around for TJ.

TJ was sitting next to Kat in a booth with their backs toward the door, looking down at something. Oops. Was she early? TJ's meeting with Kat obviously wasn't over. Should she interrupt them? Maybe she should just let TJ know she was here. Glancing at the old photographs that littered the wood-paneled walls as she walked down the aisle, she stopped at the end of the booth. Kat and TJ both looked up simultaneously and Brigid felt like she'd barged in on a personal conversation. She gestured toward the counter up front. "I'm sorry if I'm interrupting, but I just wanted you to know I'm here, TJ. I can go sit at the counter for a few minutes until you're done."

Kat took a sip of coffee and put down the mug. "No, it's okay. I should be getting home anyway."

"Oh my gosh, that's a beautiful ring!" Brigid said.

Kat looked at her hand and smiled. "Thanks, I really like it. The jeweler here in town did a great job."

Brigid gestured at Kat's hand, encouraging her to move it so she could get a closer look. "Can I see?"

TJ said, "Why don't you just sit down?"

Brigid slid in across the table from them and reached over to take Kat's hand and look at the ring. "Wow. I love this design. It's gorgeous. So, does this mean you and Joel are getting married? I didn't know that."

"At some point. It's sort of a recent development."

Brigid laughed. "I guess you weren't wearing this the last time I saw you."

"No. And you were pretty busy at the meeting anyway." Kat twisted the ring on her finger. "I heard from Sonia about the fundraising problems. She writes really long, detailed emails. I think she might be a frustrated novelist."

Brigid put her elbows on the table and leaned forward. "I know. We're not sure what to do. She's done so much work getting everything all figured out, but we have no place to hold the event. This place is busy in the summer."

"I have an idea on that. Would it be okay if I make a few calls?"

"Yes, absolutely! Go for it. Let me know if you come up with something. We may do some other smaller things in the meantime, but to say we're out of money would be an understatement. It's a good thing Dr. C offers such a generous payment plan, or I'd be in really big trouble."

"Okay." Kat looked at TJ. "I should let you guys get to your meeting. Thanks again for letting me see the photos. I really appreciate it."

TJ handed her a photograph before sliding out of the booth so Kat could get out. "Why don't you take this one?"

Kat looked down at it, then at TJ. "Are you sure?"

TJ nodded. "Take it."

Kat looked dubious. "Thank you. I'll get it duplicated, and then give you back the original."

"That would be great. I'll see you on the fourth."

"Okay. See you then." Kat waved at Brigid and walked away, looking down at the photograph in her hand.

TJ turned her attention back toward Brigid. "So, okay, we need to talk."

Brigid smiled weakly. "I don't suppose you want to discuss nonprofit organizations, do you?"

"No, and I'm sure you know that. Right now, I'm going to meddle in ways that would make my little brother want to rip my head off. But I'm going to do it anyway."

Brigid took a menu from the stand and pretended to look like she wanted something to eat. "Well, I guess I should apologize for leaving that message on your machine. I was upset and worried."

"I got that. And I'm glad you called. I left a message for him to call me back once he returned from his little nighttime romp through the forest. He did and it was all fine. But he's not."

Brigid looked up from the menu. "What do you mean?"

"I don't know what you said or did and I don't particularly *want* to know. But I want you to fix it."

"I don't think I can. There were all these rumors and then I found out they were true. I called him on it and he said I didn't trust him."

"Oh jeez, really?" TJ took a sip of coffee. "You mean all the crap about him from that letter in the paper?"

Brigid nodded. "I took Judge out of the barn, since everyone seemed to think it was so terrible."

"Wow, this is ridiculous. That was twenty years ago. Didn't he explain what happened?"

"Not really. But he was arrested for assault! I...I just can't handle that." Brigid looked back down at the menu. "My late husband was, well, violent, and I can't deal with anything like that ever happening again. I just can't."

TJ set down her mug with a thump. "I'm sorry about that. I didn't know. But Clay would never hurt anyone or anything. I told you that before."

"But he was arrested. It's even in the police database."

"That's true. But he wasn't charged with anything either time. You have to understand that things were...strange for a while after Cole died. Mom moved out for a while. She stayed with a friend named Abigail Goodman." TJ gestured toward the door. "In fact, Kat lives in Abigail's old house now."

"The log place out in the woods?"

"I spent a lot of time out there. My best friend in high school was a really good friend of Abigail's." TJ shook her head. "It's all so long ago now and this isn't my story to tell. You need to talk to Clay."

"I'm supposed to just drive out there and say, 'Hi, so tell me about how you assaulted people and were arrested' or something?" Brigid smirked. "I really don't think that's going to go over well, given our last conversation."

"All right, how about this? We always do a family Fourth of July potluck thing out at the ranch. People drop by with food. My boys love it and spend all day riding, wearing out those lazy old cow horses. Then we all eat lots of food, play with sparklers, and pass out."

Brigid smiled. "That sounds like quite a full day."

"I invited Kat and Joel and now I'm inviting you. Come out, eat food, and talk to my obnoxious brother. I can't stand him being like this, so fix whatever you did to make him so miserable. He won't go ride off somewhere if we're all around because he knows I'd kill him."

"All right. I guess I can try. Thank you for the invitation."

TJ tucked a few bills and the check into the little leather case on the table and got up. "See you Thursday."

～

After Kat left the diner, she did a couple of errands and walked down the street toward Maria's apartment. Because Kat was going to be in town, they'd agreed she would stop by after her meeting with TJ. Kat tended to park the truck in the parking lot at Maria's complex anyway because parallel parking Joel's horrible old pickup was not going to happen.

The lack of power steering on the thing made the experience akin to wedging a recalcitrant elephant into a hall closet.

Kat walked by the shops on the main street and stopped in front of the plate-glass window of the photography store, which was filled with expensive cameras. She could drop off the snapshot to be duplicated, but Maria would love seeing it. Maybe she could drop it off later, on the way out of town.

She turned and continued down the street. It would be fun to visit with Scarlett, the not-so-little kitten, again. Every time Kat saw the adolescent feline, it seemed the cat had doubled in size. The fuzzy adorableness of tiny kittenhood was becoming a distant memory.

Maria lived in an apartment building that had zero aesthetic charm. Built in the late sixties or early seventies, it was a utilitarian brick cube plunked down on a side street in Alpine Grove. Every once in a while, Maria talked about moving into one of the cute little rental houses in town, but the ugly building had the advantages of a convenient location, easy parking, and low rent, which were hard to ignore, so she stayed put.

Kat knocked on the door and looked down at the hideous hallway carpet. The gold and olive-green pattern had not improved with age. She heard Maria say, "Scarlett, cut that out...ha...*gotcha*." The door opened and Maria stood with a squirming orange tabby snuggled under her arm. The outfit Maria was wearing taxed the power of spandex. She was sporting a pink ruffly top and black Capri pants that were both about four sizes too small. "Get in here girlfriend, before this animal makes a break for it."

Kat scuttled through the doorway as Maria closed the door behind her.

Kat turned toward the small sofa in the living room and her jaw dropped momentarily. She clamped it shut again in an effort to look nonchalant. "Um, hi Fred. I didn't know you were here."

Turning to look behind her, Kat raised her eyebrows at Maria and widened her eyes in silent inquiry. Maria gave her a smug smile in return.

Fred stood up and put his hands in his pockets. Kat wasn't used to seeing him outside of the context of the dive bar or even in daylight. He looked so different without the leather vest and bandanna that it was difficult for Kat to assimilate.

He said, "I should probably be getting going now. The regulars at the Soloan take opening time pretty seriously."

Maria put Scarlett down on the floor and the small cat launched toward the bedroom while the three humans looked on, marveling at the speed of the small orange tabby.

Maria turned toward Kat and gave her the "Spock eyebrow" move, startling Kat from her state of stunned paralysis. She began edging toward the bedroom where the tiny bathroom was located, "Um, I...I need to use the rest room. It was good to see you again, Fred."

Kat hid in the bathroom, taking advantage of the facilities while she was there. Then she washed her hands a few times and combed her hair until she heard the front door close and Maria scold Scarlett again.

When Kat walked back into the living room, Maria was sitting on the couch with Scarlett. She was petting the cat's orange fur, tracing the ornate swirly designs on the tabby coat. "Hey girlfriend, sorry I lost track of time."

"No kidding." Kat sat down. "This is new. Fred? I thought he didn't meet your dental criteria."

"I confess that I'm having to adjust my standards a little. I stopped by the Soloan a few times after work. The man is a great storyteller and he hooked me like a tuna. You know how I like a good tall tale. And then I just had to find out the ending, you know?"

Kat grinned. "That's great. He does seem like a nice guy."

"I've also pointed out that it's possible for him to get his teeth fixed. Technology has advanced into the tooth arena. The fake ones are pretty good now."

"So I've heard."

"Sadly, I don't think he's going to do anything. He doesn't like that they drill into your jaw. I think he's got a pretty serious phobia about dentists."

"I can understand that. The dentist's chair is a scary place. I try to avoid it when I can."

Maria leaned back on the couch and Scarlett readjusted her lap configuration to shed more effectively on the black pants. Maria raised her hand, which was covered with reddish fur. "When I got this animal, I didn't think about the fact that cat hair reduces my already infinitesimal potential dating pool. I had no idea so many people were allergic to cats."

"You're exaggerating. Since I've lived here, I think I've only met one or two people with pet-hair allergies."

"The only people you meet are bringing dogs to your place. They are already fur-inoculated." Maria waved her hand in excitement, shaking some cat hair into the air. "Wait, in the throes of post-coital mental decline, I forgot. You need to tell me about your meeting with the woman who knew your mom...or real mom, or whatever she is."

"It was interesting." Kat reached into her bag and pulled out the photograph. She handed it to Maria. "Check this out."

Maria studied the photo. "Whoa, girlfriend. That looks just like a younger version of you. I'd think it *was* you, except for the nasty sixties fashion. Even *you* don't wear stuff that ugly."

"I know. It's kind of strange. TJ said when she saw me, it was like seeing a ghost."

"I'm guessing you freaked her out."

"Pretty much."

"Well, you told me she kept staring at you at that meeting."

"Yeah. We looked at pictures and she invited me to her family Fourth of July pot luck. Then Brigid showed up and I left."

"Uh oh, another social event for you." Maria grinned. "Maybe Brigid will bring more food for you to snarf down."

"We can only hope. I'm so *not* good in that type of situation." Kat slumped down on the sofa. "And this is with someone else's *family*. I have enough trouble with my own. Not to mention Joel's sister. He's still mad at her."

Maria poked her in the ribs. "Hey, don't speak ill of your future sister-in-law."

Kat gave her a stern glare.

Ignoring her, Maria continued, "Fred told me that all the crap in that letter that got Brigid so upset was a load of horse pucky."

"Horse pucky?"

"His words, not mine. I think he was trying not to offend my delicate sensibilities with coarse language."

"He obviously doesn't know you very well."

"Well, not yet. But I have to say that man has the inside track. It puts my powers of investigation to shame. I guess everyone in Alpine Grove eventually ends up at the Soloan and pours out their guts to him."

Kat laughed. "I suppose there isn't anywhere else to go, except the 311. I'm glad all that stuff in the letter wasn't true. I got a long email from Sonia about the whole thing. Clay seemed nice enough at the bar and he did let Brigid keep dogs in his barn. Which means they didn't stay with me."

"True. And even in the dark, I did notice the man had all his teeth. The whole Harrison Ford thing he has going is also decidedly hot. Personally, I know I have thought many impure thoughts about Indiana Jones since those movies came out."

"I get the impression Brigid agrees with you."

"Oh really?" Maria nudged Kat. "You're holding out on me, girlfriend."

"I don't know anything really. Just suspicions."

"You tend to be right about these things. I want you to give me a full report after the potluck."

"I will. That reminds me, do you think Michael would be willing to do some pro-bono advertising work for the homeless dogs of Alpine Grove?"

Maria shrugged. "Probably. He loves dogs. Even that obnoxious white furry one he's got. We just finished up the latest ad campaign for the vodka people, so he's got a little more time."

"Cool. Brigid and Sonia want to do a fundraiser, but they can't find a place to hold it. I'm thinking maybe the North Fork Lodge might work. Alec and Robin are about to re-open it. The last I heard, the restoration work is almost done. They both really love dogs and the last time I talked to her, Robin made a big point about how the place is going to be dog-friendly."

"Couldn't hurt to ask them."

"Yeah, I thought so too."

Chapter 10

Conversations

On the Fourth of July, Brigid spent most of the morning baking approximately four thousand spanikopita triangles. It was entirely possible she'd gone a little overboard, but cooking was soothing and she was beyond nervous about seeing Clay again. At least Kat would have lots to eat.

Brigid felt like she should do something nice for Kat. She owed her big-time for finding a place to hold the fundraiser. Sonia had been over the moon when she heard about the idea. Brigid and Sonia were going to have a meeting at the North Fork Lodge the next day to talk to Robin and Alec about it, but according to Kat, the couple was enthusiastic about the concept.

Gypsy and Judge watched closely as Brigid packed the appetizers into containers and put them into a paper grocery bag. She bent down to pet the dog. "I promise I'll be home long before dark. I don't think anyone will start making noise until later. And who knows, maybe fireworks don't bother you guys. Behave yourselves."

The two dogs wagged their tails and Brigid locked the dog door, just in case. She'd read too many stories about dogs ending up in animal shelters because of the noise from holiday fireworks. All of the homeless dogs of Alpine Grove were currently in foster homes, so the kennels at the station were empty. But that was likely to change after the holiday.

Brigid drove north out of town and turned at V Bar H Ranch Road. It felt like forever since she'd been there, even though it had only been two weeks. As she exited the trees and went up the driveway toward the house, she slowed, trying to figure out where to park. A gigantic white motor home was occupying much of the space in front of the barn where Judge had stayed, and cars were pulled off on the grass all over the place. TJ must have invited a lot more people that she'd let on.

Two young men were riding around in the pasture along with Clay, who was riding Hank. Barrels were set up and Clay seemed to be showing them which way to ride around them, methodically walking through a pattern.

Brigid parked up near the house and gathered her bag from the back seat. She walked up onto the porch and waved to Kat, who was standing next to an older woman with thick silver hair that fell to her shoulders.

Kat glanced at Brigid and then the older woman reached out and grabbed Kat in a hug, obviously startling her. As she walked up to the pair, Brigid smiled sympathetically at Kat's obvious discomfort.

The woman let go and Kat said, "Ellen, this is Brigid."

Brigid held out her hand and looked at the woman's face. Her eyes were the exact same color as Clay's and TJ's. "Hello, I'm Brigid Fitzpatrick."

"Ellen Hadley." She shook her hand. "I've heard quite a bit about you."

Brigid tried not to think about what *that* meant and held out the bag. "Should I put the food in the kitchen?"

"That would be good. Thank you."

Kat said, "Did you bring those spinach things?"

"I told you I was going to."

"Oh boy!" Kat snatched the bag from her. "Let me help you with that, then I need to find out where Joel went."

Kat excused herself and swiftly disappeared inside. Brigid smiled at Ellen, trying to think of something—*anything*— to say to Clay's mother. "How was New Mexico?"

"Sunny. We missed all the crummy weather here. Next we're headed up to Canada, but we always visit Alpine Grove on the Fourth to see everyone."

"That's nice. I told TJ I'd stop by."

Ellen pointed toward the pasture. "Clay is over there."

"Um, okay. I need to talk to him."

Ellen patted her on the shoulder and gave her a gentle shove back toward the steps. "Yes, you do."

Brigid turned her head to look. Clay was galloping around the barrels at full speed. "He looks busy."

"No, they're just goofing around." Ellen gestured dismissively. "Those horses are getting so lazy. Clay should be working them more. I'll talk to you later."

Brigid slowly went down the steps from the porch and walked toward the pasture. She stood at the fence and waved at Clay, indicating that she wanted him to come over. Best to get this over with so she could get back home and make sure Gypsy was okay.

Clay rode up and Hank put his head over the fence, practically smacking Brigid in the face with his huge nose. She put her hands out in front of her. "Hey Hank, easy with the big head, okay?"

Clay looked down at her and pulled on the reins, moving Hank back and away from the fence. "I'm surprised to see you here."

"TJ invited me."

"I think she's inside."

"I need to talk to you."

"What about?"

"Lots of things. Your sister told me I had to and she's very persuasive."

"I've noticed."

Brigid held her hand up over her eyes to shield them from the bright sunlight. "Could you please get down from there? I'll go blind looking up at you like this."

"No."

"No? What do you mean *no*?"

"If you want to talk to me, you'll have to get on the horse."

"Are you nuts? You know I can barely ride. Particularly not Hank. He's young and fast. And *huge*. I had enough trouble with Willy and he's old and slow."

"Climb up on the fence." He gestured toward the white slats. "Sit up there."

Brigid looked down at her flowery sundress. "I'm not exactly dressed for climbing fences."

"Okay." He started to turn Hank away. "Suit yourself."

"Wait!" Brigid reached out and clambered up the boards. She threw her leg over so she was straddling the top rail. "If I get splinters in my, um, legs, it's your fault."

"That's an interesting visual to consider." A corner of his mouth turned up. "You have my attention. Put your other leg over, so you're sitting on this side."

Brigid did as instructed and perched on the top rail. She spread her arms, turning her palms up. "Fine. Are you happy now?"

"Not quite." He moved Hank alongside the fence, reached over and grabbed her under the armpits, and pulled her off the fence and onto the horse.

Brigid squawked in protest as he plopped her in the saddle in front of him. "What are you *doing?*"

He patted her thigh. "Move this one over to the other side."

"Fine." She pulled her leg over, yanked her dress down as far as she could, and looked over her shoulder at him. "Well, great. This is just perfect. You want me to have a chat with Hank's ears now?"

Clay put his arm around her stomach as Hank moved toward the gate. "While I'll admit that Hank is a good listener, first we're going for a ride."

"We are not! I'm supposed to be at the pot luck. TJ said she'll kill you if you ride off again."

"Not if you come with me." Clay stopped the horse. "Do you want to talk to me or not?"

"I do."

"Okay, then." He bent down to open the gate, Hank walked through, and then Clay reached down again to close the gate behind them. "I'm not talking to you here with half of Alpine Grove watching us."

"I suppose you do have a point." She gripped the saddle horn with one hand and put the other hand on Clay's, which was splayed across her waist. Hank slowly strolled down the driveway and Brigid twisted to try to look at Clay's face. "I wish Hank weren't so tall, although I feel more secure with you acting as a seat belt."

"What do you want to talk about?"

"Well, TJ said I needed to talk to you about what happened. That the stuff in the paper wasn't true and there's more I need to know. But you have to tell me."

Brigid could feel his chest heave behind her in a long sigh. He finally said, "It is true as far is it goes. I was arrested. Twice actually."

"The police seem to think so too."

His arm stiffened around her. "I know that. And in a lot of ways, the story doesn't matter. Like I said, what matters is that you don't trust me."

Brigid turned to look at him again. "You said that before, but it's not true."

"I said I'd never hurt you and I meant it."

"I know."

"But you don't really believe it, or you wouldn't have given one sentence from the cops more weight than all the time we've spent together."

Brigid wasn't sure what to say. The truth of what he said settled over her like a guilty burden. He was right. She'd done exactly that. "I didn't really think about it that way. It's just, well, I heard the word *assault* and that was all I could think about. I've never really seen you get angry. And I was terrified of what that would be like. I can't go through that again."

Clay moved his hand on her waist. "Are you kidding? Of *course,* you've seen me get angry. Judy pissed me off bad when she picked up Nugget. And the last time you saw me, I was so blind furious at you, I could barely even speak. Couldn't you tell?" He let go of her stomach to gesture toward the forest. "I rode all the way to those waterfalls again."

"Did you fall in the mud?"

"No. It was past Hank's bedtime and he wanted to go home, so he wasn't in the mood for humor, I suppose."

Brigid turned to look at him. "I'm so sorry. Can we go somewhere and talk about this? I've missed you."

"Me too, honey. I can't even tell you how much." He bent to whisper in her ear. "My mother keeps harping on me that this horse is getting lazy. You sure you trust me?"

"Yes."

"Hold on because Hank's gonna work off some unsightly fat now." He held her tightly as he urged the horse into a lope. As Hank accelerated into a smooth gallop down toward the trees, Brigid whooped with delight.

∽

They rode a little way up into the woods and Clay took a side trail that led to a small clearing. They dismounted and Clay loosened the cinch on Hank's saddle so the horse could settle into some quality grazing time.

Brigid pulled up her skirt slightly and looked at her thighs. "I think I have a new understanding of the word *chaps*."

Clay pulled a rolled-up blanket off the back of the saddle, unfurled it, and spread it on the ground. "I'd be happy to take a look."

Brigid settled onto the blanket and rolled onto her back, lying spread-eagled staring at the sky. "Even if my legs may never be the same, that was great. I'll tell your mom Hank is in tip-top form."

"Thanks." He handed her a canteen of water. "Everyone's a critic."

Brigid sat up to take a drink. "Tell me about it. I'm the control-freak dog-hater."

"I'm sure it's the same with dogs as it is with horses." Clay sat down next to her and gestured toward Hank. "I've had people say my training is too soft, too harsh, doesn't work, and the best thing they've ever done for their horse. Some say you should never ride a horse bareback. Or riding bareback is the only natural way to ride. Some people think I'm brilliant and gifted—all that horse whisperer stuff. Then others think I should never get near any member of the equine species. It's all really political and everyone has their own little axe to grind."

"I guess I shouldn't have taken the letters in the newspaper so seriously."

"People have a right to their opinion."

"Maybe. But what they said wasn't fair."

Clay took off his hat and ran his fingers through his sweaty hair. "Lots of things aren't fair. What happened to you with your husband. That wasn't fair, but it happened."

"I know. And I wasn't fair to you either. I should have trusted you."

He smiled. "I suppose I should probably explain my run-ins with Alpine Grove law enforcement to you now."

"You said horse relocation was involved?"

"Yeah, that was the first time. It was at the Yearwood place, right after Cole died. Randy Yearwood was his friend. They played football together and his mother had given us a casserole after the funeral. I think most of Alpine Grove gave us food then, and I have no idea how my mother kept track of whose dish was whose. Anyway, she said I needed to return the pan to the Yearwoods and say thank you. So I went."

"What happened?"

Clay took a sip of water and leaned back on the blanket, propping himself up on his elbows. "Well, Randy and I never got along. He was, and really still is, this huge linebacker-type guy. Now he probably weighs three-hundred and fifty pounds. Back then, he was always razzing me about something. I swear to this day, he's got the IQ of a hedgehog."

"So you are not his best friend."

"Nope. But his father was worse. Like a meaner version of Randy. I think even Cole was scared of him." Clay lay flat on the blanket and stroked the back of Brigid's hand with his fingertips. "So I go over with the casserole dish and there's Mr. Yearwood beating the crap out of his horse with a whip. This was a nice horse…I'd ridden him before a couple times, and I could tell the poor creature was about to lose it. I didn't think about what I was doing. I just wanted Yearwood to stop. So I got out of the truck and ran over to them. I yanked the whip out of Yearwood's hand and threw it on the ground and then I shoved him aside, got on the horse, and rode him out of there to the neighbor's house."

Brigid smiled. "So you *are* a horse thief."

"I suppose, although I prefer to think of it as saving that moron from himself. He could have been killed if that horse had decided to fight back."

"What happened?"

"Well, Yearwood called the police and they came out. I was just hanging around next door in the Johnson's barn with the horse, brushing him, and trying to calm him down when the cops showed up. Yearwood said I assaulted him and they threw me in jail for a couple of hours."

"I guess he got over it?"

"Yeah, my father went over and gave him a piece of his mind." Clay let his fingers rest on Brigid's hand for a second. "That wasn't as bad as the second time though."

"The one in 1976? TJ said your family was having problems."

"Yeah, it was bad. I think each one of us fell apart in our own way after Cole died. Half the time, my parents were fighting. The other half they were avoiding each other. I was spending most of my time riding off into the forest somewhere."

"That sounds familiar."

"I know. If I'd been smart, I'd have gone away to college like TJ did, but I felt like I needed to stay and help at the ranch because Cole was gone. I rode a lot, but no matter how far I tried to go, I couldn't get away. One night I came home from a ride, and when I walked into the house, my parents were shouting at each other. My mom was crying and my father threw one of her little horse figurines against the wall. It smashed into a million pieces that went everywhere. I ran up and grabbed his hand before he could pick up another one, and he threw me onto the ground."

"Do you know what they were fighting about?"

"At the time I didn't, but later I found out she had told him that she was going to stay with her friend Abigail for a while. He wasn't too thrilled with the idea."

"What did you do?"

"I got back up, grabbed the figurine he had out of his hand, put it down, and held his hands away from me while we yelled at each other. I think that's when my mother called the police."

"They threw you in jail again?"

"Yeah, for a few hours while they got my dad to talk to them and my mom moved out." He shrugged. "As you probably know, the police take domestic disputes pretty seriously."

Brigid nodded. "I never called the police, although I probably should have. Your mom was smart to do that."

"Yeah and they worked it out in the end, obviously."

"I'm so sorry. That must have been awful."

"Yeah, it was. And like I said, I was kind of stupid." He shrugged. "I probably could have handled things better than I did."

"You were so young. And you didn't hurt anyone."

"No, although as you know from my recent run-ins with his horse, Randy Yearwood and I still aren't exactly friends. But many years later, Dad actually said it was okay that I got in the middle of things."

"Maybe you prevented something worse."

"Who knows? Anyway, it was a long time ago."

Brigid glanced at the sky. "I hate to say this, but I need to get home. I locked the dogs in the house in case they start setting off fireworks in town."

Clay sat up and put his arms around her, pulling her close. "Well, that's disappointing. I was just thinking about a sleepover."

Brigid kissed him and grinned. "You could sleep over at my place. I know it's in town, but we do have indoor plumbing, you know."

Clay stood up and held out a hand to help her up. "After riding around with teenagers all day, I'm completely filthy. If you have a shower and laundry facilities, I'm sold."

"A huge shower, washer, and dryer."

"Okay then, let's get my lazy horse moving again."

They rode back out of the trees and up the driveway, where it seemed even more cars were parked. Brigid looked over her shoulder at Clay. "This is quite a party."

"I'm sure it's only getting started. At least your car isn't blocked in yet."

They went toward the pasture, where TJ was leaning against the rail, watching her sons ride. She turned her head as Hank approached. "Where have you been? I've been looking all over for you."

Clay dismounted and helped Brigid down to the ground. "We went for a ride. I think you need to reacquaint your offspring with your barrel-racing skills. They're just plain sad out there. I can't believe they are even related to you."

"Hey, they only do this a couple times a year. They didn't have to spend every waking moment riding around chasing cows like you and I did."

"I'm going to town for the evening." He handed TJ the reins. "Take care of Hank, will you?"

TJ looked at Brigid and raised her eyebrows. "Everything fixed?"

Brigid nodded. "I think so."

TJ smiled as she readjusted the stirrups. "Well, okay then."

Clay opened the gate for her. "See you tomorrow."

TJ leapt up onto Hank and rode through. "See ya."

Clay closed the gate behind them and took Brigid's hand. "Let's get out of here."

～

They got into Brigid's Honda and she carefully navigated around all the other cars and left the ranch. Clay looked around the car. "This is possibly the worst-smelling rig I've ever ridden in...and I've driven cow trucks, horse trailers, and even hauled sheep and pigs a few times."

"I know. I've tried cleaning it and nothing works. I keep hoping the smell will go away, but it doesn't. Then I accidentally left the windows down a few times when it rained."

"I'm guessing that didn't help."

"No. Now it smells like mildewy old Nugget vomit."

"That's nasty." Clay rolled down the window and the wind whipped through their hair as they cruised down the highway, "I'm grateful it's a short drive."

Brigid pulled up in front of the house and they got out and walked up to the door. She unlocked the house and turned to Clay, "Home sweet home. At least for a little while longer."

They went inside and were treated to a joyous canine welcoming committee. Judge was overwhelmed by the thrilling horse scents, as if he were using his nose to vacuum aromas from Clay's boots. Clay looked around the room, sat on the sofa, and yanked at his boots. "I should take these off. This place is stressfully clean. I'm pretty sure I'm the grubbiest thing in it."

"I clean when I'm unhappy. You should have seen my last apartment. It was practically sterile."

"I never pegged you for a neatnik."

"I'm not really. It's just that when things feel out of control, cleaning the house is one thing I can control."

Brigid went to the back door and let the dogs out into the yard. Clay padded out to the patio in his stocking feet. "This is pretty here."

A banging noise rang through the neighborhood and both dogs looked up in concern. Brigid said, "Hurry up, you two."

The dogs looked more serious, got down to business, and scampered back into the house.

Brigid closed the door behind them and checked the dog door again to make sure it was secure. Clay was standing in the kitchen looking uncomfortable. She walked up to him and started unbuttoning his shirt. "Maybe we should work on cleaning you up."

He smiled and put his arms around her. "I believe the word you used to describe the shower was *huge*."

"I did. Definitely large enough for two."

Later they were lying in bed with a plate between them. Clay popped the last spanikopita into his mouth. "I don't care if you think these are the ugly ones. These things are completely addictive."

"They're supposed to be triangles, but sometimes the phyllo dough does funny things and they come out an odd shape."

Clay rolled over onto his back and sighed. "I think this may be the best Fourth of July ever."

Brigid moved the empty plate to the nightstand and curled up next to him. "I agree, although I feel a little bad taking you away from your family party."

"They'll get over it. The naked portion of the holiday has been way more fun."

"I agree, although it was sweet to see you riding around with your nephews." Brigid raised her head to look at him. "There's something I need to tell you."

He readjusted himself up on the pillows. "Well, that's a serious face all of a sudden. Is everything okay?"

"I'm fine, but I saw you with those adorable little horse-crazy girls and your nephews. You obviously love kids, so I should tell you something."

Clay sat up straight. "What? Really? But we've been so careful! Do you know how many foil packages I had to find and hide before my entire nosy family showed up? That's a conversation I don't want to have with any one of them."

Brigid laughed. "No I don't, but I can imagine. That's not it at all, although I'm glad you don't have to have the safe-sex conversation with your relatives."

"Then what is it?"

"After everything that's happened, I want to be completely up-front and honest with you from now on." She took a deep breath. "So I need to let you know that I probably can't ever have children. I know for some people that would be devastating."

Clay enveloped her in his arms and kissed her. He looked into her eyes. "I think the more important question is if it's devastating to you. Is this because of…well, something your husband did?"

Brigid's eyes widened. "No, it's not that at all. I never went to a doctor for…well, any of that. But after John died, I was run over by a shopping cart and they did a bunch of tests. I probably never needed to use all that birth control after all. It figures."

"Did you say a shopping cart?"

"It was a bad day at the grocery store."

"I'll say."

"But in a weird way, it's what caused me to decide to move here."

"I'm glad of that. And so you know, I'm okay with just being the ornery old uncle people aren't quite sure what to do with. To be honest, it's kind of a relief my nephews are finally just about grown. Twin boys are a handful."

Brigid ran her fingers down his arm. "I don't think you're ornery. I bet you're a great uncle. I like to think I'll make a pretty good aunt someday."

"I'm sure you will."

"On that note, I can't believe I finally did it, but yesterday, I called my mom and my sister."

"That's interesting. You haven't talked about your family much. Heaven knows you've heard enough about mine."

"I guess I was thinking about them and how even after all the terrible things that happened, you don't hate each other." She gestured toward the window. "Your parents even came up to Alpine Grove for the potluck."

"Yeah, they always do that. Probably making sure the place is still okay and I haven't screwed anything up."

"No, it's because they're your family and they love you. When I got married to John, I burned some bridges with my family. A lot of bridges. Like a huge, blazing inferno."

Clay laughed. "You have a bit of a temper sometimes."

"Yes, well, it was bad. And then I was too…I don't know…embarrassed, after all the things I had said, to get back in touch. After they found out John died, they tried to reach me, but I was sure they'd just say 'I told you so' and I never called anyone back. I didn't want to speak to them. But yesterday I called my mom and we talked for a long time. My sister seemed sort of surprised, but she even wished me a happy Fourth."

"That sounds promising."

"It's a start. My mom is a nurse and we talked about compassion fatigue. I told her what I was doing here with the dogs and she brought it up. Nurses tend to suffer from burnout and she suggested that it could happen working with animals too. I forgot how smart she is. Anyway, it was a great conversation."

"Sounds like it."

Brigid moved closer alongside him and placed her hand on his chest. "I missed talking to you so much."

"Yeah." He crooked an arm behind his head. "At the house, I kept thinking I saw you everywhere. Sitting at the kitchen table, it was so lonely all of a sudden. And that makes no sense, since I was alone there before. But I kept looking around, thinking that I just couldn't stand to go through this again…living in a house full of ghosts."

"What do you mean?"

"I was thinking of leaving. Sell off the horses, throw Hank in the trailer, and go."

Brigid sat up and looked into his face. "You can't leave! The ranch is your home. I can't imagine you not being there."

He smiled. "Well, I didn't live there for a long time. Fifteen years or something, traveling all over. It's not like I couldn't do it again."

Brigid put her palm on his chest again. "You're not going to leave, are you?"

"No. I asked TJ if she and Jim might want to retire to a slightly used ranch. The boys just graduated, so I figured they might want a change."

"What did she say?"

"She just about tore me a new one."

"I can imagine." Brigid giggled. "That must have been when she called me."

"Maybe so." He put his hand over hers on his chest. "I'm glad you accepted her invitation."

"I am too." Brigid moved onto her stomach to face him. "I love you and I don't want you to go anywhere."

Clay pulled her closer to kiss her. "I love you too, honey. You know that."

"I was thinking about everything you told me and there's just one thing I still don't understand." She ran her fingertips along his jaw. "Why does Judith Alistair dislike you so much?"

"Remember how I told you the day he died, Cole was late to meet his girlfriend?"

"Yes."

"Judith, or Judy as we used to call her, was the girlfriend."

Brigid rolled onto her back and leaned on the pillows, staring at the ceiling. "Wow, this really *is* a small town isn't it?"

"Yup, and the longer you live here, the smaller it gets."

~

Brigid woke up feeling warm and content, snuggled up to Clay, who murmured something unintelligible and wrapped an arm around her. She glanced at the clock and jerked upright out of his grasp.

"I'm late!"

Clay groaned and rolled over on his back, "Late for what?"

"I have a meeting out at the North Fork Lodge this morning with Sonia. But I don't have time to drive you back to the ranch, get back here, and meet her."

"You don't have to."

"Yes I do! It's for the fundraiser. Kat suggested the lodge and the people sound so nice, I can't just ditch this meeting."

"That's not what I meant. Go meet. I'll stay here and hang out with Gypsy and Judge."

"But your whole family is waiting for you."

"They can wait a little longer. Do you know how long it's been since I've had a day off?"

"No."

"Neither do I, which is just plain sad. The idea of lying around here doing nothing and being shamelessly lethargic sounds great. I might even take a nap."

"Okay. Make yourself at home."

Clay stretched his arms above his head. "I sure hope there's a coffee maker somewhere."

"I'll get it started."

After an accelerated morning routine, Brigid left for her meeting. Everything went extraordinarily well and by the time she came home, she was bursting with news. She walked into the house carrying a garment bag, and the dogs came running in from the back porch, followed by Clay, who smiled and pointed at the bag. "Did you go shopping too?"

"No, I'm broke, remember? Robin gave me some evening dresses to try on. She got them at a mega-sale when she worked for a catalog company in Portland. If they don't fit me, she thought they might fit Kat." She folded the garment bag over a chair and looked him up and down. "Speaking of which, you seem to be going for casual Friday here."

"Serious lethargy doesn't include pants." He pointed at the back door, "And you have a tall privacy fence, so I'm not scaring the neighbors. Practically speaking, boxer shorts are almost the same thing as a bathing suit. I worked on my tan."

"You fell asleep out there, didn't you?"

"Yeah, it was great. Gypsy and I hung out on that chaise for a while. I started in on one of those self-improvement books, decided I really could stand some work, and passed out."

Brigid put her arms around his waist, enjoying the feel of his sun-warmed skin. "I think you're pretty great just the way you are."

He inclined his head to kiss her. "That's good because I didn't finish the book. I think you're stuck with me like this."

Clay sat down on the sofa and put his bare feet on the coffee table. He picked up a book off the end table and looked at it. "I guess it makes sense that the first time I laid eyes on you, it was in a bookstore. There are books everywhere here. What's *Funds to the Rescue* about?"

Brigid picked up the garment bag and unzipped it. "That one has fundraising ideas. It's from the library. My book-shopping habit ended when I started handing all my money over to the Alpine Grove Veterinary Clinic to get dogs spayed and neutered."

"Hmm, ideas for raising money." He looked up with a smile. "Guess you need that."

"No kidding. Sonia found the book, and then had me check it out too. We have a whole list of possible stuff to do. The "Fur Ball" we're doing at the lodge is one of the ideas in there."

"That sounds like something where you have to dress up. Please tell me it's not."

"Well, you would have to dress up, but it's going to be great! I'd love to see you in a tux." Brigid held up a sapphire-blue evening dress in front of her. "Check this out."

"If you can slide yourself into that slinky thing, I might be convinced."

Brigid started stripping off her clothes. "I doubt it will fit. Robin thinks because I'm short, this size will work, but the dress is sort of the wrong shape for me."

Clay made a dubious face. "I'm not sure that particular configuration of fabric is going to cover what it's supposed to cover."

Brigid stepped into the dress and made an effort to get it on. "Wow. Not even close."

"I like it, but I have a particular fondness for the parts that are exposed. You might cause a very public scandal."

"I don't think partial nudity is the look I am going for. Drat. I really love the color. Maybe it will fit Kat."

"She's somewhat less well-endowed than you are. There could be hope."

Brigid pulled another long dress out of the bag. "Maybe this one. Robin said she only paid three dollars for these dresses, but they have to be worth hundreds. I guess the catalog company sells the stuff that's returned or used for photo shoots to the employees for cheap. They're all small sizes though, which is good news for those of us who are short."

Clay flipped through the fundraising book while Brigid extracted herself from the blue dress. He held up the book in front of him. "Hey check this out—walk naked. That's a good one. Kirby Russell likes you, right? Maybe he'd do this, if you asked nicely." He turned the book around, so she could see the page.

"I do seem to have a better relationship with the members of local law enforcement than you do."

"Very funny."

Brigid pulled the sleeves of a green dress over her shoulders. "It wouldn't hurt to ask the Chief. If doing it increased donations like it did for that animal shelter in Nebraska, it would certainly be worth it."

"You've made a lot of other things happen that no one thought to do." Clay looked up from the book and threw it aside, "Okay then, *that* dress definitely fits in all the right places."

"You're willing to get all dressed up for the event, right? It's just one night and it would mean a lot to me if you were there."

"Hey, I'm all about supporting charity and homeless animals." Clay pulled her into his arms and kissed her. "Especially if you're dressed like that."

"I'm going to be busy the next few weeks getting ready for this event, but I'm really excited. The lodge is beautiful and I think it's going to be great. Robin is an organizing machine. Oh, and Kat knows someone who has agreed to design posters and ads for us too. For free!"

Clay ran a fingertip down her neck. "So are you busy right this second?"

"Not really, but I suppose I should probably make some calls. A couple of stray dogs came into the station—a miniature pinscher we named Pete and another little black-and-white dog we called Kermit. Some volunteers are already lined up to walk them, but I was thinking I should check in."

"Can the calls wait? Because I'd like to take that dress off of you and enjoy the last of my partially clothed vacation day."

"I think I can work that into my schedule."

Chapter 11

Fur Ball

The night of the Alpine Grove Fur Ball, Kat glared at herself in the mirror as she attempted to deal with her hair. Putting it up was always an exercise in frustration. She braided, tucked, squished, and approximately four-hundred and seventeen bobby pins later, her tresses seemed willing to stay put. After dousing it with a noxious cloud of hair spray, she declared the coiffure complete.

She crossed the hallway into the bedroom, where Joel was sitting on the edge of the bed fussing with a cuff. He looked up at her. "Whoever came up with the idea of cufflinks had a really twisted sense of humor. You think you've got the little thing lined up, then you drop it on the floor. Then repeat. It's like a loop in programming."

Kat laughed. "Only you could compare a male fashion accessory to something so incredibly geeky."

"Hey, you're wearing makeup."

"Try not to look so appalled. I can do the girly thing every once in a while."

"It's just startling. I'm used to the *au naturel* you."

"Now I have to see if I can get into this dress. It fit when I tried it on at Brigid's house, but it was a little dicey."

"This could be fun. Can I watch?"

"Only if you promise to help and not distract me. Brigid will kill me if we're late and miss the announcements. I have to wave when she names the new board of directors."

Joel gave her a mock serious face and made an X across his chest. "I will be good. This is like getting dressed up for the prom."

"I'll take your word for it." Kat slid the blue dress up over her body. "Could you zip this over here?"

"This dress is an architectural marvel. I don't understand how it stays on."

"You're getting distracted."

"I'm conducting an analysis." Joel hooked his index finger into the bodice and peered down. "Why doesn't it fall off?"

"According to Brigid, Robin told her it has interior structure. She said it has spiral steel boning in the corselette."

"I have no idea what that means."

"Me neither, except it won't fall off. Everything I've got is supported and wedged into place."

"Nice." Joel ran his hand across her bare back. "I like this. I can stand around looking like I've just got my arm around you, but really be imagining you're naked."

"You're getting distracted again."

Joel put his jacket on while Kat continued to readjust various body parts within the structurally advanced dress. She looked up at him and gasped slightly. "Wow."

He looked down. "What? Am I already covered in dog hair? I hope everyone realizes that's going to be a problem at this event."

"No. You look like you'll probably look when we get married. It was like a flashback, except into the future."

"A flash forward? I suppose we'll have to get dressed up for that too."

"Probably. How do you feel about eloping?" Kat smiled. "Although I think Maria would hunt me down and kill me if we run off like that."

"Whatever you want to do is fine with me."

"You do realize that after the squeal, every woman is going to ask us *when* we're getting married, right?"

"What's the squeal about?"

"It's the ring. Women squeal about engagement rings."

"Interesting."

Kat put her arms around his waist. "You think I'm making this up, but I'm not. You should have seen Brigid. She practically tore my hand off trying to get a look."

"I guess that whole thing about diamonds being a girl's best friend is true." He ran his hands across her back and pulled her closer. "I like this dress a lot."

"You're getting distracted again. I can't wait to see the pugly puppies. The photograph Michael took of them for the posters was adorable."

"Making it look like a movie poster was a good idea. 'The Alpine Grove Fur Ball, featuring Shelby and the Puglies!'"

"I know. And the word *pugly* is fun to say." Kat stepped back and smoothed the front of her dress. "I think this is as good as I'm going to look. We should grab your dog and go."

"You think Lady is the best option?"

"Well, she's the least bad option. Tessa the hyperactive nutball or Chelsey the shy weird dog are obviously not candidates. Linus's size freaks people out and Lori has been known to eat things she shouldn't. Since you'll be there, Lady will behave herself."

"That sounds like a plan."

When they arrived at the North Fork Lodge, the buildings, trees, and even a boat in the cove were strewn with little white twinkly lights that reflected on the water, making the lake look like it was sparkling in the twilight. Joel held Lady's leash while Kat got out of the truck and discreetly checked to made sure all of her assets remained securely contained within the blue fabric of her dress. She took his hand. "Okay, we're good."

They walked down the hillside, where crowds of people were standing around under a huge white tent that had been set up on the lawn. Many people had brought dogs and there was lots of laughing and chatting. Kat nudged Joel and pointed, "Who's that guy with your sister?"

"I'm not sure. Is it the electrician who worked on the kennel?"

"Really? That's surprising. Maybe..."

"Don't say it."

"What?"

"I know where you're going with this. I don't want to hear the words *turn on*, *electricity*, or *electrical impulse* in relation to my sister."

"I would *never* say that." Kat turned and looked down toward the lake. "Oh, look at Dixie! The tiny adorable puppy is all grown up."

They walked up to a couple with a fuzzy brown dog and the woman smiled and let go of the necklace she'd been fiddling with. "Kat, Joel! I'm so pleased to see you here."

"Hi Beth. Hi Drew." Kat bent to pet the dog. "I can't believe how big Dixie is now. The last time I saw her, she was able to curl up in my lap."

Beth squealed and waved her hands, "Wait, I forgot…my mother informed me! Let me see the ring."

Kat stepped back from Dixie, held out her hand, and gave Joel an I-told-you-so grin. She turned to Drew, "I loved your latest novel."

Before he could answer, a woman ran up to the group with a small shepherd mix in tow and tackled Kat in a hug. She let go and said, "Kat! I heard you guys are getting married. I have to see the ring!"

Kat held out her hand again and the woman uttered a small squeak as she leaned over to examine the ring. Kat said, "Hi Becca. Where's Jack? Didn't he come?"

Becca let go of Kat's hand. "He's here somewhere." She pointed and quickly rattled off locations of trees on the lodge property. "There were some cedars he wanted to look at over there too. After he finishes his tree-viewing excursion, I'm sure he'll turn up. Joel, we wondered if you could stop by. Jack said something about a tree out behind the Shack that he wants to remove. But he wants to make sure it's okay with you."

Joel nodded. "I'm sure it's fine."

Becca said, "But it's your house."

"I'll talk to him." Joel put his palm on Kat's back and she glanced up at him. He arched a single eyebrow at her and she tried not to giggle at the suggestive glint in his green eyes.

At the sound of the microphone being tapped on the stage, everyone turned around. The owner of the lodge, Alec Montgomery, thanked everyone for coming and introduced

Brigid, who said a few words about the newly formed 501(c)(3) nonprofit, Alpine Grove Animal Adoptions, and named the board of directors, who were welcomed with hearty cheers.

Brigid then introduced the Chief of Police Kirby Russell, who took the microphone and praised her efforts to help the homeless dogs in the community. He also encouraged everyone to reach into their pockets and make a donation. Pointing to a big thermometer display on the stage, he proclaimed that if they reached the lofty financial goal, he would walk naked down the main street of Alpine Grove. The police would close off the thoroughfare for an hour redirecting traffic, and he'd let it all hang out.

Along with everyone else, Kat burst out laughing. "I'm not sure I *want* to see that. I had no idea the police chief was a closet nudist."

Joel traced an intricate design on her back with his fingertip. "You just never know when nudity will be on the agenda."

"You're getting distracted again, aren't you?"

"I have a very active imagination."

Chapter 12

Epilogue

A week later, Brigid stood in front of the bookstore next to Clay, clapping along with everyone else in the crowd at Kirby Russell, who was walking down the middle of the street waving at the spectators along the sidewalks of Alpine Grove.

In front of him on a leash was a dog that appeared to be a Labrador retriever mixed with Great Dane. The police chief was dressed in his formal dress uniform, and the big dog was wearing a dog vest with "Naked" emblazoned on it. Strutting proudly, the dog seemed thrilled by all the attention, his long tail wagging merrily behind him.

Clay nudged Brigid and bent to whisper in her ear, "So what's the dog's real name again?"

"For today, he's Naked, but really that's Ziggy. His foster mom already took him to be neutered and he has a permanent home all lined up when he's done showing off here."

"Kirby is loving this too. What a ham."

"He has a great sense of humor. And he was thrilled when he found out we made enough money to start setting some aside for building a shelter. I'm going to drive out and look at how Kat's kennels are being constructed."

"You are a planner."

After the event was over and the crowds had dispersed, Brigid and Clay walked back to her house. She opened the door and they were greeted by Gypsy, who toddled over wagging her tail. It seemed odd to not have Judge galloping around barking at them, but he had gone to his new permanent home. Brigid picked up Gypsy and ruffled her ears. "So do you want to help with some more packing?"

Clay stroked the dog's head. "I should get back and return to my task."

"How is it going?"

"Cleaning out the bunkhouse reminds me how disgusting those ranch hands were. The cows left less of a mess in the barn. You don't want to know."

"You're right, I don't. But I appreciate you letting me rent the space after my lease here is up. My many books and I will have somewhere to live this fall."

"I'm assuming you'll be spending lots of time at the house as well."

Brigid grinned as she put Gypsy back down. "I anticipate many sleepovers."

"I certainly hope so. Waking up next to you is part of my morning routine now. Even more important than coffee."

Brigid looked at the clock and set a box of books on the table. "Could you take this with you? I don't really have time to get anything else done. I should get back to the law office and get to work. Larry's files make your archaeological filing system look downright organized. I told him I was taking a long lunch, but I may be pushing the envelope here."

"So has he hit on you yet?"

"No. I think you scared him the other day when you stopped by. You obviously did not have legal matters on your mind."

"I am not scary."

"When you stand there all silent and intimidating, looking like a cowboy, people don't know what to do with you."

"Well, you certainly figured it out."

"Someone once told me that it's all in the eyes. And yours are so warm and kind—not scary at all."

Clay looked into her eyes and grinned, "Well then, maybe it's just the hat."

Thanks for Reading

Thank you for dedicating some of your reading time to *The Good, the Bad, and the Pugly*. I hope you enjoyed Brigid and Clay's adventures. I'll be writing more books that will feature Kat, Joel and various other residents of Alpine Grove who bring dogs to the new boarding kennel. The eighth book, *The Treasure of the Hairy Cadre* is available along with ten other books in the series.

If you would like to be notified by e-mail when I release a new book, you can sign up for my New Releases e-mail list at SusanDaffron.com.

I know that not everyone likes to write book reviews, but if you are willing write a sentence or two about what you thought of *The Good, the Bad, and the Pugly*, I encourage you to post a review at your favorite book vendor site or share a message with your social networking friends.

If you would like to share your thoughts about the book with me privately, you can reach me through the contact page on the SusanDaffron.com web site.

I look forward to hearing from you!

~ Susan C. Daffron

Acknowledgements

Writing a novel is never easy and I'd like to thank my husband James Byrd for his support and encouragement throughout the publishing process.

I'd also like to thank my alpha and beta readers for their eagle-eyed reading and great feedback:

- James Byrd
- Dian Chapman
- Adele Hudson
- Kate Turner
- Clare Cinelli

A number of readers also shared their adopted dog stories on my blog, which provided inspiration for many of the dogs in this book. Each person whose story was selected receives my undying gratitude, and I am donating copies of my nonfiction books *Funds to the Rescue* and *Publicity to the Rescue* to the pet rescue group of their choice. Thank you all!

Reader	Dog	Rescue Group
Sue Ingebretson	Shelby	CampWannaQ
Jacqueline Simonds	Lewis	Southern Nevada Beagle Rescue Foundation
Stacey Ambrose	Layla	Piece Of My Heart Rescue
Adele Hudson	Nugget & Ziggy	The Greyhound Project, Inc.
Susanna Perkins	Gypsy	Papillon Care and Rescue Trust
Margaret Moore	Scout	Suntree-Viera Pet Rescue
Harriet Higgs	Pete & Kermit	Schertz Animal Control

About the Author

Susan Daffron is the author of the Jennings & O'Shea series and the Alpine Grove romantic comedies, a series of novels that feature residents of the small town of Alpine Grove and their various quirky dogs and cats. She is also an award-winning author of many nonfiction books, including several about pets and animal rescue. She lives in a small town in northern Idaho and shares her life with her husband and three really cute dogs.

Made in the USA
Middletown, DE
10 January 2018